The Last Servant

handwritten inscription:

Brenda,
thank you very
much for let me
stay at your
place for Break
signing at Jenkintown
hope to see you
again later
take care of
yourself (+ thine)
Stevie

A novel by
Stevie Platt

American Literary Press
Five Star Special Edition
Baltimore, Maryland

The Last Servant

Library of Congress
Cataloging-in-Publication Data
ISBN 1-56167-915-1

Library of Congress Card Catalog Number:
2005907823

Published by

American Literary Press
Five Star Special Edition
8019 Belair Road, Suite 10
Baltimore, Maryland 21236

Manufactured in the United States of America

To Aunt Dot,

Thank you very much for your help in correcting everything in *The Last Servant*. I hope that the novel will be successful after it is published.

Love,
Stevie

Chapter 1

In downtown Raleigh, North Carolina, the street was full of wagons carrying fresh meat, fruit, vegetables, and a few chickens in their cages. People looked through the wagons and bought items they needed for their homes. A young woman with her five-year-old daughter named Joy walked along the street. Joy liked to escape from her mother for no reason. They went to the wagon with two different kinds of sugars.

"Ma'am," the salesman greeted. "What kind of sugar are you looking for?"

"Yes, I want brown sugar please," the woman answered.

"Yes ma'am." The salesman smiled, looked, found a bag of brown sugar, and brought to her. "This is for you."

Joy was bored with her mother shopping in the market every day. She saw a few cages with chickens next to the wagon. She looked at her mother, who was checking the sugar. Joy walked to the cage and put her finger into it. Her mother saw Joy doing that.

"Joy," her mother called out. "Please do not bother the chickens."

Joy looked at her mother, stood up, and put her hands together so that she would not touch the cage.

"Why?" Joy wondered.

"The chickens will bite you if you try to bother them," her mother warned.

Joy looked at the sugar and then looked back at the cage, sneaking a look at her mother to see she was not watching. Joy had a plan to play with the chickens. Joy put her finger into the cage. At that moment the chicken bit Joy's finger very hard. She tried to pull her finger out of the cage but it was stuck. The cage fell down to the road and Joy screamed out loud, nearly scaring her mother to death.

"I am sorry about my daughter's behavior," the woman was embarrassed to say to the salesman.

"The children always like to play." The salesman smiled.

The mother came to Joy and pulled her finger out of the cage. The worker put the cage back. The mother and Joy went back to the wagon and paid for the brown sugar.

The clouds moved in a flow that covered the sun. The people looked at the sky expecting that rain would soon come down. They had to rush to buy their food. The clouds became dark and started to thunder with lightning and rain. The people left the market street. The worker used blankets to cover the vegetables and pushed the wagon. The street became empty and quiet. A half hour later the rain became even stronger.

Robert Blackburn and his younger brother Ron were lawyers and had worked together for almost four years. They worked hard and won some cases in court. They had a small office with two rooms full of books on the shelves and only three small windows. They could see over the roof because they were on third floor. Robert worked at the case on his desk and looked at the ceiling. He could hear the rain hitting the roof and was feeling frustrated that he could not use such force on his case.

"Please stop the rain now," Robert sighed.

He looked at the case on his desk and started to read carefully.

In the narrow street paved with bricks, a few people ran out onto the sidewalk and crossed the street. They rushed into the stores or other businesses. Ron ran on the sidewalk, stopped and looked each way for the horses that might be coming. Just as he ran across the road a horse came. He ran and jumped across the puddle, trying to avoid getting his shoes wet. Finally he arrived on the opposite sidewalk from his office. He was relieved the horse had not hit him. He came to the door and entered the building, closing the door behind him. He leaned on the door and thought about what a bad day it had been.

Ron walked from the door to the lobby. He forgot to shake his long black coat to get the water off before going up the stairs. He looked at the small stairs and at his shoes. He was supposed to walk slowly so that other people in the offices would not be bothered by his shoes making noise. Ron started up the stairs slowly. He looked up to the second floor and saw no one. He walked to the rail and looked down to the small lobby. He felt better and again began walking upstairs. He got on the second floor and then walked to another level, but he gave up on walking slowly. He wanted to hurry to his office, so he started to run quickly. Other people in their offices could hear Ron's feet on the stairs. They opened their doors and looked at him as he ran to the third floor. Mr. Collins from the first floor knew who was making all the noise. He stood up from his chair and walked out the door to the middle of the lobby so he could see Ron on the third floor. He did not appreciate what Ron was doing making noise on the stairs.

"Mr. Blackburn," Mr. Collins pointed. "Your feet are sup-posed to be quiet when you step on the stairs. Now you can see people coming out on the stairs and looking at you!"

Ron heard Mr. Collins's angry voice. He stopped and looked around. He saw people on the second floor. The people looked at Ron and did not like what he had done. They pointed down to the lobby. He blinked his eyes and knew that Mr. Collins was angry at him for making noise. He looked back at Mr. Collins on the lobby.

"Yes, Mr. Collins," Ron muttered. "I am sorry I made you get upset about the noise in the hall. Well, I'll try my best to control my feet and walk more properly."

He turned back to his office. The people in the hall looked back to Mr. Collins. Mr. Collins sighed, then walked back to his office and closed his door. The people looked at each other, shrugged their shoulders, and went back to their offices.

Ron came into the office and shut the door quickly. He felt foolish about the stairs. Robert looked at Ron as he leaned against the door. Robert wondered what was wrong with his young brother.

"What is your problem?" Robert asked.

Ron did not answer Robert's question. He walked to a small closet, took his coat and hat off, and hung them up. He went to his desk next to the window.

"Ron, did you hear me?" Robert puzzled.

Ron looked at Robert quickly.

"Nothing," Ron sighed. "I hate the weather! I want to finish the case."

Ron opened the file and looked for the crime section. Robert nodded and went back to his work.

The rain became lighter, then stopped. The clouds moved to the west until there was clear blue sky and sunlight. In the office even the dark walls were bright from the sun. The hard wood was reflecting sunlight all around the room. It almost hurt their eyes. Robert could not see well at all, so he walked to the window and pulled the curtains close. He rubbed his eyes to stop the discomfort.

"My eyes got blurry from all the light," Robert complained.

"Yes, my eyes hurt from that, too," Ron giggled.

Robert stopped rubbing his eyes and looked at Ron, wondering why he thought the glare of the sun was funny.

"Don't make fun of me." Robert was upset. "I will beat you up!"

"That's fine with me, go ahead," Ron laughed. He got up from his chair. "Make your day!"

He chased Ron around the table in the middle the room.

"You are a brat, boy!" Robert yelled.

"Yes, I am a brat, man!" Ron laughed.

Robert tried to catch Ron. In his mind he thought that he should jump over the table and catch Ron. Robert looked at the table; Ron was puzzled about what he was doing. Robert jumped on the table and caught Ron suddenly, causing the two of them to fall to the floor together.

The man from downstairs looked up at the ceiling. He knew that Robert and Ron always played together like that. He hit the ceiling with a broom to tell them to stop playing around.

They knew the man from downstairs wanted them to stop fighting. They stood up, wiped off the dirt from their clothes, and went back to their desks, intending to sit down at their chairs. At that moment, the door opened. There was a short, older man with a white beard. He had a flushed face. That was his natural skin color, suggesting that he might be Irish. His name was Mr. Wright and he was the owner of a hotel near the capital. He smiled at Robert and hugged him and Ron. They were puzzled and looked at each other. Mr. Wright laughed and took off his coat and hat, then put them on the hook on the wall.

"I am so tired." Mr. Wright yawned. "I need to sit and rest for a while. I want to talk with both of you."

Ron rushed for a chair and brought it to Mr. Wright. Ron came back to his desk and looked at Robert.

"Can I do something for you today?" Robert asked.

Mr. Wright looked at Robert's eyes for a second, then looked at Ron's eyes, then went back to Robert again. He smiled and took his wallet from his vest. He opened the wallet and handed a check to Robert, who wondered why Mr. Wright had done that. Ron came to Robert and looked at the check.

"That's a lot of money." Ron was shocked and looked at Mr. Wright. "Why did you give us so much money?"

Mr. Wright put his wallet back in his vest. He stood up and came to them to hug them again. Robert and Ron were surprised that he gave them so much. Mr. Wright came back and sat down and looked at them.

"Both of you did a good job," Mr. Wright said with a smile. "We won the case. They found the murderer guilty."

"You gave us five thousand dollars?" Robert asked.

"Yes." Mr. Wright nodded. "I think it's better for me to go now."

Robert gestured to Ron to give Mr. Wright his coat and hat. Mr. Wright was surprised that Ron was helping him put the coat on.

"Thank you very much," Mr. Wright told both of them. "You two, both of you, have my best wishes."

He opened the door, then turned and looked back at them with a smile. "You have a nice day." Mr. Wright waved. "Goodbye!"

He closed the door. Robert and Ron waved and looked at each other for a second, then screamed and hugged. Mr. Wright was already in the hall but still could hear Robert and Ron's screaming. He laughed and went down. Ron jumped on the table and danced with the check. Robert ran and pulled up the window, stuck his head out and screamed for anybody passing by to hear.

"I got five thousand dollars with me!" Robert yelled.

Ron jumped off the table and took Robert back from the window. He pushed the window down.

"You are so crazy." Ron laughed and pointed his finger at Robert's chest. "Someone will shoot you and get the check!"

"They will not get my check!" Robert giggled.

He hugged Ron and started to dance again on the way to the door. They stopped by the door and then pranced back to the window. The man from downstairs looked up at the ceiling and again hit it hard with his broom. That made Robert and Ron stop dancing. They took their coats, hats and briefcases with them and went out of the office. Robert locked the door and looked at Ron's face. He looked downstairs, and Robert started to laugh. They both knew that they should make some noise while they ran downstairs. They agreed and began to run downstairs. The people from every office heard the noise and they all opened their doors and looked at Robert and Ron running down. They arrived at the lobby at the moment when Mr. Collins's door opened. They kept on running. Mr. Collins tried to catch them but they were already out on the street.

"I told you many times," Mr. Collins yelled, "you are not supposed to run downstairs. That will bother other people in the office!"

They had left the door open. He was disappointed and closed the door shut. He walked back to his office, looking up at the open stairwell where the people were standing and looking at him. His fists were at his hips.

"Go back to your offices right away!" Mr. Collins told the people.

The people looked at each, walked back to their offices, and shut the doors. Mr. Collins sighed and walked back inside his office, closing the door behind him.

Robert and Ron were excited and laughing, running along the road and jumping on the sidewalk. People heard the men's voices and came out to look at them. They were running to the park and through the woods, passing the foundation and the lake. The owner's dog was a greyhound. When he saw them running, the dog started to run after them. He saw his dog and tried to catch up with him.

"Larry! Come back now!" the owner called.

However, the dog ignored the call and kept on running with the men. Robert saw the dog following along behind Ron's back.

"Look at that dog!" Robert pointed and laughed. "Better watch out! He will bite your leg! You had better run faster than the dog does!"

Ron tried to run faster than the dog, but it was still close behind. Ron made a right and then a left. That made the dog tired and it finally gave up and went back to the owner. They ran to the street where they lived in an apartment with a decorative margin of red brick and white stone on each side of the window. Ron saw his wife, Rosemary, who was wearing a trim of white lace around her chest and shoulders, opening the window of their apartment.

Rosemary saw Ron and Robert running. She waved at them, and they waved back to her. She turned her head and looked at Robert's wife, Lily. She was sitting on her bed and sewing a dress.

"Lily," Rosemary called. "Hurry up! Come here right away!"

Lily looked at Rosemary and wondered what she was pointing at outside in the park. She put her dress on the bed and went to the window. Rosemary pointed to Ron and Robert; they were running on the sidewalk toward their home. Lily looked at Rosemary and wondered why they had come home so early.

"Why did they come home so soon?" Lily was puzzled.

"I don't know what they are doing today." Rosemary shrugged.

Rosemary pulled at Lily's hand and they left the bedroom, walking fast through the hall toward the door. She opened the door and looked downstairs. Robert and Ron came into the lobby and ran upstairs to the door. They had not expected that their wives would have already opened it for them. Lily came to Robert.

"Did you come home early?" Lily asked.

Robert nodded, looked at Rosemary, then turned his head toward Ron. He pulled Rosemary and Lily by the hand through the hall and into the living room. Ron closed the door, took his hat and coat off, and put them on hangers. He ran to the living room. The women went to sit on the sofa and waited for what Robert would announce. Ron and Robert pulled up chairs for themselves to sit on.

Rosemary turned her head to Lily. "What are they doing here?" she wondered.

"I don't know," Lily said softly. "I will ask my Robert. Maybe he plans to tell me something about his job."

Robert heard Lily's voice; he looked at her and thought about what he would say to her.

"Robert," Lily said. "What are you going to tell us?"

"Well," Robert said softly, looking first at Ron and then back to Lily again. "We would like to tell both of you that our client has given us a check."

Lily and Rosemary moved their heads to hear what Robert said.

"Can you tell me how much he paid you?" Rosemary was curious.

Robert smiled, then pulled the check out of his coat pocket and showed it to the women. They looked at the check, opened their eyes wide, and looked at each other.

"That's a lot of money!" Lily was shocked.

"What do you plan to do with all that money?" Rosemary asked.

Robert looked at Ron. He had not made any plans for using the check. Robert nodded and looked back at Rosemary. His facial expression indicated that he didn't have a plan.

"I have no idea about it," Robert said. "Maybe we should get out of this town and move somewhere. What we really want is to have our own business."

"What kind of business?" Ron asked. "Wouldn't we work as lawyers anymore?"

"Maybe we could work with a different one," Robert nodded. "I really want to run our own business."

Lily was puzzled as to why Robert wanted to set up a new business. She thought he might be better off buying a new house for his family.

"Robert?" Lily said.

"What darling?"

"What are you planning?"

"I am not ready to make a decision yet," Robert said. "Let

me think for a while and then I will tell everyone what my goal might be."

Robert stood up and left the living room. They watched as he walked away and tried to figure out what he might be planning. Robert came into his office, pulled the chair from the desk and sat down. He thought about possibly buying some land somewhere in the South. He felt that he could start a new business there. He took some paper and ink and began writing down a plan. He would buy land first, then build a house, a barn, and a few small houses for slaves. They would also need a place to live.

In the living room, Lily felt uncomfortable about what Robert's goal might be in setting up a new business. She thought she ought to be face to face with Robert. She stood up and left the room. Rosemary looked at Lily while she went to the hall.

"Where are you going now?" Rosemary said.

"I ought to be talking with Robert right now," Lily said. She kept on going to the hall.

Rosemary sighed and left the room quickly. Ron did not like being alone in the room. He thought he might try to follow Rosemary to the hall.

"Lily, please don't disturb Robert," Rosemary said.

Lily stopped walking and looked at Rosemary. She came back to speak to her.

"He is my husband," Lily said. "I have to talk with him."

She turned around and walked into Robert's office. Rosemary followed her. Lily stood in front of the desk. Rosemary and Ron came in together; they felt they had to watch Lily because she might get angry with Robert for some reason. Robert kept on writing down his plans. Lily put her hands on the desk to get Robert's attention. Robert noticed Lily's hands in front of him and sat back in his chair.

"Do you want to tell me something?" Robert sighed.

"I was wondering what you are planning?" Lily asked. "Why did you choose the South to live?"

"I want to do a different kind of work," Robert said. "I don't want to keep on working for the court. You know it is not an easy job. It gives me stress. I think it's best for me to get out of here and get a new life. Maybe we can start a new family like Ron and Rosemary are doing."

Robert looked at Ron and Rosemary standing next to Lily. Rosemary looked at Ron for a moment.

"Are you sure about having a new family?" Rosemary asked. "When we settle down in a new place, then we can start having a family?"

"Yes, that is what I hope to do in the South." Ron nodded.

Rosemary looked at Lily and wondered if she would accept what the men had been planning. She came close to speak in Lily's ear.

"What do you think of the men's idea?" Rosemary whispered.

"I think that it is OK for them to move." Lily nodded. "We will be able to have a new family when we get settled down in the South."

Rosemary was surprised that Lily already had accepted what her husband suggested. She looked at Robert with a smile.

"That's great. We can go ahead with your goal." Rosemary was smiling, too. "Now, can we talk about the plan before we go for sure?"

Robert felt better that Lily and Rosemary were beginning to accept his plan.

"Can we talk right here?" Lily asked Robert.

"Yes, you may work with us if you wish." Robert smiled.

Lily nodded and took the chair from the wall to bring it closer to Robert's desk. Ron went to another room and brought two more chairs to the office. He put the chairs close to Robert's desk. Rosemary and Ron sat and talked about their plans for the South.

Robert checked the paper on which he had written the list for a plan. It was ready enough for him to tell them about it.

"Now, I have this list of what we need for the plan," Robert explained. "First, I want to look for a large plot of land so we can grow plants and sell them to earn more money."

Lily was surprised that Robert wanted to become a farmer.

"What kind of plant would you sell?" Lily asked.

At that moment, Robert realized that he had not thought yet about an answer to Lily's question.

"I guess maybe cotton," Robert answered.

"Robert wants to plant cotton?" Lily was puzzled and looked at Rosemary.

Rosemary shrugged her shoulders, not knowing what Robert might be talking about in his plans. She looked at Ron.

"Are you planning to plant cotton?" Rosemary asked him.

Ron looked at Robert quickly. His facial expression showed that he was puzzled and did not know what the plan was supposed to be.

"Are you sure that you want to farm cotton?" Ron asked Robert. "Is that a joke?"

"No, I am not joking," Robert replied.

Rosemary looked at Lily and spoke into her ear.

"Maybe we will leave this state," Rosemary whispered.

Lily looked at Rosemary quickly and stood up.

"How did you know that?" Lily was shocked.

"Well, as far as I know, cotton comes from the South," Rosemary explained. "I believe that the best kind is supposed to be in Louisiana."

Lily looked at Robert; she did not want to leave her family and friends. She became upset and ran out of the office to her bedroom. Robert rolled his eyes, moved the chair away from the desk, and stood up.

"She is going to mess up our plans," Robert sighed. "Damn it, Rosemary! Why did you tell Lily where we would be going to plant the cotton?"

"I thought Lily was supposed to be willing to accept your plan," Rosemary said. "But it was not what she must have expected to happen to her. I'm sorry that I upset her."

Ron stood up and stepped between Rosemary and Robert.

"Please don't get mad at my wife!" Ron said seriously. "She is trying her best to help you and your wife."

Robert was silent and left the office. Still angry, he kicked his feet on the wall in the hall, then went toward his bedroom. He came in and saw Lily on the bed. Her face was down on the pillow and her hands were behind her head. She was crying. He knew that she did not want to leave town. He sighed and came to sit beside her on the bed to try to talk.

"Lily, I am trying to explain to you about our plan," Robert said softly. "I know how you feel about being apart from your family. We will just have to get used to that when we go south."

Lily turned her head to look at Robert, then put it back down on her pillow.

"It's not possible to move so far away from our family in North Carolina," Lily wept. "We don't know any other family so far south. Maybe we would have to make a new life."

Robert answered, "Yes, I think we would have to do that. Being married to each other is a whole new life, isn't it? And you did want to do that, didn't you?"

She picked up her head and smiled, taking his hand.

"If it's what you are planning for us, then it must be right."

"He was surprised that she might really be more willing to go than she had admitted so far.

"What are you saying?" Robert asked. "Are you sure that you feel it is possible for us to go to the South and make a new life there?"

"Yes, Robert," Lily nodded slowly. "I have to follow your heart and say farewell to our old life."

Robert felt relief that Lily would accept his plan to move. He kissed her forehead and hugged her.

"Lily, thank you, thank you." Robert was happy. "You will get used to it when we are settled somewhere. Can you come with me to discuss the plan with Ron and Rosemary please?"

Robert stood up and pulled Lily's hand to get her up from the bed. Lily told Robert that she needed to wash her face before going to the office with the others. Robert nodded and let her go. Lily came to the drawing room, where there was a white bowl with a pitcher. She poured the water into the bowl until it was filled. Then she put the pitcher on top of the chest of drawers. She put her hands in the water and splashed at her eyes lightly. She did not want her hair or dress to get wet. Robert took the towel and gave it to Lily. She rubber her eyes, hung the towel on the chair and walked out of the bedroom with Robert. They went through the hall to the office. Rosemary and Ron were sitting there waiting for them to arrive.

"Are you all right?" Rosemary was concerned.

Lily nodded. She came to a chair and sat down. Robert came to his desk, sat down and moved the chair in close. He looked at Ron for a few seconds.

"Now we can begin to discuss our plans," Robert said. "The first thing I ought to do is to contact a person who knows about the planting of cotton in the South. Somebody like that could help me find the best place to live there."

They talked about the plan for a few hours. The clock above the fireplace was chiming. Rosemary heard the sound and looked at it. She did not realize that it had been such a long discussion. She told the others that it was midnight. They moved the chairs back, kissed each other, and returned to their bedrooms.

Robert knew where the factory in Raleigh was. The company made handkerchiefs, dresses, nightgowns, diapers, sheets, pillowcases and bath towels all from cotton. Robert went to the factory and came into the front office. He saw a young man at a desk and came over to him. The man looked at Robert as he stood there.

"Hello, I am Mike Kirby," Mike introduced himself. "May I help you, Mr. . . .?"

"Robert Blackburn," Robert introduced himself. "Can I

speak with any manager who knows about cotton farming in the South?"

"I know one of the managers," Mike said. "Mr. Russell is in charge of ordering cotton and bringing it to our factory every month. I will talk with him about whether he can help you. Please have a seat right here."

Robert nodded and sat on the chair. Mike went into the office and told Mr. Russell that Robert would like to talk with him. He asked Mike to bring Robert to his office. Mike went back to his desk and called Robert's name.

"You can talk with Mr. Russell," Mike said. "Follow me to his office."

Robert followed Mike through the door and went into the office. Mr. Russell stood up and came over to Robert and Mike.

"Thank you for coming here, Mr. Blackburn." Mr. Russell shook Robert's hand. "Please have a seat over here."

Robert sat on the chair in front of the desk. Mike left the office and pulled the door shut behind him. Mr. Russell sat down on his leather chair at the desk.

"What can I do for you, Mr. Blackburn?" Mr. Russell asked.

"Yes, Mr. Russell," Robert said. "Where do you get your cotton from?"

"I order cotton from New Orleans, Louisiana, every month," Mr. Russell answered. "Cotton will be sent up to our building every month. That is a long trip to bring cotton from the South by wagon."

"Do you know anything about the farmer who plants cotton in the South?" Robert asked.

"Umm," Mr. Russell nodded. "The best place to grow cotton is in Mississippi and Louisiana. In my experience, I am not aware about how you could get in touch with people who would talk to you about plantations."

"What is a plantation?" Robert questioned.

"It is a farm," Mr. Russell answered.

"Oh, it is a farm," Robert said. "That's new to me. I guess

I have to get used to the way they say things in the South."

Mr. Russell nodded and wondered why Robert had asked him if he could find a plantation.

"Can I ask you a question?" Mr. Russell said. "Do you have a job now?"

"Yes, I am a lawyer," Robert answered. "I am planning to go into a new line of work. I want to grow cotton in the South as a plantation owner."

"I see," Mr. Russell said. "It is a good idea to start with that kind of work if you can do it well. First you are supposed to find a place to live. You will need a big house and a large area of land for planting. You will need to purchase slaves to gather the cotton. You will need to provide a place for them to eat and sleep."

"How much is the usual cost for the land and a suitable number of slaves?" Robert asked.

"I can't say exactly what the prices are for land and slaves," Mr. Russell said. "I think it would be better for you to check those questions out with the people in the South after you go down there. If you can spend the time with them and learn something, then you can move on."

"Do you think five thousand dollars would be a good enough amount to do that?" Robert asked again.

"I have no idea about the money," Mr. Russell sighed. "My suggestion is that you should inquire about that when you are in that area."

Robert nodded and stood up. Mr. Russell was puzzled about the whole conversation but he stood up too.

"I suppose I could talk with a few of the plantation owners and see if anyone is interested in selling." Robert sighed. "Mr. Russell, thank you for explaining to me what a plantation is."

"I am sorry, Mr. Blackburn." Mr. Russell shook Robert's hand and opened the door. "I wish that I did know more about how to run plantations and plant cotton in the South. Good luck in your new venture."

Robert left Mr. Russell's office and walked out of the factory to return to his home. He found it difficult to think about how to buy land and get some seeds and whatever else might be needed to grow cotton. He decided anyway that he was ready to go ahead and take the risk on behalf of both families. He would be taking Lily, Ron and Rosemary to the South to find a place to establish themselves in their new business.

The Blackburn's quit their jobs as lawyers, packed their things from the office and went home. They all packed their personal things and moved their furniture into the wagons. They had a chance to speak with and hug their family and relatives, then they left Raleigh.

A week later, they arrived at Greenwood, Mississippi, and looked for a hotel to stay in for a few days before they would start to Louisiana for the last leg of the trip. They went downtown and found a restaurant next to the bar on the corner. Inside the restaurant, there was a narrow dining room with one plain white wall and a few round tables and chairs. They found an empty table, where they sat and waited for the server to come. A woman with a white, long dress came to take their orders.

"What would you like to eat today?" she asked.

"Well, can you bring each of us a bowl of soup with a few slices of bread, please?" Robert said softly.

"Yes, I will get some food for you all." She smiled and went to the kitchen.

Ron was hungry. He looked around the room at the people eating their food. Just then, he overheard two men at the next the table. Both were about forty years old. They were talking about a plan to sell a big house with land to anyone who wanted to buy it.

"Robert, I just heard what the men at the next table are saying," Ron said quickly. "They are considering selling a big house with land."

"Does the house have cotton planted there?" Robert asked.

"I have no idea whether they have cotton plants," Ron said. "I think it would be better for you to talk with the men before they leave here. You can find out if they have room to plant cotton."

The woman brought the soup and bread to the table. She gave the soup to each person and put the bread in the middle of table. "I'm sure you'll like it. We have really good soup today," she said with a smile.

They ate the soup and bread for a few minutes. The men from the other table stood up and began to walk out of the restaurant. Rosemary told Robert to catch the men before they went outside. Robert ran and caught them outside.

"Sir, wait a minute!" Robert shouted to the men.

The men stopped in the middle of the road and looked at Robert standing in front of the restaurant. They were puzzled, but came back to talk to him.

"What do you want from us?" the man asked.

Robert felt uncomfortable that his behavior might make him seem impolite. He really needed to talk with them about whether the house had possibilities for planting.

"Are you planning to sell a big house?" Robert asked immediately. "I wonder if there is space there to plant cotton. I want to be able to do that and then sell the crop."

The men were surprised that Robert had heard their voices from the other table where they had been talking about selling their house. They looked at each other. Robert felt that there might be something wrong with him. The man looked back at Robert and laughed.

"Yes, we are planning to sell the big house," the man chuckled. "Of course, there are 2,000 acres planted with cotton. We have lots of slaves, too. I know most of the slaves are very good workers. I suppose you would want them, too."

"You will sell the house with the slaves?" Robert wondered.

"Yes, you can take it for your business." The man nodded.

"I am Kevin Mason and my friend's name is Glyn Pace. What is your name, please?"

"Robert Blackburn," Robert said. "I am a lawyer from Raleigh. My wife and my young brother and his wife are in the restaurant."

"You are a lawyer?" Kevin asked, surprised. "Why do you want to become a plantation owner here?"

"Well, it's a long story," Robert said. "The others are still in there waiting for me to come back now."

"Yes, sure, we can go back in there with you again!" Kevin laughed.

They went into the restaurant. Lily saw them on the way back to the table.

"Rosemary, Ron," Lily pointed to the men. "Look at that. It's a good thing that Robert caught those men before they left."

Rosemary and Ron looked back at the men. They all came to the table.

"My wife, Lily, and my young brother, Ron, and his wife Rosemary," Robert introduced them all. "This is Kevin Mason and this is Glyn Pace."

The men took chairs and brought the other table over to theirs. The server came to the table. She saw the men that she had thought were finished and leaving the restaurant.

"Are you still hungry?" she asked.

The men laughed at her question and slapped their hands on the table. They didn't think she was serious about it.

"No, we are not hungry," Kevin said. "Mr. Blackburn caught us outside. He may want to buy our big house."

"Oh, no wonder," she nodded. "Sir, are you planning to buy a house around here? I can tell that you are not from around here. Are you coming from another place to do something like that?"

"Yes, we are here from North Carolina," Robert said. "We are hoping to buy a house and go into the cotton-growing business."

"Good to hear that," the waitress smiled. "I hope that all of you will come here whenever you are hungry. You can call me Sally. I wish you very good luck in your new business."

"Thanks, Sally, I take much pleasure in that!" Robert smiled.

Sally collected the dishes and glasses from the table and walked to the kitchen. Robert looked at Kevin and felt good that he might well have found the right step to achieve his goal.

"Kevin, can you explain to me how to run the business," Robert asked. "For myself, I really don't know how to work with a plantation. I didn't have to know about that to get to be a lawyer."

"I will be glad to show you," Kevin agreed. "I would like you to come over to the house and let me show you around the place. There are plenty of things to do. Are you ready to leave here to look at the house now?"

"Yes, please! I would like go with you right away!" Robert was excited.

They left the restaurant and walked to their wagons. Lily was confused. Robert was supposed to be settling in Louisiana, but now he seemed ready to change his mind and stay in Mississippi. She wanted to ask Robert which one he preferred, to live in this state or to go on to Louisiana.

"Robert, I want to know for sure if you are planning to go on to Louisiana or not," Lily said. "Your first plan was supposed to be living in Louisiana, but now you have changed that plan. Are we going to stay here since you heard from the men about selling their house here?"

"Lily, I had not expected the big house would be for sale here," Robert answered. "Yes, this happened to change my mind. You never know when it will happen that you find a good place to live. We might stay there for now, Lily. OK?"

"I see. I guess I accept your plans," Lily nodded. "Maybe it will be better for us to live in the big house. Nevertheless, I want to see whether the house looks good. If it's not good then we go on to Louisiana?"

"Yes, that's why I want to see it, to find out if I like it," Robert agreed. "What you want is to see inside the house. If you like it, then I will buy it. Ron and Rosemary will tell me if they like it or not, too."

"Yes, we will look at the house," Rosemary said. "I will tell you if we like it or not. If we don't all like it, then we will go farther South again."

Lily nodded and climbed up into the wagon. Rosemary went into their wagon and waited for Robert and Ron to talk a little longer. They went in their wagon and followed Kevin and Glyn, who were riding their horses. They were a little bit scared and excited. Could they trust what the men had said? It was a dangerous possibility that they could all be robbed and possibly even killed for no reason.

After about half an hour, Kevin and Glyn finally turned left and led them to a dirt road with plenty of cotton planted all over the land. At last they could see the big house. It was made of white wood and had black shutters. There were three stories with a long balcony on the second floor and a porch on the ground. Lily felt awed and put her hand on Robert's shoulder. He looked at Lily.

"Do you think that we can buy this house?" Robert asked. "First we will look around for awhile before we make the decision whether to buy it."

Lily nodded and jumped out of the wagon. Rosemary jumped out and ran to Lily. They walked toward the house together. Ron jumped off and came to Robert.

"The dream has come true," Ron said. "Now we can start to work on planting the cotton and the business of selling. Maybe Kevin and Glyn can explain to us how to run the business."

"I hope that they will teach us how to use things," Robert said. "We will have to get along without those guys after we buy the house. Maybe we can spend some time with them for a while. Sound good to you?"

"Yes, Robert," Ron agreed. "I think that we will need them

to be very helpful with us in learning how to run the business of planting cotton."

Kevin and Glyn took their horses and hitched them to a post in front of the house. They came over to Robert and Ron, who were standing near the wagons.

"That building is a big surprise to me already," Robert admitted. "I already like it! However, we do not know how to run the business with the plants, the cotton and the slaves. You know that I never lived in such a house before. Would you be willing to teach us if you can? Please?"

"Yes, sure," Kevin chuckled. "Glyn and I will teach you how to work on it. We live near here, not too far away. We will bring our wives over too. They are about the same age as your wives. I hope that they will teach them how to deal with the slaves in your house."

"They are allowed to use our house?" Ron asked Kevin.

"No, they are not supposed to live in your place," Kevin said, shaking his head. "They are to serve you, for cleaning, cooking and bringing things to you that you ask for."

Ron understood Kevin's point. Glyn saw that Lily and Rosemary were already up on the porch trying to open the door because they wanted to see inside the big house. Glyn slapped Kevin's shoulder and whispered in his ear that the women wanted to go into the house.

"Hey, ladies," Kevin shouted. "I have a key with me. Please just wait and I will unlock the door and open it for you to come in."

The women were looking through the front windows, but they did hear Kevin's voice. Lily and Rosemary nodded to him and then waited to see inside.

"Do you want to go inside?" Kevin asked Robert. "I have keys with me now. Your wife wants to see what's in there. Let's go now."

Kevin and Glyn walked to the big house where the women were excitedly waiting. Ron followed them, but Robert did not move. He was still feeling a little bit shocked that his plan seemed to be coming along in such perfect time. Ron had planned to talk with Robert while they were on the way to the house, but Robert was never close by. Ron sighed and came over to Robert. He pulled his arm to come along with them.

Kevin pulled the keys out of his pocket and put one in the keyhole. The women grew more and more excited as Kevin unlocked the door. He pushed the door open and raised his hand as a welcome to the women. They came into the house first, followed by the men. Robert and Ron had stopped on the porch for a second. Glyn told them to come in.

Robert looked at the stairs, which were made entirely of wood. A railing went up to the second floor. Ron looked in the lower room and told Robert that there was furniture.

"Robert, they have nice furniture," Ron said, pointing to the formal living room. "It is very beautiful and expensive furniture. We won't have to buy new furniture."

"I did not know about all of that," Robert said. "Are you planning to give us all of the furniture?"

"Yes, you have it now," Kevin said. "The family that lived in this house have all already died out, the last ones just a few weeks ago."

Lily and Rosemary came into the foyer and heard what Kevin said about the recent family death. They felt scared and not entirely safe to be living in the big house. Maybe someone would kill them.

"I don't feel so safe here since you told us about the family death." Lily was scared. "Can you tell me what caused them to die? Was somebody trying to murder them or what? If you can't tell me the truth about why they died, then we will leave here to go farther south. Kevin, please, will you tell me?"

"Nothing is wrong. There was never any murder of the family here," Kevin assured her. "It is a long story about what happened with that family. So far, all I know is that they had lots of problems with each other, not with the slaves, and none of it was our fault. The only son died after being sick for a long time. His wife had killed herself, and he was depressed and killed himself, too. Now I am telling you the truth and you do not have to worry about anything bad happening in this house."

Lily nodded and looked at Robert. He was not bothered by Kevin's story about the family deaths. Robert nodded and wanted Lily to forget about what had happened with the family. Lily understood and came into the formal living room. She looked around the room and at the sofa with the red and white stripes and brown wood along the top and on the feet. She sat on it and looked at the rest of the people in the foyer.

"I want this big house. This is a very fine home." Lily smiled, but felt tears in her eyes at the same time. "Robert, are you sure you want to buy this big house? I can see outside that there are still plenty of cotton plants around here. Kevin, where are the slaves?"

"Yes, I will show you and Robert and take you to meet the slaves," Kevin said. He walked to the back door of the house. "Only two women have worked in the kitchen in the past two years. I think you might like them and will find they cooperate well with you. The other slaves work at picking the cotton outside the house."

Kevin pulled the door open and took them outside to the slave quarters, where there were about fifty black people. They were all very quiet, planning to work at picking cotton and saving whatever they could for the next new family. Kevin called out the name of one of the slaves, "Sonny." The man was inside his house with his family and heard Kevin's voice coming from outside. He told his wife to stay in the house, walked to the door and opened it. He looked at Kevin and the other people, then went outside in front of his house, closed the door, and walked to Kevin.

"Yes, master, can I do something for you?" Sonny asked Kevin in a very respectful manner.

"Yes, Sonny, I want you to meet your new master, Robert

Blackburn," Kevin said. Sonny's wife came out of the house and looked at the people standing outside. Kevin saw her on the small porch and went over close to her. "This is Betty. She works in the kitchen and serves in the house. Where's Joyce, Betty?"

Betty pointed inside the house and she called out, "Joyce!" Joyce was in the kitchen and heard her name, so she walked through the doorway to stand with Betty on the porch outside. Kevin came over and pulled her by the hand off the porch to meet the Blackburns. They waved to Joyce and she waved back to them.

"Joyce is very shy," Kevin said. "She works at the big house too. Most of the time she works on what Betty asks her to do."

Lily came and looked at Joyce. She nodded to Robert to indicate that she would accept Joyce for service in her house. Robert pointed to Betty on the porch. Lily looked at Betty, and then turned her head to look back at Robert again.

"Thank you for coming outside and meeting us," Lily said to Joyce and Betty. "My friend and I will work with you in our new house. My husband, Mr. Blackburn, is planning to buy the house today if he can."

Lily came over to Robert and told him that she wanted the sale to happen. Robert smiled and said that he would try to buy the house right away. He walked to Kevin, and they both went back inside to the office in the house. Robert followed Kevin to the room. Kevin pushed the door open and let Robert and Ron come in and look around. The room was bigger than their office in North Carolina. Kevin came to the desk and pulled out the chair.

"Robert, this chair is for you," Kevin told him. "You can sit here and we can discuss the terms for buying this big house today."

Robert was surprised that Kevin was ready to discuss the sale right away. He told Ron that the women could be looking around the house or the formal living room if they wanted to.

Ron came out to Lily and Rosemary in the hall. The women looked at Ron as he was on the way to them.

"Are they planning for us to buy this big house?" Lily asked.

"Yes, we are planning to buy it today," Ron said. "Robert told me that you and Rosemary can walk around the house or just stay in the formal living room until we come out of the office and let you know what has been decided."

He went back into the office and closed the door. Then he walked over to sit in the chair next to Glyn.

"Now we can discuss how much the house will cost," Robert said. "I have only five thousand dollars in this check that I have with me. Is that an acceptable price for this house, or more than the amount you expect? Can you tell me the exact amount?"

"Well, this house does not belong to me," Kevin said. "Mr. Jeffery Duchesne represents his daughter, who is the former owner of the property. You can talk with him when we go back to Greenville this afternoon."

"Can we meet Mr. Duchesne today?" Robert asked. "You know where he is, right?"

"I am sure that he will be staying at his house," Glyn answered.

"Then let's go back to Greenville right away," Robert said, standing up and leaving the office. "I can negotiate with Mr. Duchesne for a price for the big house and the slaves."

Lily and Rosemary were in the formal living room and heard Robert's voice in the hall. They came over and looked where he might be. Robert came to Lily.

"We are leaving here for Greenville now," Robert said. "We will meet Mr. Duchesne in his house, if he is still at home."

"Who is Mr. Duchesne?" Lily asked.

"His daughter was living here with her family," Robert answered. "We had better leave here right now so as to try to catch up with Mr. Duchesne this afternoon."

Robert rushed out of the house with Lily. They got into the

wagon and Ron and Rosemary went to their wagon. Glyn went to his horse and Kevin locked the door and went to mount his horse.

When they arrived in Greenville, Robert asked Kevin to lead him to Mr. Duchesne's house. Kevin nodded and went in front of Robert. It took about twenty minutes to get there going north from downtown. They arrived at the house where Mr. Duchesne lived. Kevin got down from his horse, came to the front door, and knocked. The door opened slowly and Mr. Duchesne came out and looked at Kevin standing there. He could also see the people sitting in their wagons and looking at his house. It was a middle-sized building built entirely of wood with black and white painted framework shielding each window.

"Who are those people here on my land?" Mr. Duchesne wondered. "Kevin, can you tell me who they are and what they are doing here?"

Kevin looked at Robert, who was waiting on the wagon for Kevin to come over and bring him to meet Mr. Duchesne. Kevin raised his hand in the air, beckoning to Robert to come over. Robert gave the reins to Lily, stepped down from the wagon and walked over to Kevin.

"This is Mr. Robert Blackburn," Kevin introduced him. "He wants to buy your daughter's big house and slaves. Would you like to talk with Mr. Blackburn today?"

Mr. Duchesne accepted Kevin's request and told Robert to come into the house saying, "welcome," but not with great enthusiasm. Robert did not feel sure that Mr. Duchesne was a friendly person. He seemed to be in a bad mood. Robert thought maybe he should refuse to come in the house. Kevin sighed and pushed Robert into the house, and Mr. Duchesne followed them. Robert walked through the foyer to the hall and stopped there.

"Kevin, will you please go outside," Mr. Duchesne ordered. "We will work this out together today."

He walked past Kevin, who nodded, turned back to the

door, and went outside alone. He closed the door, then went back and told the people there to wait to come into the house after Mr. Duchesne and Robert had finished discussing the plan to buy the house. They looked at each other and wondered why Kevin had to wait outside the door.

Robert was standing in the hall alone and was not sure where he was supposed to go. Mr. Duchesne came to Robert, who looked back at him and waited to be told what to do.

"You can go in to my office right there," Mr. Duchesne said, pointing at the doorway. "And just sit down and wait for me. I will get some things and be right back in a second."

Mr. Duchesne passed by Robert, who looked at Mr. Duchesne, and then walked into the office. He looked around the room. There were some shelves filled with books and a long basket filled with cotton balls on a side table. He went to the desk and glanced at the papers on it. In a moment he heard the sound of Mr. Duchesne's boots and knew that he was on his way back. Robert hurried over and sat down on a chair. Mr. Duchesne came back into the office with a bag that he had brought with him. He put the bag on his desk, then picked up the papers and put them away. He sat down at the desk chair and could see that Robert was staring at the bag.

Robert looked back at Mr. Duchesne and could see that his eyes seemed angry, almost demonic. Robert's heart was beginning to beat a little bit faster.

"Are you afraid of me?" Mr. Duchesne chuckled. "I don't mean to scare you to death. I just want you to tell me who you are and where you come from …"

"Well, I am not that scared," Robert said softly, "But, yes, I am a little nervous. I am fine … I am a lawyer … I have come from Raleigh, North Carolina, with my wife and my brother and his wife. All of us will be moving here."

Mr. Duchesne sat back in his chair. He was wondering why Robert had come over and asked to buy his daughter's house with the cotton plantation. Did Robert know how to run a plantation and supervise slaves? How could such work compare with his job as a lawyer? He needed to ask Robert what he expected to get out of such a risky business.

"Mr. Blackburn, can I ask you," Mr. Duchesne said, "why you want to buy a plantation? Do you know how to run the business of planting cotton and using slaves? Can you tell me, why do you want such a thing?"

"I do not want to continue as a lawyer," Robert said. "I like to learn different businesses, and a new life is what our family should have. However, I will need someone to teach me and my brother Ron how to run this kind of business. Will you please look up someone who will be able to help me? I have a check for five thousand dollars with me."

Mr. Duchesne nodded and considered what Robert was saying.

"Do you think that the check is enough for the house plus the slaves?" Robert asked. "If it is not enough, what do you suggest?"

"I think that would be a good deal with your offer as it is." Mr. Duchesne nodded. He stood up and came over to Robert. "We can help you out. There are some people who live near my daughter's house. They will be glad to teach you. The men will teach you how to run the business and their wives will teach your wife how to handle the service problems with the colored women."

He motioned for Robert to get up and they walked out of the office to the hall. Robert was confused. He had not understood clearly what Mr. Duchesne had said. He stopped walking. Mr. Duchesne heard Robert's footsteps stop. He looked back at Robert standing there. He came over talk to him.

"What are you thinking?" Mr. Duchesne was puzzled. "Maybe you feel you are not ready to be become a plantation owner? We will help you. If you did not understand or are not used to dealing with the slaves, then just ask me, Mr. Blackburn?"

"No, Mr. Duchesne," Robert said, shocked. "I was surprised that you accepted my offer and plan to help us learn how to run the business. My dream is coming true. We can move right along now. Thank you, Mr. Duchesne."

Robert shook Mr. Duchesne's hand vigorously. A woman came into the hall and stood with them. Robert saw the woman and stopped shaking hands with Mr. Duchesne. He was puzzled as to what she might want to say.

"Mr. Blackburn, this is my wife, Therese," Mr. Duchesne said. "This is Mr. Robert Blackburn; he is buying our daughter's big house. He came here from North Carolina. He is a lawyer specializing in ..."

"Criminal law," Robert said. "I worked with people who were fighting against killers. It's nice to meet you, Mrs. Duchesne."

"Yes, nice to meet you, too, Mr. Blackburn," Mrs. Duchesne responded. "Welcome to Greenwood. I hope that you will like it here. My daughter's neighbors and their wives are close friends of my daughter's. I hope that they will like and be friends with you and your wife. I am sure that both of you will like them right away."

"Yes, I'm sure my wife Lily will be glad to meet new friends," Robert smiled. "You will meet my wife outside with my brother and his wife. They are all waiting right outside your front door."

Mr. Duchesne had no intention of staying in this place much longer. He told Therese that they ought to leave right away. They left her alone for a minute, but then he changed his mind, remembering that he was supposed to take his wife to meet Robert's wife and his brother. He took Therese with him and they followed Robert to the door. Mr. Duchesne opened the door and let Robert go outside first.

The people outside heard someone walking out of the house and looked at Robert, Mr. Duchesne and his wife coming out of the house onto the front steps. Ron told Rosemary to stay there while he talked to Robert. He jumped off the wagon and went over to them.

"Is everything done for now?" Ron asked. "What did Mr. Duchesne say about our buying the house from his daughter?"

Robert nodded and turned his head to look at Mr. Duchesne, who was still standing with his wife at the front steps. He looked back at Ron.

"Yes, everything is being set down," Robert said. "They will help us learn how to run the business. I would like you to meet Mr. Duchesne and his wife, Therese."

Robert pulled Ron over to meet Mr. Duchesne.

"This is Ron and that is his wife, Rosemary," Robert said. "My wife is Lily. I will explain to them that you have a plan for them to learn how to work with the servants in the house."

Robert told the women to come there and meet the Duchesnes. The women stepped down from the wagon and walked over to the porch together.

"My wife, Lily, and my sister-in-law, Rosemary," Robert introduced them. "This is Jeffery Duchesne and his wife, Therese. They will help us out at our new house and show us things about planting cotton and using the slaves."

"Have you bought the house already?" Lily was surprised.

"Yes, I did," Robert smiled. "May I have a key for the house today? And I also need to know when we can start to work with you and the other men to teach us how to run the business?"

Mr. Duchesne looked at Kevin and told him to give the key to Robert. Kevin tossed the key to Robert, who caught it and looked at it.

"I am glad that you are buying the house." Kevin smiled. "My wife Joan and I will come over to your place and begin to teach you how to run the business."

Kevin shook hands with Robert and Lily, and then with Ron and Rosemary. Mr. Duchesne came over to Robert and shook his hand.

"Thank you for buying my daughter's house," he said. "We will bring some food for your first dinner tonight, and Kevin and

Glyn will ask their wives to bring some food over, too. See you later."

Mr. Duchesne went back inside with Therese.

Glyn went back to his horse. "I will help you learn how to use the gin for making bales out of the picked cotton," he said. "You can come into the cotton house next to the barn to see what it looks like."

"Thanks, Glyn," Robert said. "I will look into the cotton house when we get there."

Glyn nodded and waved to Robert and the other people up in the wagon again. They waved back. He left to return to his home. Robert jumped up and sat on the driver's seat of his wagon.

"Now we can go to our new home!" Lily said excitedly.

"Yes, we are on the way home." Robert smiled and looked at Ron and Rosemary in the other wagon. "We are going home now."

"Yes, Robert," Ron said. "We can't wait to get there. Let's go right now!"

Robert laughed and started to move his wagon out on the road to leave Mr. Duchesne's place behind.

On the dirt road, Robert looked up at the clear blue sky and wondered how he had been so lucky that he could buy the big house so easily. His dream was coming true. They wanted a new life and now they would have one in their new home.

Robert and Ron brought some things out of the wagon and carried them into the house. They had some furniture from North Carolina, but they soon found that they would not need to use it since the house had a complete set of furniture in all of the rooms. They decided to give some of the old furniture to the slaves if any space could be found for it.

Lily and Rosemary went to the kitchen and also looked at another service room. Robert told Ron to come with him to see the cotton house. They went into the cotton house and saw a big wood factory machine called a "gin." Ron walked around the room and looked out through the window. He saw an unfamiliar wagon parked beside the big house. He told Robert that someone had come to visit them already. He was puzzled and wanted to find out who was there.

They went out of the cotton house to the big house and found out that the visitors were Kevin and his wife, Joan. They were talking with Lily and Rosemary outside on the porch. Lily waved and showed Robert a basket of vegetables that Kevin's wife had brought.

Chapter 2

The rooster was walking though the chicken yard, a good distance away from the chicken house. He went to stand on a pole along the fence and began to call for the morning. Robert and Lily had been sleeping in their bed when they were awakened by the rooster's voice coming in loudly from outside. They wondered where all the noise was coming from. They tried to go back to sleep, but Ron came into Robert's bedroom and woke them up again.

Robert looked at Ron, who was pointing at the window. It was already broad daylight. Robert wondered what he wanted. Maybe he really just wanted to know what kind of bird made that much noise.

"Robert, do you know what that rooster is yelling about?" Ron asked. "That is for us to wake up to go to work. Now we aren't lawyers anymore."

Robert had not realized that the sounds had been coming from the rooster. He told Lily to get up before people from the neighborhood came over to the house. Lily agreed with what Ron was saying and got out of bed. Ron had left their bedroom and gone back to his own room. Robert wanted to sleep some more, but Lily told him he must get out of bed. Robert blinked his eyes a few more times to wake himself up and then tried to stand up slowly. He was not used to geting up so early to work on the plantation.

Lily went to her dressing room and closed the door. She poured water from the pitcher into the bowl and washed her face, then put on her clothes. She came out of the dressing room to the bedroom and saw Robert standing and looking through the window to the outside. He had not changed his clothes to meet the people from next door. Lily was upset at him for being so late.

"Robert, don't you know that the people from next door are coming to our place so that they can teach us how to run the business?" Lily asked. "I think it would be best for you to go and shave your face and put clothes on. They will be here any minute now."

Robert nodded and began to shave. Then he splashed on some water to take the cream off his face and dried himself with a towel. He put on his clothes and boots, then left his dressing room for the dining room.

Lily went to Rosemary's bedroom and knocked on the door. Rosemary heard her at the door and came over to open it.

"Good morning, Rosemary," Lily said. "Are you ready to come down with me to cook breakfast?"

"Yes, I'm ready. I'll come with you right away." Rosemary smiled.

Lily and Rosemary went downstairs to the kitchen. They were not used to this room. It was a very big kitchen compared to the one in their old apartment. That one had been very small. In this house, there were several cabinets made of pine wood on the walls. The fireplace had two different places for cooking that could be used at the same time. The smaller-sized cooking area was a kind of oven, which could be used for baking bread or to hold pots or bowls of vegetables and meats to keep warm. There was also a much larger metal grill for large pots and for meat to be heated directly above the flames.

There were big ice boxes on the outside porch for storing food. The doors were heavy and latched to keep out animals or any colored people who might try to get at them.

"Rosemary, can you find some plates and glasses for the dining room?" Lily asked. "I am going to look for a pan to cook the eggs and some saucers to put them in."

"Yes, I was planning to look for them!" Rosemary laughed. "Are you reading my mind?"

"I didn't know that you were planning to get them." Lily pretended to be surprised. "Maybe you are right that I can read your mind."

They were laughing while they looked inside the cabinets for the breakfast things. Rosemary was trying to decide which one of the cabinets would have the plates and glasses. She guessed the right one, opened it, and found a full set of white plates inside.

"Lily! I found the plates. This is the right cabinet!" Rosemary said.

Lily was in the storage room and heard Rosemary's voice. She came over to see what she had found.

"Oh, that's great!" Lily was pleased, taking one plate off the top of the pile. "It looks nice and not so old, but maybe these are still dirty. I don't know how long it has been since they were used. I think that we should wash everything before putting them on the table in the dining room."

"Yes, I think so, too," Rosemary agreed.

They collected some plates and put them into the steel sink near the window. Lily could not find a bucket to fill with water.

"I don't know where the bucket is. Do you know where they kept it?" Lily asked Rosemary.

"Excuse me, we just moved in here yesterday afternoon. Don't you remember that?" Rosemary puzzled.

"Oh, that's right, I didn't think about that." Lily had forgotten. "I am sorry. I was still thinking we were using the kitchen of our old apartment."

Rosemary nodded and laughed, then went outside to the porch and looked for the bucket. It should be somewhere near the door or the window. At that moment, she heard a sound and caught sight of a colored woman who was standing beside the fence. Rosemary knew that she had been working with the former master's wife in the house. She went over to the woman.

"I am sorry, but I forget what your name is?" Rosemary said.

"I am Betty, and what should I be calling you, ma'am?" Betty answered.

"Rosemary, that will be all right with me," Rosemary answered. "Betty, do you know where the bucket is? I need some water to wash the dirty dishes. I need some to serve breakfast this morning. Can you help me find a few things today, please?"

"Yes, I know where the bucket is," Betty said. "The bucket was in the closet when the family was here. I can show you where the well is, too."

"Yes, please do that. Thank you very much, Betty!" Rosemary smiled.

This was the first time Betty had ever met a woman who spoke so kindly to her since she had been working as a servant with that family. They walked back to the porch and she showed Rosemary the buckets that were hanging on hooks on the wall in the storage area.

"Do you need two buckets?" Betty asked.

"Well, it doesn't matter to me," Rosemary said softly. "Maybe it would be better for me to take two buckets in case we need more water."

Betty took the two buckets and they walked together to the well. There was one for the slaves and another one for the master. Betty showed Rosemary the well that was near the small barn where the horses were kept. Betty pulled a rope with a bucket out of the well and poured the water into one of the buckets they had brought with them. She then did it again, filling the second bucket.

Rosemary had planned to carry one of the buckets, but Betty told her that she would not need her help. Betty carried the two buckets full of water to the house quite easily. Rosemary was not used to having a servant. They went back to the house and came into the kitchen. Betty put the buckets on the table near the sink. Lily saw Betty in the kitchen for the first time.

"Rosemary, why did you go over to her house for help?" Lily asked.

"I did not ask for help," Rosemary explained. "Betty stopped by our house and asked me if we needed help with anything. I asked her where the bucket was. We went to the well near the barn and then we brought the water over."

Lily didn't say anything about what Rosemary had said. She looked at Betty.

"Betty, do you know where the pans are?" Lily asked. "I can't find them around the kitchen. Please, you can find some for me?"

"Yes, I know where the pans are. They are back here in the storage," Betty said, pointing back to the storage pantry. "But I just wrap the pans with cloths to keep the iron from rusting. Nobody used them for a long time since the family done gone."

Betty brought a few pans to the kitchen. Lily and Rosemary helped Betty unwrap the cloths off the pans. Rosemary took the bucket and poured the water into the metal sink to wash the pans and dishes.

"Rosemary, you didn't have to wash those for me," Betty protested. "I will wash every one of them for both of you."

"Oh well, I have the habit of doing what I did when we lived in a small apartment in North Carolina," Rosemary said. "OK, Betty, I will try my best to stop helping you out with things around the house."

Betty laughed at Rosemary talking about her bad habits from her earlier life. Lily was puzzled at how Betty was behaving, but after that she began to laugh, too. Rosemary walked over to a chair, pulled it out, and then sat down and let Betty do the serving for her.

Lily was still laughing. She came over to Rosemary and sat at the table. Rosemary looked at her and felt that it was not the right place for Lily to sit. Rosemary decided to push Lily off the table. Lily was shocked at what Rosemary was doing to her.

"How dare you try to push me off the table!" Lily was surprised.

"You know better than that. The table is not a chair!" Rosemary answered. She pointed to a chair right beside her. "You are supposed to sit on the chair."

"OK, I will sit on the chair," Lily said. She pulled it out and sat on it. "Now, Betty, you can start cooking the breakfast for us."

Betty was beginning to laugh at them because they were acting like little girls. She put the pan on the counter and went to the storage cabinets where the food was kept.

Robert was still thinking about his new life as a master. He came out of his bedroom and walked to Ron's door. It was open. He was wondering if Ron was in his bedroom.

"Ron, where are you now?" Robert said. "I am ready to go downstairs."

Ron had been in the dressing room when he heard Robert's voice. He came out of the room and saw Robert at the door looking around for him.

"Yes, Robert, I was over here in the dressing room," Ron said. "I am coming down with you now."

Ron came over to Robert and they went downstairs together. They could smell the breakfast in the kitchen from the foyer. The scent really made them hungry.

"I know that our wives are cooking breakfast for us," Robert said with a smile. "That smell is giving us an appetite."

They came into the kitchen and saw the food on the table. There were eggs, bacon, sausages and toast. Robert picked up a piece of bacon and ate it.

"That's a lot of food for our first breakfast!" Robert said. He saw Betty standing by the fireplace with a pan. "What is that woman doing in our kitchen?"

"Robert, you need to know that she is our servant for the housework," Lily said seriously.

"How do you even dare to come into this kitchen?" Rosemary joked.

"Rosemary, you do know why they are coming into the kitchen, don't you?" Lily asked. "They are men and they are very hungry. Please, will you go into the dining room and sit down and wait for us to finish cooking. Then we will bring the food in."

Robert and Ron followed Lily's orders and left the kitchen for the dining room. They sat on their chairs and waited for somebody to bring some food for breakfast.

"It will be good for them to learn how to be patient with us," Rosemary laughed. "You did the right thing in ordering them to get out of here."

Rosemary came over to Betty and asked her where the knives and forks were. Betty pointed to a wooden box in the second drawer of a chest. Rosemary pulled out the drawer and picked up the wooden box.

"Rosemary, I will set up everything on the table for you," Betty said.

"Oh, I am sorry about that," Rosemary said, putting the box on the table. "Of course, I can wait for you to set things up for us."

"OK, I will get it for you right away," Betty said. She came over the table and took the wooden box with her as she left the kitchen for the dining room. She put it on the table and told the men what it was for.

"I will be right back," Betty said.

She went back to the kitchen and took a large wooden tray out of the top shelf of one of the cabinets and put it on the kitchen table. Then she placed several plates filled with eggs, sausages, bacon and toast on the tray. Lily brought two pitchers, one with water and one with milk. Rosemary brought the plates. Lily came back into the kitchen again and brought some glasses for everybody. Ron poured from the pitcher to fill each of the glasses. Robert was planning to put some food on each plate, but Betty didn't want him to do that. She said she would put the food on the plates for them. Robert didn't say anything to Betty and sat back in his chair. Lily and Rosemary were sitting in their chairs and waiting for Betty to set things up for them.

"Here's the breakfast. Now it's ready for you to eat," Betty said in a friendly way.

She took the tray with her back into the kitchen. Robert guessed that was she was finished serving.

"This is our first breakfast in our new house," Robert said. "Now we can eat this good food."

They were eating and talking about some of the plans for the day. At that moment, they heard some noises outside in front of the house. People were talking and laughing outside on the dirt road. Ron told the others that he would go and check whether somebody was on their property. He walked fast and opened the front door to look out. He saw people coming. They were on the way to the house. Ron couldn't see their faces because they were too far away from him. When they came closer he could see that it was Kevin and Glyn along with their wives. The women were bringing baskets. He was wondering what they might hold. He remembered that the neighbors had been planning to teach them how to work the plantation.

Ron came back into the house and walked into the dining room. "Kevin and Glyn and their wives are coming," he said. "I remember that they are planning to work with us today. But I did not know that the women were bringing baskets of something."

"Do you think they are bringing more food for us?" Rosemary asked.

"No, I have no idea what they have," Ron answered.

There was a knock at the front door.

"I will go to the door," Ron said. He left the dining room.

"I think we ought to take all the dishes and bring them to the kitchen before they come into the house," Robert said.

"No, you don't need to clear the table," Lily said. "I will

call Betty to come in and pick up the dishes and glasses for us."

Lily pushed the kitchen door opened and called to Betty. Betty came into the dining room with her tray to collect everything, but Rosemary did help her by putting the glasses on the tray. Lily also began to get some of the dishes and took some into the kitchen. Betty was starting to laugh about Lily and Rosemary trying to help her. Robert was puzzled about what was wrong with them and followed them to the kitchen.

Ron went to the front door and opened it.

"Good morning, everyone." Ron smiled. "Won't all of you please come in?"

"Good morning, Ron, how are you today?" Kevin greeted him. "Anna and Joan, may I present our new neighbor. Anna is Glyn's wife, Ron."

"I am happy to meet you, Mr. Blackburn," Anna said. "Kevin has told me that you and your brother bought this house yesterday. We are all pleased that you have decided to become the master here."

"Yes, thank you, madam, my brother Robert and I are now joint owners of the property."

"Please come in and sit in the living room," Ron said. "We will all be joining you in a few minutes."

"Yes, we will be glad to," Joan smiled.

"Welcome to Greenwoods," Anna added. "We are very pleased to be able to be of help to your family. We can show you how to run your business in the same way we do."

The women sat on a very long sofa against one wall. A large painting decorated the wall behind the sofa.

"Robert, where are you now?" Ron was calling his brother.

"I am in the kitchen with these three women," Robert said.

Ron thought it would be better for him to come into the kitchen. He saw that they were all helping Betty put the dirty dishes and glasses in a large metal pan.

"Where are the visitors now?" Rosemary asked.

"They are in the living room waiting for us," Ron answered.

"All of you better go to the living room right away," Betty suggested. "You are not supposed to help me while I am cleaning in the morning."

They all left the kitchen and walked straight to the hall. Rosemary and Lily stopped by the mirror to check their faces and hair, then they went into the living room. Kevin and Glyn stood up as they entered.

"Good morning, ladies, this is Glyn's wife, Anna, and I think you have already met Joan," Kevin said to them. "They will teach you the things you may need to know about running the house."

"Nice to meet you, Anna," Lily greeted her. "This is Rosemary, my sister-in-law. Robert and Ron will be here in a minute. Oh, yes, here they come."

Lily and sat down on a love seat beside Rosemary.

"Good morning, Robert, this is Anna, Glyn's wife," Kevin said, turning to Anna. "This is Robert Blackburn. He is the man that I met at the restaurant yesterday afternoon before he bought this house."

"Yes, my husband told me about it," Anna said. "Congratulations, Robert, on your purchasing this house and on your plans to go to work in the cotton business."

"Thank you very much for your kind words," Robert said. "So, Kevin, please tell me what we are doing today?"

"Yes, Robert, I am planning to talk to all of you first," Kevin explained as he sat on a chair near the fireplace. "Many planters have a thousand acres for growing cotton. They sell cotton to Britain, to North America, and to several other places which are interested in buying cotton."

"Everyone wants to buy cotton, no matter how far they have to go to get it?" Ron was surprised. "I would like to have more information about other places that might want to buy what we grow."

"Yes, Ron, people buy cotton for making clothing, sail cloth, and many other things," Kevin explained. "We harvest the cotton and send it on to New Orleans."

"How long does if take before the cotton grows?" Robert asked.

"It takes about six months from planting to harvest," Kevin answered. "You will see the cotton planted in your back yard completely ready twice a year. But there are still plenty of ways to grow more cotton and earn even more profit. You are on the right path to find wealth. What you need is more land than what you have now."

"I see. I would like it if you could begin to teach us how to run the business today," Robert said hopefully.

"Yes, Glyn and I will explain things," Kevin said, indicating the women sitting on the long sofa. "Joan and Anna will teach Lily and Rosemary about how to run the housework. They brought two baskets with lunch for all of us for later."

"That sounds very good to me." Robert smiled. "We are ready to learn whatever you want to teach us."

"All right," Kevin said as he stood up. "Joan and Anne, please go ahead with your part of the work."

"All right," Joan said. "Lily and Rosemary, the first place we should start is in the kitchen, and then I will show you something else."

Kevin, Robert and Ron went over to the office between the living room and the door. Glyn came over to the desk and pulled the chair back.

"That seat is for the master," Kevin said. "Either you or Ron can sit and work at the desk when you need to."

"Kevin, can you tell me what I am supposed to do when I'm working?" Robert asked.

"You are the manager of the cotton planting," Kevin explained. "You need to know about the money and the slaves."

"I think it will be difficult for us to order slaves around," Ron admitted.

"No, there won't be any difficulty with the slaves," Kevin answered. "They know they are supposed to cooperate with the master. If they don't do what you ask, of course, the master must give them a punishment. You need to do that."

"How are we supposed to punish the slaves?" Robert wondered.

"That depends on what the slaves are doing. If they don't cooperate with your orders, or if they try to leave the plantation at all without permission, then you will have to get tough," Kevin said. "But you will find that most of the plantation's slaves will not be any problem. They are usually willing to work hard. This place is their home, too, and they want to keep on living here."

Robert and Ron understood what Kevin was saying. They went outside to the fields, where rows of cotton had been planted. There were colored people working at picking the cotton by hand. Ron noticed that each of the slaves had a long cloth bag.

"Kevin, what they are carrying in those bags?" Ron asked.

"That is a cotton sack," Kevin answered. "I will show both of you what happens after they have filled the sack with the cotton they have picked. To the gin office."

Robert and Ron followed Kevin and Glyn to the small building, a shack about sixteen feet square. Robert thought it seemed too small for the colored people to come in and drop the bags of cotton balls off.

"Kevin, I don't understand what that is for." Robert felt confused. He pointed at the gin office.

Kevin nodded and took Robert into the gin office. He showed him a weight that was hanging from a bar with a cotton sack hanging from the other end.

"This is a 'poise' scale. We call it 'pea' for short," Kevin explained. "The pea will tell you by weight how much cotton each bag holds, and you can get the total for the day."

"After they finish with the weighing, what comes next?" Ron asked.

"I am planning to show you that next." Kevin smiled, walked out of the gin office and pointed across the field. "That is the factory building. I will show you how it looks inside and how it works to compress the cotton from the sacks into bales. That's where we hold the cotton until we send it somewhere else in this country or to other countries."

They went into the factory and Kevin showed Robert and Ron what a bale of cotton looks like. It was about five feet tall and three feet wide, with a brown cloth wrapped around it to cover the cotton so that it would not fall away. Each bale had three metal bands to hold it together for shipping.

Meanwhile, Joan and Anna were teaching Lily and Rosemary how to prepare things so that the slaves could do their jobs for the inside of the house. They started in the kitchen by showing Lily and Rosemary where the things were that the servants would need. Betty and Joyce came into the kitchen and watched and listened to Joan and Anna talking with Lily and Rosemary. Joan noticed them beside the door.

"This is Betty and Joyce. They are your servants," Joan introduced them. "Either of you can order them to do whatever you need them to do for you in the house."

Rosemary raised her hand to ask a question.

"Yes, Rosemary, do you want to ask me something?" Joan wanted to know.

"Yes, I would like to ask you some questions," Rosemary said. "Are the servants supposed to take our dirty clothes and bed sheets out to wash and dry?"

Betty nodded and said, "Yes, ma'am, we will do all the laundry for you."

"What did Betty say?" Joan asked Rosemary. "I missed that whole thing between you and Betty."

"Betty said yes, she does expect to wash our clothes and bed sheets for us," Rosemary said.

"I see," Joan said. She looked at Betty. "Betty, you got ahead of me and answered Mistress Blackburn's question before I could."

Betty started to smile slowly and looked at the floor. Joan

laughed kindly and stopped for a minute.

"They will do quite a good job for your family," Joan said. "I am sure that they will always do things however you want them done. Now, I would like to show you around, but I suppose you may be a little bit familiar with the house already since you moved in yesterday afternoon."

"No, we haven't walked around the house much yet," Lily replied. "We are used to living in a small apartment. I am not used to being in a house this big. I suppose I will get used to it in time."

Anna nodded and went out of the kitchen with them. The two colored women did not know if they should come too. Joan went back into the kitchen and told them to come along. The colored women went with them around the house to tell what they knew about where things were supposed to be.

A little colored girl was on the front porch of her house looking up toward the sun in the middle of the sky. She knew by the sun that the time was noon. She came into the factory where the men were still talking. She came over to Kevin and waited for him to finish what he was saying. Robert and Ron noticed that the little colored girl was standing there beside Kevin. Kevin was puzzled about what they were looking at. He hadn't noticed she was there.

"This is Betty's daughter, Renee," Kevin said, picking her up. "She is almost four years old. Do you know why she comes into the factory? That is to tell us it's our lunch time. We can go back over to your house now."

Kevin was still carrying Renee as they walked out of the factory building. Robert and Ron were wondering why he was still holding the little girl. Glyn had expected to go out with Kevin, but he noticed that Robert and Ron were not moving at all. He felt that they seemed uncomfortable about what was happening.

"Are you uncomfortable with Kevin holding the little colored girl?" Glyn wondered. "She has short legs and can't walk so far from her house to the other house where her mother works."

"No, we aren't bothered about the girl," Robert said. "I was just wondering how she knows about the plans for lunch?"

"I think that she is part Indian," Glyn guessed. "Either her father or her mother is part Indian, or they know that the sun can tell what time it is. That's what I think. Let's go now. I am getting hungry!"

Robert and Ron were laughing as they went outside with Glyn. They arrived at the house and came into the kitchen with Kevin. Joan saw Kevin was coming in the back door with Renee. When Renee saw her mother, she was in the process of getting the lunch ready to serve.

"Mama, Mama!" Renee squealed.

Betty was scared and looked at Renee, who was still on Kevin's shoulder. He put Renee down and let her go. She ran and hugged her mother. Joan did not like that Kevin had brought Renee into the house. She felt that it wasn't mannerly.

"Kevin, you should not have picked up that little colored girl and brought her in here," Joan said seriously. "Her mother needs to work now. She should wait until she finishes this job and then go back to the quarters and feed her daughter there, not here."

Kevin did not say anything about Joan's complaint about Renee. He told the men to go with him into the dining room.

Betty was holding Renee protectively. She was not sure if Kevin was possibly going to do something to hurt her daughter. Joan sighed and came over to talk to Betty.

"He isn't supposed to do that," Joan said kindly. "But it is late and we will let Renee stay here for a while. When you finish serving up this meal for us, then you can eat with Renee outside on the back porch."

Betty nodded and told Renee to sit on a chair and wait for her to finish her job, and then she would take her to eat on the porch. Renee went and climbed up on the chair. Joan looked back at the women standing beside her.

"Now, we should all go to the dining room and sit down," Joan said. "Let the servants bring in the food to the dining room when they are ready."

The women pulled the chairs out and sat down. The servants brought in a tray with several bowls full of corn, beans, carrots and roast ham. They put the tray on the table and then served the food in portions. After that, they went back into the kitchen. Everybody was very ready to eat by that time.

A half hour or so later, when they had finished eating, they went to the living room and had some hot tea to drink. They were talking about their new lifestyle. The newcomers felt as if they should be wearing a fine fashion, dressed the way people do in Europe. Lily and Rosemary asked Joan what they were supposed to teach their future children. Joan told them that they must teach their children to practice strict manners and be as perfect in them as if they were living in Europe.

Kevin told the men it was time to leave the living room. They walked out through the hall and to the back of the house again. He saw Renee outside with her mother, Betty. She was telling Renee to go back home. Kevin told the men to come with him, and they followed Renee. They went over to the slaves' home area, which Ron and Robert soon learned was called "the quarters." Renee heard Kevin's footsteps, so she knew he was there and looked back at him. She ran to Kevin.

"Please carry me to my house," Renee begged.

"Yes, Renee." Kevin smiled.

He laughed and picked her up. They walked through the cotton fields to the small houses with a wood fence all around them. Kevin put Renee on the ground and she ran back into her house alone. Robert could see the chimney, so he knew that there had to be a fireplace. That meant it must be possible for Renee's family to cook and keep the house warm inside.

Chapter 3

After five years had gone by, the Blackburn's had children of their own, all of them between two and four years old. They played in the fields and collected bits of cotton from the ground that sometimes fell away from the plants. They put cotton in their pockets and down inside their dresses, then they ran into the gin office. The picker would carry a sack to Ron and he would put it on the pea scales, then Ron would tell him the weight of what he had picked that day.

"That's 265 pounds. You got lots of cotton today," Ron told the picker.

The white children came into the building and took cotton out of their pockets and dresses and gave it to their father. Ron laughed and put it into the picker's cotton sack to add to the weight.

"You have only a one-pound gain for today," he laughed.

The picker knew what Ron was doing and laughed.

Ron knew the guy worked very hard. He went to the field early in the morning before the other slaves came. They all picked the cotton very carefully to avoid getting their fingers hurt by the metal bandits on the bales, which were as sharp as the teeth of a garfish. Robert and Ron figured out that on average, most of the slaves could pick about a 100 to 150 pounds a day. There were only a few men who could sometimes average as much as 265 pounds a day.

Before dinner time, the pickers stopped work, brought their sacks to the gin office and waited on line to hear the weight.

Robert put the sack on the pea scale and announced the weight that the picker had brought in that day. He wrote the number down on the record. After the slaves left the gin office, they went back home for dinner with their families. Robert and Ron took cotton into the factory to compress it into bales.

Ron saw Renee leaving the back porch of the house with a basket. He knew that the basket held her baby sister. He told Robert that he wanted to see Renee's new baby and came over to talk to her.

"Can I see your new sister?" Ron asked Renee. Robert came over to them and also looked at the baby. Renee pulled the cloth open to let them see the baby. "What is her name?"

"Shana," Renee answered. "My mother wants me go home now and put Shana in the crib and let her sleep. I will wait after that for my mother to come home. She'll be here when she finishes cleaning up after your dinner."

"OK, you can go now," Ron said.

Renee did not say anything more and turned away. Robert and Ron went to their house. Renee went through the field to make a shortcut to her home from the master's house. When she got home she took Shana out of the basket and put her into the crib.

Robert and Ron came into the foyer. Robert told Ron that he wanted to go with the bookkeeper back to the office. Ron went to the dining room and ate with his family there. Robert went to the office, showed the bookkeeper to his desk, then went to the dining room with his family. When he got there, his two sons, who were three and two years old, were excited to see him. They came over to their daddy and hugged him. Lily had been sitting next to her sons and tried to call them back.

"John and Tom, please will you come back and sit down," Lily said. "It's time for dinner now."

The boys went back to their chairs and took napkins to cover their laps to prevent food from spilling on them. Ron's oldest daughter, Margaret, was four years old and had a one-

and-a-half-year-old brother, Gerry. The cousins were all very close in age. Both families ate dinner at the one large table. Betty gave each of the children a bowl of peach pie with warm milk in it. That would help to make the children sleepy and ready for bed time.

Lily and Rosemary took their children upstairs and changed their clothes for sleeping. Then they went to the living room and sat on the sofa and read books. Robert and Ron went back into the office and talked more about the business. Sometimes they had a hard time putting work down, the family and business affairs being so mixed.

"You and I sometimes have problems with the business being right here in the house," Ron tried to explain to Robert. "Sometimes I think about living on my own with my family. It is hard to have just one place for business and both families."

"Why didn't you say something about that problem before?" Robert wondered. "I did not realize that we were having any kind of problems with our business."

Ron did not like Robert's attitude. He seemed to be talking down to him for no reason. He had tried to get right to the point, but Robert did not seem to understand what Ron was trying to tell him.

"I think that you did not understand my idea," Ron sighed. "We each need more space. A single family should not have to live with any other family."

At that moment, what Ron was saying hit Robert very hard. He did not like what Ron was telling him, that he needed to be on his own. Robert did not want to tell him to move out of the house. He was sure his brother would fight back if he could.

"Excuse me, how do you dare tell me this?" Robert was shocked. "Do you expect me to move out of this house with my family? You will take all of this as your own business? Would you try to kick your own brother out of this house?"

"Well, I did not say that you are supposed to move out of this house." Ron was almost almost speechless.

Robert was becoming more and more angry. He stood up from his chair.

"What is wrong with you?" Ron tried to be a little nicer to him. "I did not want anything like this to happen."

"I want you to come outside and fight," Robert said, really angry now. "Whoever wins this fight will take over the house."

"Yes, as you wish, if what you want do is fight." Ron nodded, went to the door and opened it.

Ron walked out of the office. Robert followed him into the kitchen. Betty was putting a tray with two cups of hot tea on the table and looked over her shoulder at Ron. He went to the door and slammed it open. Robert followed him outside. Betty had a hard time believing it, but she could see that they were getting ready to fight. She thought that she should inform Lily and Rosemary that the men were rushing outside with their fists clenched.

She hurried upstairs; Lily and Rosemary were in their own bedrooms. Betty thought that she preferred to inform Rosemary because she liked her more. Betty entered Rosemary's bedroom and closed the door. Rosemary was on her bed reading a book. She looked at Betty, who stood against the door by herself.

"Betty, what do you want to tell me? Is there something wrong?" Rosemary was concerned.

Betty was having a hard time telling her that the brothers were in danger.

"Robert and Ron done gone outside and they are going to fight," Betty said, pointing outside.

"OK, I will go over to Lily's bedroom," Rosemary said as she got off her bed.

Betty went back downstairs. Rosemary went to Lily's bedroom and informed her that their husbands were in a fight outside.

They rushed through the kitchen and opened the back door. They could see the men outside over near the barn where the horses were kept. Lily saw Robert and Ron, both with their hands up in fists, facing each other. She could see that they were planning to fight.

Ron began to hit Robert's face, looking as if he was trying for a knockout. Rosemary felt shocked to see that Robert was actually hitting her husband right in the mouth.

"Oh no! You had better be careful or you will get hurt!" Rosemary called to Ron.

"Robert! You better not fight your brother," Lily shouted, but he was not listening to her. He continued fighting with Ron. "Don't fight! I think both of you better stop that right away!"

Lily stepped down off the porch and tried to stop the fight by coming between them, but Robert pushed at her and she fell down. Rosemary was shocked and ran to help Lily. The slaves were standing around watching the two men and wondering why they were fighting. What reason could they possibly have?

Betty was on the porch and was very upset. She did not understand why they were fighting. Was it about the business? At that moment, a drop hit her cheek. She looked up at the sky, but she could not see anything in the dim light of early evening. She felt another drop on her other cheek and knew that rain would be coming soon.

The sky turned darker and louder. People looked up and could see that it had started to rain. They were spread out on the porch and in the barn. They could see outside that the men were keeping on with the fight. Betty ran out and brought Lily and Rosemary back with her to the porch. The rain became heavier and the men kept on fighting. Lily and Rosemary were hugging each other and crying. Betty tried to calm the women down, but they were feeling terrible about what their husbands were doing.

Robert hit at Ron's nose once more and he fell down in the mud. Robert stayed standing and watched Ron, who was not getting up. Lily and Rosemary were frightened, wondering what was wrong with Ron. The slaves looked at each other and didn't dare to say anything. Finally, Ron came slowly to his feet. Robert was preparing to fight with him again, but Ron was not going to fight anymore.

"I don't want to fight with you again," Ron said, giving up. "Now you can have the whole thing here. I will move out with my wife and children."

Leaving Robert standing there alone, Ron came over to his Rosemary on the porch, and they both went into the house. Robert hadn't finished fighting with Ron, he thought. He was surprised that Ron had given up and called him the winner of the house and the cotton plantation. The slaves were quietly looking at each other. They went back to their houses as the rain became lighter.

Lily was upset with Robert for beginning the fight with his brother. She went over to Robert and tried to tell him she was sorry for what had happened between him and his brother. Betty was still standing on the porch and thought that she had better come back into the house and leave them alone outside. She went inside, emptied the tea pot and washed it.

"What were you doing with your brother?" Lily asked seriously. "I don't understand why this happened?"

"I really don't remember what caused it," Robert sighed.

Lily didn't want to hear that sadness in his voice, so she went into the house. Robert tried to tell her something more, but she left him out there alone.

In their bedroom, Ron and Rosemary were feeling very frustrated and worried about their future. They would have to find a place to live with a separate cotton field. They would have to move out the next day.

Ron was in the dressing room. He sat there covered with mud. Rosemary came into the room and stared at him with a sad face.

"What's wrong between you and your brother?" Rosemary was beginning to sob. "Why have you become enemies!"

Ron heard Rosemary's voice and realized she was right

to say that he and his brother had become enemies after what had happened.

"I guess you are right. We really are enemies now." Ron nodded. "So we have to move out tomorrow by noon. We'll just pack some things to take with us and then ride in the wagon to go south again. I guess maybe we could live in Louisiana, if I can find a good place with plenty of cotton planting going on."

Rosemary had a hard time leaving her sister-in-law because she had been very close with her since they were married. They had lived together in the apartment and then in this house for a very long time. She went over to Ron and tried to tell him that, but Ron wanted to get out of there, so she had to agree.

"Do you want us to leave here for Louisiana?" Rosemary asked. "I guess it would be better for us to go. We'll just have to forget about the past."

She left the dressing room, then came right back to tell Ron that she would go get a bucket of warm water for him to wash the mud off his face and hair.

Ron did not say anything more to his wife. He looked at an oval mirror on the wall. He could see he looked very bad. He felt anger against his brother for taking this place away from his family.

Chapter 4

The next morning, the slaves went to the field with their sacks and started to pick cotton. They were wondering why the masters were doing such wrong things the night before, but they did not say anything, not even to each other. They were waiting to hear what would happen next.

Ron had a bad dream during the night. He awakened and tried to forget the past. He got up from his bed and walked over to the window. He knew that he was supposed to leave the house right away. He looked back at Rosemary. She was still in bed asleep.

Ron went over to Rosemary and tried to wake her up. Rosemary began to wake up slowly, then looked at Ron. He had a bruise on his left cheek that had swollen a lot since the night before. She tried to touch Ron's cheek, but it hurt him badly.

"Ron, your face looks awful. I will go get some ice for you," Rosemary said sadly.

"You don't have to get ice for me," Ron said.

"Are you sure?" Rosemary was concerned. "I think that your cheek won't swell as fast with ice. If we don't use it, the healing will take longer, maybe a week."

"I don't care about that, Rosemary," Ron said. "I want you to pack something so we can start to move out right away."

Rosemary nodded and stood up. She went to her dressing room and looked in the mirror. In her mind, she knew that time was passing and there would be more risk for their family if they didn't move out of Robert's house, but the main thing she was thinking about was how much she would miss Lily.

Ron and Rosemary began to pack their clothes in bags and in a big wooden trunk with metal bands. They managed to move their things to the wagon by themselves. A few of the slaves helped by bringing a wagon over to the front of the house.

Lily was standing at the window of her bedroom watching what was going on outside. She was sad that Ron and Rosemary were moving out. She looked back at Robert on his bed. He was still wearing his dirty clothes from the night before. He was still angry with his younger brother, Ron. He would never forget what had happened before they began to fight.

Lily sighed and came over to talk to Robert. He looked at Lily's face and knew that she already missed her sister-in-law and the happier times they had when they lived together in the small apartment in North Carolina.

"Robert, why did you start to fight your brother?" Lily cried, and she slapped at his face. "I still don't understand why you did what you did last night."

Lily ran away from the bedroom and went downstairs. Robert could not say anything in answer to Lily's question. He stood up from his bed and walked toward the window. He looked out at Ron and Rosemary, who were putting their things into the wagon with the help of the slaves.

Just as they were about to leave, Rosemary jumped off the wagon. Robert wondered what she was doing. Lily came out and ran to Rosemary and they hugged each other. Ron and the slaves looked at the women. Some of the slaves were crying, too. Robert knew that Lily did not want to see them be separated from the family.

Ron looked up at the second-floor window where Robert's bedroom was and could see him beside the curtain. Robert would have avoided it if he had known Ron could see him. Then Ron looked back at Rosemary and Lily. They were still hugging and crying.

Ron sighed and jumped from the wagon. He came over to the women and tried to talk to Rosemary, who looked at Ron with tears in her eyes. She wiped them away with a kerchief.

"Yes, Ron, do you want to tell me something?" Rosemary was almost wailing.

"I want you to choose any servants from the house that you want to take to our new home," Ron said. "I will talk with Robert and tell him that I want to choose a few pickers for our fields, too."

Rosemary nodded and left Lily alone. Ron followed her into the house.

Lily wondered if they would be able to get some colored people for their new home. She followed them in.

"You can go to the kitchen, where the servants are working," Ron said to Rosemary. "I will go upstairs and talk with Robert in his bedroom right away."

"Ron, you better not start fighting with Robert again, please …" Rosemary begged.

Ron did not say anything in response to Rosemary's concern. He looked back at Lily. She was starting to walk in the house, and they both knew that she was already feeling that she would miss them a lot.

"Lily, I am going into the kitchen to get some servants for my new home," Rosemary said. "Ron will get Robert and they will go outside and pick some slaves for the field, too."

"Which ones will you choose for your new home?" Lily asked Rosemary.

"I don't know. I will see who I want to have come," Rosemary answered.

She went into the kitchen and Ron went upstairs to Robert's bedroom. Lily found it hard to decide which one she was supposed to go with. Finally, she thought it would be better for her to go to the kitchen. She did not want Rosemary to take Betty with her, because she was a very good worker.

Lily rushed through the dining room and pushed the door open. She saw Rosemary with Betty. She knew that Rosemary certainly wanted Betty, too.

"No, Rosemary! I want Betty to stay here!" Lily shouted. "You can't take Betty! She is supposed to be my servant for my whole life!"

Lily went in and blocked Betty from Rosemary to indicate that she would not allow her to take Betty with her. She pointed to Joyce, who was standing behind Betty.

"You can take Joyce with you!" Lily was angry. "I want to keep Betty. Please, Rosemary!"

Rosemary was shocked and confused that Lily was telling her to take Joyce instead of Betty. Rosemary was upset, but she felt she really needed to take Betty away from Lily.

"Lily, I am sorry, but I do want to take Betty with me," Rosemary said. "You have Joyce to be your servant. Betty, you can go home and start packing your things right away."

Betty didn't know what the rules about this should be. She wondered if she would be allowed to take her children and her husband with her if she went with Ron and Rosemary to their new home. Would it be somewhere in this area or far away from this place?

"Can you take my daughters and husband with you for your new place?" Betty asked Rosemary.

"Yes, you can bring your daughters with you," Rosemary said. "But I am not sure if my husband will get your husband from the field."

Betty nodded and hugged Joyce.

"I will miss you and your family," Joyce said.

"Yes, I will miss you, too. I think it's better for me to go right now," Betty said.

She waved to Joyce, whose face was very sad, then pulled the door open, walked out on the porch, and ran across the field. The pickers in the field looked at Betty and wondered why she was going to her home at that time of day.

Ron went upstairs and came in to Robert's bedroom. Robert looked back at Ron as he stood near the door.

"Do you want to tell me something?" Robert asked.

"Yes, I want to get some slaves from the field for my new home," Ron said.

Robert nodded and came over to Ron. They went downstairs and outside through the back of the house. They climbed down off the porch and went to the fence, where there was a big bell at the top of a pole. Ron pulled at the bell to call in the slaves from the field.

The pickers heard the bell ringing, so they put their sacks on the ground, left the field and came over to the house. They looked at Robert and Ron, who were standing in front of the porch with sad faces. They were wondering what was wrong with the masters.

Robert had a hard time telling the slaves what he had to say. Finally, he moved back a little to the porch steps.

"Ron and I are not getting along anymore," Robert announced. "He and his family are planning to move to a new place. He is going to choose from among you who he wants to join him there."

The slaves were surprised and looked at each other. Robert walked back and let Ron step up on the steps so he could look out at the slaves in the yard.

"I want to call your names, and then you must come over here," Ron said, pointing to the place near the porch where the slaves should stand. "I want Sonny, Willy, Louis, Marvin, Bo and Andy, with their wives, to come over here."

The colored men began to walk over to the porch, and then the colored women followed their husbands. Ron went down the steps to the ground and looked at the slaves he was not choosing.

"I want the rest of you to go back to work right away," Robert said.

The slaves left the back yard and went back to the field. They picked up their sacks and put them back on their shoulders and started to work.

"I want all of you to pack your things in bags and start to leave here within the next hour," Ron told the slaves, and they left to go get ready. Then he went back to the porch and pushed the door open. "That's all the slaves I want for my new home."

Ron went into the house and closed the door. Robert was still angry inside. He wanted some of the slaves that Ron had chosen because they had been doing very good work in the fields. Now Ron would have lots of good slaves and he would not have as many.

Sonny was on the way back to his house. He came into the cabin and saw that his wife, Betty, was packing her clothes in a bag. Renee was in another room and saw her father standing beside the door and looking at her mother. She jumped off the bed and ran to Sonny. Betty looked at Renee and her father.

"Daddy, we are going with Ron, the master, today," Renee said. "Are you coming with us, too?"

Sonny was surprised that Rosemary had chosen Betty to be her servant. Betty came over to talk to Sonny and wanted to know if he would be coming with them.

"Yes, the master chose me, too," Sonny said. "We have to pack all of our things, and then we will be leaving here in an hour."

"Good! I am so happy that you are coming with us!" Betty was excited. "I am packing Renee and Shana's clothes in the bags. I haven't packed your clothes at all."

"I will pack them and we'll leave right away." Sonny smiled. He rushed to the bedroom and took his clothes out of a drawer and put them into the bag with Betty's clothes. "I can't believe that the masters were in that big fight last night. I feel sorry for them."

Betty nodded and went to get some the girls' things that they would need for the new place. After they had finished packing and taken the bags outside on the porch, they could see that there was a wagon in front of their house for all of the slaves.

Who would be leaving? Louis was on the front seat and waved to Sonny.

"We are going with Ron, the master, to this new place some-where. I don't know where," Sonny told Betty.

Louis stopped the wagon right in front of the porch.

"I want you and the girls to ride on the wagon and I will take a walk behind it on the dirt road."

Betty took her bags and walked out of the cabin. She looked at her home and felt that she would miss this house for a long time. She could see the other people on the wagon. She handed her bags to somebody, then climbed up into the wagon. Sonny helped his daughters up to be with Betty.

"You are the last ones we stopped for, so we are ready to leave right away," Louis said with a smile. He was going to ride one of the horses.

Sonny started to walk with the other men. Together, they went around to the front of the main house and waited for Ron and Rosemary to be ready to leave.

Robert was in the office. He wrote a check to Ron for his share of their partnership. Ron would have to find a new place to settle down, build a new house and begin a new cotton plan-tation. Robert gave the check to Ron, who left the office and kept on walking to the front porch.

Ron told Rosemary they would be leaving right away. Nei-ther of them said a word to Robert and Lily. Ron jumped into the first wagon and Rosemary took her children with her to a second wagon. The slaves in the third wagon followed them away from Robert's property.

They continued southward for a few days. Finally, they ar-rived at a small town in northeast Louisiana called Providence. Ron looked around for a factory that would send cotton to other cities. He saw a man picking up cotton and putting it on a wagon. They followed him to a factory, where Ron asked a man in the office for information about finding land to buy for planting cotton. The manager told him to go to City Hall and ask someone there to find land for him.

Ron went to City Hall and found an office with a list of land available for cotton planting. He saw two thousand acres of land for sale about three miles away from town, so he looked for the name of the person who was selling the property. Ron found the seller and asked him if he could look at the land.

When they arrived, Ron jumped off the wagon and looked around. There were a few acres of woods near the road and he could see about a mile from the road to a river. Ron asked his wife, Rosemary, what she thought about the land.

She said, yes, she thought it would do.

Ron bought the land, and they began to build a new house with a porch along the back. From the upper floors they would have a nice view of the river and the fields as well. They also began to build a few small houses for the slaves to live in near the fields. They planted some seeds into the ground and were able to grow cotton in six months.

Within a year, the cotton was growing plentifully in the fields. Ron was selling the cotton well, and his new business was a success. Ron and Rosemary were very happy now that they and their family had their own place to live.

Chapter 5

In 1861, the armies of the North were beginning to travel as far south as Vicksburg, Mississippi. From there they would go across the Mississippi River and down to Louisiana.

The planters decided to join the army for the Civil War. Their wives, who were familiar with the operations of the plantations, ran them for two years. They were doing what they could with substitute supplies and materials. There were many difficulties, partly because of the blockade of international trade during the war.

A year later, loyal Southerners, increasingly angry, decided to set fire to plantations still planting cotton in some areas of Mississippi and Louisiana. The Northern armies walking on the roads could see heavy black smoke over the entire area. They wondered what could be causing that, and decided to go where the fires had been started.

The soldiers went into the factories, but all they saw were a few bales, ashes and rusted metal. The federal government of the North had wanted to take over the plantations as plunder. Traders and schemers had wanted to operate them because the prices were high, making the value of cotton almost equal to that of gold. The stock market rose and many investors were trying to cash in on war profiteering.

In February 1863, the Union armies and engineers arrived at Providence. They worked to connect the Mississippi River with the Tensas River, which would allow river traffic to bypass the Confederate guns at Vicksburg.

The plantation owners knew that the Union armies were coming to their area. The Emancipation Proclamation had been issued, ordering plantation owners to a give slaves their freedom. Many plantation owners wanted to keep some colored people living near them. They were very good workers and understood the needs of their households. The owners began to pay out something in salary to keep those who were loyal and willing to stay.

Early in the spring, Adjutant General Lorenzo Thomas announced that there would be a new policy and that some of the free colored men could join the army. There was a training camp for them established south of Providence.

Chapter 6

In downtown Lake Providence people could go shopping on Lake Street. There was also a small park at the end of a road near a high hill. The road ended because it had been blocked by flooding from the Mississippi River some years before. The children played with their balls and jumped rope. The people sat on the bank at the waterway under the trees and heard the birds sing in the springtime. A boy ran over to the other boys in the park.

"I saw a pro baseball player on TV!" he said excitedly.

"Where did you see that?" another boy asked.

"The TV in the front of the store over there across the street." He pointed at the store window.

"Let's go now!" the other boy said.

All of the boys followed him and ran over to the store, leaving the park. Their mothers sat on the river bank and watched the boys leaving. One mother called out her son's name, "Where are you going?" The boy answered his mother, "We want to watch the TV at the store." The mother accepted that plan and let the boys go to watch the TV. They went across the street and ran down the sidewalk to the store.

Vic Stadden, a short, elderly man, had worked as an editor for the *Lake Providence Sentry*, a newspaper that had been published for nearly forty years. He got out of his car and saw the boys running past him to the big window where the new black and white TV stood. They were enjoying watching the baseball player on TV. Mr. Stadden sighed, knowing that the boys' parents could not afford to buy TV sets for their homes. The boys would only be able to watch TV this way. He walked next door to his office, went upstairs, and walked past his co-workers at their own desks. They kept on typing and answering calls. He came into his office, dropped his briefcase on his desk and took off his coat to hang it on the rack. His secretary came into the office.

"Good morning, Mr. Stadden," the secretary said. "How was your day?"

"Good morning, Miss Cooksey," Mr. Stadden smiled. "I am doing fine! What about you?"

"I am fine, thanks." She smiled. "I have something for you. Here's today's paper."

She gave the newspaper to Mr. Stadden, then left the office and closed the door. He picked it up and opened it to the front page. Some pages dropped on the desk. He opened the newspaper and read through it until he got to the obituaries on the last page. He noticed in bold type the full name of Mary Waters. She passed away from natural causes at her home.

He knew Mary; she had worked as a servant with Mrs. Margaret Rhodes for many years. He read through the story and found out that her granddaughter, Nancy William, had come to town from Indianapolis, Indiana. She had been taking care of her grandmother until she died.

The funeral for Mary Waters was set for early the next morning. He would like to do an interview with Nancy, but his co-workers were all white males and had not wanted to talk with colored people since the Civil War. He felt uncomfortable that no one wanted to talk with Nancy.

After a moment he thought of one of his coworkers, Billy Vangslia, who came from Minnesota. He was used to getting along with colored people. Mr. Stadden felt that Billy would be glad to do the interview with Nancy William after she buried her grandmother. He went out of his office and walked among the desks to Billy Vangslia's desk at the corner of the room.

There were two windows on each side from which it was possible to see outside. Billy looked at Mr. Stadden with his wide, blue eyes.

"Good morning, Mr. Stadden," Billy said. "Can I do something for you this morning?"

He nodded and then told Billy to come with him to his office for a moment. He had no further words to say, so Billy felt that something was wrong with his boss.

Billy stood up and walked over to his office with Mr. Stadden. The coworkers at the other desks watched them go and wondered what might be happening. Billy came into the office and sat on a chair. Mr. Stadden closed the door and came over to his own chair behind the desk.

Billy's hands started to sweat. He was afraid that his boss might be going to fire him for some reason.

Mr. Stadden put his hands on the desk and looked at Billy for a second. Then he opened his mouth.

"Mr. Vangslia, I would like to talk with you a moment," Mr. Stadden said softly. "I want to know if you would like to do an interview with Nancy William. She is a colored woman. I thought that you might be comfortable talking with her."

"I don't mind interviewing Miss William," Billy said. "I am used to talking with colored people in my hometown in Minnesota. Where does she come from?"

"She came here from Indianapolis, Indiana," Mr. Stadden answered.

"Umm, I see," Billy said. "When can I meet Miss William for the interview?"

"Tomorrow morning," he said. "You might want to wait outside the church for the colored people to finish praying for Mrs. Mary Waters. After the burial service you can go up to Miss William and ask her if she would be willing to join you for the interview. I hope that will be good."

"Where can I find the cemetery for colored people?" Billy asked.

"The cemetery is about two miles away from downtown," Mr. Stadden said. "You'll see the cemetery on the left side, but you need to make a left turn before it starts and just keep driving for a mile until you see the cemetery for colored people on the left side of the back road. You can pull out, park your car on the right, and then wait for them to bury Mrs. Mary Waters. When the ceremony's done and they all start to leave the cemetery, then you can come over to Nancy William and ask her if she can come with you."

Billy nodded and wrote down the plan to meet Miss William the next day.

"Yes, Mr. Stadden," Billy said. "I will be there tomorrow morning and hopefully I'll be able to talk with Miss William after the burial of her grandmother. I guess we could even spend the whole day together if she has enough information about her grandmother's early life."

"I hope so. It will most likely work out." Mr. Stadden smiled. "I am glad that you are willing to talk with Miss William. I'd like the feature story to run about two days from now, but you have to be careful. If either colored or white people see you and Nancy together, just walk away and find someplace comfortable you can talk with her. Mr. Vangslia, watch out for people who might get ugly seeing you do that, OK? Thanks, and you have a good evening."

Mr. Stadden shook hands with Billy, then opened his door and watched Billy walk to his desk. He was glad Billy would attempt the interview with Miss William. He was sure the story would be interesting if she would tell Billy about her grandmother's life, when she had lived and served with her mistress as a slave.

Chapter 7

The clock rang at 5 a.m. and Billy woke up. He stopped the alarm and went back to sleep for a while. He had wakened in the night and worried that Miss Nancy William's relatives would not allow her to join him for the interview this morning after her grandmother's funeral. His wife, Vicky, was still asleep. He was supposed to get up and shower, but he didn't.

Vicky turned her body to the side and looked at Billy. He looked back and she blinked her eyes.

"Billy, I thought you were in the shower," Vicky said. "Don't you feel like going to work this morning?"

Billy did not answer her question. He was afraid that if he told her the truth about the interview with a colored woman, she might be worried about what would happen if someone saw them together. They could hang him, she might think. He decided he had to tell her no matter what she might say.

"Vicky, I hope that you are going to understand," Billy muttered. "Yesterday, my boss called me in and asked me to interview Mrs. Mary Water's granddaughter from Indiana today."

Vicky did not understand what Billy was talking about. She had no way of knowing what Billy was asking of her about the woman.

"Can you tell me more clearly please," Vicky asked. "I don't understand why you don't seem to like that your boss ordered you to interview this particular woman."

Billy was silent. He did not tell Vicky that the woman he was going to interview was colored. He had a hard time admitting to her what his boss wanted him to do for the newspaper.

"OK, Vicky," Billy sighed. "I am planning to interview Miss Nancy William."

"It's fine with me, whatever your boss wants you to do for your job," Vicky said, rolling her eyes. Then she turned her body around to face the other way and go back to sleep. "You better get in the shower now. I don't want to see your boss get mad at you for not doing the interview with her. I forget what her name is. I am sorry, but I do need to get some sleep now."

Billy knew that he had not finished talking with her. He moved his head closer to Vicky's ear.

"I am doing the interview with Miss Nancy William," he said softly. "She is a colored woman."

At that moment, Vicky woke up. She was shocked to hear him say that he planned to interview a colored woman. She stood up and turned on the lamp on the night stand. She looked at Billy with a shocked face.

"Billy, are you joking with me?" Vicky felt confused. "Are you sure that your boss wants you to interview Miss … that colored woman? I am sorry, what is her name, what did you say again, please?"

"Miss Nancy William," Billy answered. "She is a student from a college somewhere in Indianapolis. I guess that it will be easier for me because she lives up north and is used to socializing with white people. Things are not the same there as here. Do you remember that we came here from Minnesota, Vicky?"

Vicky nodded. She got up off the bed, walked to the bathroom and closed the door. Billy sighed and thought that he should not have told her about the interview. He stood up and went to the door of the bathroom where Vicky was.

"Vicky, I have to tell you the truth," Billy said, standing close to the door to make sure Vicky would hear him. "This is my job. I know that there is some risk if someone sees me with a colored woman somewhere."

He heard the flushing of the toilet and then the water running. He knew that she had just been shocked for a moment.

He went back to the bed, sat on it and waited for Vicky to come out of the bathroom. In a few minutes, he heard the door open. He looked at Vicky as she came out, but she didn't look confused or shocked. She just seemed tired.

"Darling, are you all right?" Billy asked. "Are you worried about the interview?"

"That is your job," Vicky nodded. "I understand your point about the colored woman, that she comes from Indiana. But you ought to think about her relatives that live here. Maybe they won't allow Miss Nancy William to go with you for the interview. I would like to know why the boss asked you."

"Her grandmother passed away a few days ago," Billy explained. "Her name is Mrs. Mary Water, and she worked as a slave for Mrs. Margaret Rhodes for many years."

Vicky nodded again, then came and sat next to Billy on the bed. She found it hard to believe what his boss wanted him to do for his job in a southern town. It was very dangerous if other white men saw Billy out with a colored woman. They might even want to hang him.

"Billy, you better be careful," Vicky said, concerned. "If anything happens at all we might have to move out of town. We would have to leave everything here and travel to Minnesota before the KKK comes into our house and takes you out of here to hang you."

"Yes, that might be a good plan," Billy agreed. "Pack our clothes in a bag and collect any important paperwork in a box so we can take a trip to Minnesota before anybody can catch me here."

Billy kissed Vicky's cheek and went to the bathroom. He pushed some toothpaste onto his brush and brushed his teeth. He shaved and then took a hot shower. He went out of the bathroom and put on a nice suit for the interview, but his heart was still beating rapidly.

Vicky was in the kitchen putting bread in the toaster. She took a kettle from the stove, filled it with water, then put it back on the stove and turned the gas on. Then she got a cup and put some instant coffee in it. The bread came out of the toaster nicely done. She put it on a small plate and put grape jelly on the top.

Billy came into the kitchen and sat on the chair. Vicky gave him the toast. When she heard the whistle from the kettle, she turned the gas off and poured a cup of black coffee and brought it to him. He ate half a slice of the toast and drank the whole cup of coffee. He took his notepad and pen with him. He kissed and hugged Vicky, which made her tearful about this risky job he was undertaking.

"Be careful, and watch out for any other white men," Vicky said sadly. "If anything happens, run away from her, drive straight here, and we'll get out of here, OK?"

"Yes, I will do my best, especially if I need to run," Billy promised. "Please try not to feel so stressed about it, OK, Vicky? See you later."

He kissed her and went out to his car. He started the engine and drove away.

Billy's heart was still beating a little too fast as he was leaving. He took a box of cigarettes and a lighter out of his suit pocket, then took a cigarette out of the box. His hand was shaking enough that he dropped the cigarette on the seat beside him. He picked it back up and lit it.

When he saw the road on left side, he turned and kept on driving until the town views began to fade into a bare country landscape. He nervously kept on smoking as he drove along. The road was so smooth and quiet that he wondered if it was the right one for the cemetery where he was supposed to meet Miss William.

In a minute, he saw a few dusty cars parked beside the road. He slowed down, then parked his car on the other side of the road. He got out and looked at the people across the roadway, where there definitely was a funeral going on for Mrs.

Waters. The people were standing and looking at a plain pinewood coffin. He could see a colored woman with a dark green jacket and long black skirt. She was about five foot five and very thin, probably weighing less than 125 pounds. She had a silvery clip in her hair to hold it up and away from her face. She saw him across the road, then turned her head back to listen to the minister.

Billy was almost sure that this must be Nancy because her hair and clothing were in a different style than what most black women here wore. He began to smoke again and waited for the mourners to leave the cemetery. He looked for Miss William to see if she was coming out with the other people, however, he was not sure anymore which one she was.

There were several other young colored women. As Mrs. Mary Waters' relatives hugged each other and left for their cars, Billy kept an eye on the one he was fairly sure was Nancy. He waited until the last person had hugged her and the minister had finished talking with her.

Nancy finally moved away from the minister and walked with her relatives to a car. Billy checked the roadway for approaching cars, then rushed across the road. He was still a little nervous and walked fast so he could catch Nancy before she got in the car.

"Are you Miss Nancy William?" Billy asked.

Nancy stopped when she heard Billy's voice. She looked back and saw Billy, who was feeling a little timid about what Nancy's relatives might think of him. They did stare at him because he was a white man. Nancy saw them and told them to "calm down." She came over to Billy, acting in the same manner that a white person would.

"Yes, sir, that is me," Nancy said. "Who are you and what do you want to talk to me about?"

"I am Billy Vangslia," Billy said in a low voice. "I work for the press as a reporter from the hometown newspaper here."

"I am sorry, but I cannot hear you Mr. V…?"

"I am Billy Vangslia, a reporter from the newspaper," Billy said in his normal voice.

"OK, Mr. Vangslia." Nancy smiled. "What do you want, just to talk with me?"

"Yes, I would like to do an interview with you," Billy said, "if you are willing to tell me about Mrs. Mary Waters, your grandmother, right? She worked for Mrs. Margaret Rhodes here for many years. I would like to know if she told you any stories about her life when she was raised in the big house."

"Yes, my grandmother told me everything she remembered about that before she passed away from this life."

Nancy's relatives and friends felt uncomfortable with Billy because he was white and was asking Nancy for an interview about her grandmother's life. Mrs. Dorothy Datson was Mrs. Mary Waters' friend from the years in service at Mrs. Margaret Rhodes' house. She was a small-sized woman who had taken very good care of Nancy for whole summers at a time when she was a little girl. Mary's daughter and her family visited in this city every year. Dorothy told Nancy to go and talk with Billy.

Nancy listened and went with Billy. They walked across the road to Billy's car. He opened the door for Nancy. One of Nancy's cousins kept an eye on Billy, watching as they got in the car and drove away.

"Dorothy, why did you let Nancy go away in a car with a white man?" Nancy's cousin asked.

Dorothy looked at him and raised her hand to get him to calm down.

"You remember that she comes from Indiana," Dorothy explained. "She must be used to being with white people. It is not the same as here. You have never been to visit there, have you?"

He understood her point and got into the car to leave.

Billy was driving back to town and looking for the best place to talk. Nancy saw the lake named after the Mississippi River.

"Mr. Vangslia," Nancy pointed, "we could go and sit and talk over there by Lake River. That sound good to you?"

"Yes, we can go there," Billy agreed. "I will find a place to park my car near the water."

He saw a spot to park, put his car there, and they both got out. He was still nervous and looked around for people, but no one near them saw them at all. Nancy did not care what people thought about what they were doing. She would have ignored any other people anyway.

"Mr. Vangslia," Nancy said, "you don't have to worry about other people. I have been in this kind of thing before. When I talk to a white person, I just have to act like a white person. Some people would listen to me and some people wouldn't. I know that it is hard to get used to how different things are here than they are at home."

Billy was surprised by what Nancy was saying. They kept walking to the Lake River. They found a wooden table without a bench, so they decided to sit on the table.

Nancy felt relaxed. The air smelled so fresh from the river. She felt good and healthy. Where she lived in the big city, the air was less fresh. Billy was still nervous, feeling that he needed to begin by talking with Nancy about the surface of her personal life.

"Miss William, can I ask you something about yourself," Billy asked. "It won't be deeply personal, OK?"

Nancy looked at Billy and nodded. She wanted to reassure him that he did not have to use special care with her because she was black.

"Can I call you Billy?" Nancy asked. "You can call me Nancy. I don't want to use my formal name. That is for business only, not here, OK?"

Billy was surprised that Nancy's personality was not the same as that of other colored women in Lake Providence. He believed that he could be comfortable with Nancy.

"Nancy, you certainly can call me Billy," he agreed. "Well,

I am not used to talking with colored women from the north."

"I understand that," Nancy giggled. "It is hard for me to change and follow the ways of most colored women from the South. I don't really like to do that, but I do have to do it when I am visiting here for vacations with family and friends. So, what did you want to ask me about?"

"Yes, Nancy," Billy said. "Why do you presently live in Indianapolis?"

"I was born and raised in that town," Nancy answered. "Now I am a junior at Marian College. My major is social work with children. Maybe I will fly across the ocean to Africa and learn their way of living. I know that is a very different culture from ours in this world."

"I can imagine that," Billy replied. "How often did you visit here?"

"Well, when I was a little girl, my family came here every year," Nancy said. "I stopped visiting here when I went to college for the first year. When my grandmother got older, it seemed as if we would never know when her life would end. I felt like I had to come down here and get some more information about my family tree. My mother had not told me anything about it. Perhaps she was not interested in how her own mother had lived. That's why I decided to come down here and spend time with my grandmother. I was here for three months before my school started at the end of August last year."

"I am sure that you did the right thing to come and visit your grandmother before she passed away," Billy said, surprised.

"Yes, you are right about that." Nancy nodded. "I told my mother that I am glad that I was able to get all of the family history from the time when my great grandparents came here from Africa more than a hundred years ago."

Billy was listening to Nancy's voice. He took a cigarette and his lighter out of his suit pocket and started to smoke. Nancy saw that and felt like asking Billy for a cigarette.

"Billy, can I have one please?" Nancy asked.

"Do you smoke?" Billy was surprised, but he gave a cigarette to Nancy.

"Yes, I began doing it when I was under pressure at college," Nancy answered.

They both smiled, remembering that kind of moment. She was recalling what her grandmother had told her in stories about her family and the Rhodes family when she was in service at the big house.

"My grandmother told me about the mistress's family history, too," Nancy mentioned.

Billy looked at Nancy, not understanding at first that her grandmother had been telling her about the Rhodes family and not her own family history.

"Didn't she tell you about her own family history?" Billy asked.

"Yes, she told me about herself between her memories about the Rhodes family," Nancy nodded. "The person she served under was named Mrs. Margaret Rhodes. She always liked my great grandmother, ever since she became the owner of the plantation."

Billy was glad that her grandmother had told her about her own family, but he did not understand why she also told Nancy about Mrs. Margaret Rhodes' family history. It was not part of the history of Nancy's family, related to her by blood. He guessed it could be possible, of course, that some of the children had come from a great grandfather who was white and raped one of the slave women.

"Nancy, did your grandmother tell you about Mrs. Rhodes's father?" Billy said. "Do you know if he raped any of the slave women?"

"No, she did not tell me anything like that," Nancy said. Her eyebrows rose at the thought.

Billy did not understand why her grandmother told Nancy about the two different families. He thought that the story would certainly be of interest to the newspaper.

Chapter 8

The Civil War was over and the plantation owners had to give the slaves in their service their freedom. They had always worked at picking the cotton by hand. Ron's area had to be reduced to forty acres from the 2,000 acres he had once owned. Once the slaves were freed, most of them decided to move out of state to cities in the North. However, Rosemary wanted to keep Betty to serve in the big house with a salary. Ron, his daughter, Margaret, and the sharecroppers who took over worked together to collect the cotton every day.

Ron, Rosemary, Margaret, and her husband, John, were all in the dining room eating together at the table. They were having a good conversation. Ron was laughing at a joke John was telling him, when suddenly he felt ill and stopped laughing. He walked out of the dining room. They did not know what might be wrong. John told them that he would check on him to find out if he was all right. John thought that Ron had probably gone to his bedroom. He went upstairs and walked into Ron's bedroom, but he was not there. John looked all around the room, but no one was there. John knew that Ron had intended to go to his office downstairs after dinner. He was sorry that he had gone upstairs to find Ron for no reason. He went back downstairs to the office. He stopped in front of the door to the office. It was dark inside and he could not see anything in the room. He thought that Ron was probably outside.

John went back to the dining room and told Rosemary and Margaret to come with him to find Ron somewhere outside. They went out and looked for Ron in the barn and another small house around the back of the main building. They could not find him at all. John felt that Ron must be somewhere around inside the big house.

Rosemary told John that Ron must be in the office taking a nap on his chair. John agreed that it might be possible and went back into the big house. John took a lighted candle from the dining room into the office. He lit another candle on the wall to make the room brighter. John put the dining room candle on the desk and then saw Ron on the floor. He was lying near the window. He went over to Ron and bent down to listen at his chest, but the heartbeat had stopped. Rosemary asked John if Ron was alive. John said, "No, I can't hear any heartbeat at all."

Margaret and John took over the plantation. Margaret had a bookkeeper named Eloise Taylor who worked with her after her father died. Her mother, Rosemary, still lived with them and took care of Margaret's son, Nelson, because the rest of the family worked outside every day.

Mary was born in 1880 in the small house next to the big house. She had a younger brother named Sam. They would play together outside and pick a little of the cotton with the sharecroppers. Sometimes they had fun collecting and playing with bits of cotton from the grass and dirt road where some of it had blown away from the plants. Her mother, Shana, was also a servant, and her grandmother, Betty, was still cooking and cleaning with her daughter for Mrs. Margaret Rhodes in her big house.

Margaret went to the sewing room and picked up a light blue and white strip of cloth with small red flowers on it from the table. She rolled up the piece of yard goods and brought it with her, going downstairs toward her office. She came in the office and showed the cloth to her bookkeeper, Eloise.

"Mrs. Taylor, do you want some yard goods," Margaret asked. "You can use it to make a dress."

"No, thank you for asking," Eloise answered.

Margaret decided that she would give the yards to Shana and Betty. They would probably like to make a dress for Shana's daughter, Mary.

"OK, I will give this to Shana and Betty," Margaret said. "I will be right back in a minute, Mrs. Taylor."

Margaret left the office with the piece of goods. Eloise nodded her head and had nothing to say about giving the material to the servants. She went back to her paperwork, estimating the price per pound and the number of bales to be sent to a resale agent in New Orleans.

Margaret went downstairs to the kitchen. She looked in there for the two colored women but neither of them were there. The kitchen was very clean. All the dishes and glasses that had been on the table and in the sinks had been put away. She knew that they had gone to their house for a break for a few minutes after they cleaned up this room.

Margaret went outside and over to the servant's cabins. It was a short walk, just a few steps away from her big house to theirs. The small kitchen with faded yellow paint on the wall had a fireplace for them to cook their meals. A French cabinet was full of dishes, glasses, and small paper bags.

Shana was sitting on a chair and sewing a new dress for Mary. Betty was cooking in a big pot in the fireplace with her granddaughter. Margaret tried to open the door but it was stuck. Inside the kitchen, they looked at the door and realized that something wrong. The person who was trying to open the door couldn't get in. Finally, the door did open and Margaret came into the kitchen. She put the goods on the table. Shana looked at the material next to the fire so that she could see what it looked like.

"You can use this for you or for Betty and Mary," Margaret said, "to make a dress for your church or somewhere else you might like to wear it."

"Yes, thank you, ma'am," Shana smiled. "I am making a nice dress for Mary to wear to church."

"You are welcome. I'll see you later," Margaret smiled.

She was leaving the kitchen, but at that moment, Mary saw Margaret, and followed her outside. Mary ran after Margaret and stopped her. Margaret looked down at Mary standing in front of her.

"Yes, Mary, what do you want?" Margaret smiled.

"I want to work with you," Mary said. "Like my mother and grandmother are doing now, working with you in your big house."

Margaret was surprised to hear Mary asking her for this work. Betty heard Mary's voice and what she had said. Shana was shocked that Mary was asking the lady of the house to give her work when she would be grown up enough to do it. Margaret never had asked Mary to become a servant like her mother and grandmother; the Civil War was over. She looked at Betty and Shana. They were silent, choosing not to say anything about what Mary had asked. Margaret looked at Mary, and in her mind it was very difficult for her to tell Mary the truth. Mary was only eight years old and still did not understood what her mother and grandmother's life as servants for the white people had been like.

"Mary, that is nice of you to ask me to hire you to help out and work with me in my big house," Margaret said, trying to explain it to Mary. "I don't know about that yet. Let me think about it, OK?"

Mary nodded and went back to the fireplace with her grandmother. Margaret sighed. She felt sure that her mother and grandmother did not want Mary to be a servant like them.

Shana and Betty stared at Margaret. She was so innocent, and they had never talked to her about what might happen later on in their lives.

Margaret decided to leave them alone. She closed the door

behind her and worried about whether they would get angry at her. She didn't know what they might have wanted her to say in answer to Mary's question.

Chapter 9

It was a quiet night. Shana's husband Henry brought a cotton sack with him and hung it on a hook on the porch. He could see through the window that the dining room light was on. He wondered why she was staying there so late. He came into the house, walked through the kitchen and pushed the dining room door open. He looked around and saw that Shana was sitting on the floor beside the table. Henry walked around the table. He was puzzled by why she was polishing Mrs. Rhodes' silver candlesticks and other things. She was supposed to get off work at eight o'clock, but she was still there at eleven.

"Shana, do you know what time it is?" Henry asked.

Shana looked at Henry and refused to answer his question. She just went back to work cleaning the silver candlesticks. Henry suspected that something was wrong with Shana. He decided to leave her alone. He went back to his house and went to bed to wait for the next morning.

After an hour or so, Shana had enough of polishing the silverware and put all of it back into the French cabinets. She stood up slowly. Her back was sore from bending all those hours. She came into the kitchen with the polish and the dirty towels. She walked around and checked to see if anything was in the sink or on the counter that was clean and needed to be put away. She left the house for their small house just a few steps away.

Shana came up onto the porch. She was upset with her daughter Mary. Mary wanted to become a servant like her mother and grandmother and just work for Mrs. Rhodes. Shana sighed and went into the house. She came into the kitchen area and looked at the fireplace; the fire was low. She shoveled the ashes over the logs to stop the fire. She looked around for mice in the kitchen. They might be trying to hide somewhere. She knew that her mother, Betty, was not cleaning up the dirt on the floor so well. That was why the mice were coming into the house and eating some of the food on the floor. It was still pretty clean tonight.

She saw the yards on the table that Margaret had given to her that morning. She did not want to remember that. She put them away in the cabinets. She kept an eye out for mice in the other room on the same floor. She went upstairs and checked on her daughter and son in their grandmother's bedroom. They were asleep and quiet. She went into her bedroom, closed the door, and looked over at Henry. He was asleep in their bed. She sat by his stomach and made Henry wake up. He looked at Shana's face and could smell the silver polish on her hands.

"What's wrong with you, Shana?" Henry asked.

Shana refused to answer his question and walked away from him.

"Shana, I don't like what you are doing to me!" he yelled at her.

Shana stopped in front of the door of the bedroom and then looked back at Henry. She came over to the bed slowly and tried to tell him about Mary.

"Shana, will you please sit right here." Henry spoke more softly now, and she came over and sat on the bed next to him. "Can you tell me what's the matter with you?"

Shana had a hard time telling him what had happened that morning. Henry did not understand what was wrong with Shana. She was supposed to tell him whatever was on her mind. She looked at Henry and her face was sad.

"You need to know this about Mary," Shana muttered. "This morning, Mrs. Rhodes came into our house and brought yards for us in the kitchen downstairs. Mary went to Mrs. Rhodes and told her that she wanted to work for her as a servant, so that she could become a woman like me and my mother."

Henry was surprised that Mary had told Mrs. Rhodes that she wanted to work for her when she was grown up. He did not like it at all that Mary had as a goal for her future job to be a servant.

"Henry, what do you think about what she said?" Shana asked.

"I don't like that," Henry said. "But I cannot control her life, so if she wants to do that, then she has to go ahead with her life. You know that we were slaves, but now we have some freedom and could earn more money."

"Do you think that earning more money would be enough for you?" Shana asked. "The white people would earn more money than colored people would all the time! Damn it!"

She left the bedroom and started to cry about what Mary's life would be like. She did not want Mary to become a servant the way she and her mother had. She wanted Mary to get out of this state and try for a new life in Indiana. Mary's only goal was to work for Mrs. Rhodes when she grew up.

Ten years later, Mary had grown to be eighteen years old. She was thin and tall, almost five feet seven inches. Her hair was long and curly and came down to her elbows when she let it hang loose. She worked with her father in the fields to pick cotton, and sometimes she did work with her grandmother in the house. She was not getting along with her mother, who had turned a very cold shoulder to her for a long time, even when she was a little girl. Mary took along her younger brother, Sam, and they often went to the store together, sometimes with other friends from school.

There was a heavy rain and wind outside. Shana was not happy with her job in the house working for Margaret. They did not get along and often started to argue about things that happened over the years. Shana just gave up with Margaret's latest order that she should wax the floor of the foyer. She poured lukewarm water into the bucket, mixed it with wax and brought it in. She had dared to pour water from the bucket onto the floor, then dropped the bucket on the floor, not caring that it sounded really loud.

Margaret and Eloise were working in the office on the same floor and heard the noise. Margaret knew that Shana was having some problems. She gave up on doing her paperwork for New Orleans. She stood up and left her desk. Eloise followed her to the foyer and they looked down at the floor where Shana was. The job was not going properly.

"What is wrong with you, Shana?" Margaret asked.

"I am tired of this damn old ugly floor," Shana said with a nasty attitude. "That floor is very damn old and I just can't wash any dirt off of it at all!"

Margaret sighed and looked at Eloise standing beside her. She told her to leave them alone. Eloise respected Margaret's orders and went back to her desk.

"Shana, why did you drop the bucket on the floor?" Margaret was upset. "That scared us to death. I don't appreciate it when you do things like that."

Shana did not care what Mrs. Rhodes' feelings were about it.

"I don't care what you say," Shana said. She removed her apron and dropped it on the floor, rolling it up with her foot. "I am going to quit. We are planning to move out of here to go up north where my cousins live."

Margaret was shocked that Shana was saying this to her. Shana walked down the porch stairs outside and called out to Henry. He was in the field, but he could hear Shana's voice. She had never called him by his name before. He told the men at the field that he needed to go see about his wife. He walked out of the field with his cotton sack and hung it on the tree branch. He went up to Mrs. Rhodes' house, but Shana was not there. She probably had gone home. He came into his house and heard Shana and her mother talking in the bedroom. They were arguing about something that had gone wrong. He knew that Shana was always arguing with her mother about some small thing or other. He came upstairs and was going to go right into the bedroom, but he stopped outside by the door. He could hear what Shana was saying to her mother.

"I am giving up my job; we'll have to leave here for Indiana, where my cousins live," Shana was saying. She was packing her clothes into a bag on the bed. "Time is up for me now. I've had enough. What are you going to do now, Mammy?"

"No, I won't leave here," Betty said. "I like to work here and I like having a place to live in."

Henry was shocked at what Shana was telling her mother. She had already quit her job and wanted to leave this place to move north. He had no choice, he decided. He would have to give up his work too. He came into the bedroom. Shana and Betty both stared at him.

"Shana, are you sure that you want to move to Indiana?" Henry asked.

Shana was surprised that he had already heard what they were saying in the bedroom before he came into the room. She came over to Henry and begged him to leave with her from Mrs. Rhodes' place.

"Yes, I want to leave here right away," Shana told him seriously. "I am tired of these damn old things with Mrs. Rhodes! Sam will come with us. Mary is not going to go with us. She already asked Mrs. Rhodes if she could stay and work with her like I did. Now Mary and my mother can just stay here and work at Mrs. Rhodes house."

Shana kept on packing her clothes in the bag. Then she walked to the window, pulled it up, and called to Sam. He was playing with his friends, rapping a stick along the fence, when he heard his mother's voice. He told his friends that his mother needed him back at their house.

Sam ran over to their yard. He saw his mother still at her bedroom window.

"Mammy, what?" Sam asked, playing with his stick on the grass.

"I need you to pack your clothes in the bag with your things, whatever you want to take with you," Shana said. "We will leave here on the train to Indiana pretty soon. You better hurry up to pack your stuff right away."

Sam was surprised and confused by what his mother was saying about a last-minute plan to leave their home for Indiana. He dropped the stick on the grass. He felt bad about not getting to stay in Louisiana. He had a lot of friends and his school was here. He did not want to move to Indiana just for his mother's sake.

"Mammy, I don't want to go to Indiana with you," Sam begged her. "I won't even have a chance to say good-bye to my friends. This is just too last-minute to have to leave here."

"I am sorry, Sam," Shana sighed. "I don't want to work here any more. Maybe you will like it when you are in Indiana. I want you to go to the bedroom and start packing your things into a bag right now."

Sam nodded and came into the house. He began to pack whatever he had into a bag in the bedroom all by himself.

Mary was collecting some flowers for her grandmother and walking along the dirt road to her house. She saw her father out front. He was putting bags and boxes into a wagon. She wondered what he was doing with those things. She came over to her father.

Henry looked at Mary and his face was sad. That made Mary feel scared because she thought something might be wrong with him.

"Daddy, what is happening?" Mary pointed to the bags in the wagon.

"Darling, I want to tell you," her father sighed. "Your mother is not working for Mrs. Rhodes anymore. She wants to move to Indiana and live with our cousins."

Mary found it hard to believe that her mother had already quit the job for good. She knew that her mother had not been getting along with Mrs. Rhodes for a long time. She had known that even when she was a little girl. Mary realized that they must be leaving for Indiana.

"Are we leaving here now?" Mary asked. "Is Grandmamma planning to go with us?"

"No, your grandmamma and you are going to stay here," her father answered. "If you want to stay here, you don't have to pack your things and come with us to Indiana. Your mother and Sam and I will go to the station now. You can come along with us, but just to say good-bye."

Mary had a hard time believing what her father told her, that they were already leaving here for Indiana. She heard something inside the house and saw her mother came out with a big brown case. She saw Mary standing next to her father. Shana brought the suitcase to Henry and come over to talk to Mary.

"Mary, we are planning to leave right away." Shana sighed. "I guess your father told you that we are going to Indiana today."

Mary nodded slowly and looked at her brother Sam. He was standing there with his grandmother and crying because he did not want to leave his home and friends. He came over to Mary and hugged her.

"I don't want to go to Indiana!" Sam yelled. "I want to stay with you and grandmamma here, but mammy wants me to go with them. I am sure going to miss you and grandmamma."

"Sam, I'll miss you, too," Mary was upset. "I didn't expect this to happen so fast. Maybe I will visit you in Indiana, if I have enough money to buy a ticket to ride a train. OK, Sam?"

Sam nodded and felt better after hearing what Mary said. He jumped into the carriage. Mary started to cry as her family began to ride away and leave her behind.

"I want you and your grandmamma to ride with us to the train station, OK, Mary?" her father said.

Betty came over to Mary and told her to come with them so they could drop the others off at the train station and say good-bye. Mary agreed and climbed up to sit on the wagon with the rest of the family. Mary was wondering if Mrs. Rhodes was feeling upset that her mother had not wanted to keep on working as a servant in the big house. Mary knew that she would be the next to go and work there now that her mother was leaving.

They were rushing to the train station. Mary looked at the sky and saw that the clouds would soon become dark and cover the blue sky. She knew that the rain was going to come sometime soon.

"We are coming to the train station!" Henry said, pointing up ahead.

Shana looked at Mary's eyes. She knew that Mary must be shocked that her family was leaving their home for Indiana at the last minute this way. They arrived at the front of the train station and Henry pulled the horse to a stop. He jumped off the wagon and tied the rope to the pole.

Shana and Sam got off the wagon and took their bags with them into the station. Henry held Betty's hand to help her step down to the ground from the wagon and avoid a fall. Henry took some of the bags and rushed into the station with Betty.

Mary was the last person left in the wagon alone. She did not like it that her family had left her and her grandmother alone in the house, but she had to find a way to get used to being without them. Sam came out of the station and saw Mary sitting alone on the wagon seat.

"Mary, please come down here now," Sam begged. "We don't want to miss saying good-bye before we get on the train."

Mary nodded and got down from the carriage. She walked over to Sam, and he opened the door to let her come into the station. She looked around inside. There were only four wooden benches in the middle of the room. There was another door and a window on the other side, where the train was going to come. She had never seen inside the station before.

"Mary, please, will you stay here and watch the bags?" Henry asked. "I need to go and get three tickets at the booth."

"OK, Daddy, I can stay and wait for you." Mary nodded.

Her father kissed Mary's cheek and then went to the small booth with Shana and Sam.

Mary sighed and felt that she might be going to vomit. Her grandmother came over to her and held her hand tightly.

"Mary, I will not leave you alone," Betty said softly. "I am still going to stay here with you and work for Mrs. Rhodes without your parents and brother."

Mary nodded her head slowly and watched her family as they waited in line to get tickets.

A couple of people got their tickets and left the booth. The man working in the booth put some paperwork away and then looked at Henry in the line.

"Next!" the man called.

Henry heard the man and stepped up to the booth with Shana and Sam.

"Where are you going to?" the man asked.

"I need three tickets for Indiana today," Henry said.

"Are you planning to come back from Indiana?" the man asked again.

"No way! We are not coming back here again ever!" Shana yelled at the man in the booth.

"Shana! Please don't yell at him." Henry calmed Shana down and then looked at the man. "I want three tickets going one way to Indiana. We are not coming back at all. Thank you, sir."

The man did not say anything against that because they were colored and needed to leave Louisiana. He respected them for wanting to do it and he made out the three tickets for one way. He set them up and brought them over to Henry.

"Here are the tickets. The total is \$1.80 for one way to Indiana," he said.

Henry smiled, took a small bag out of his pocket, and poured some coins out. He counted out \$1.80 and moved it over to the man.

"I counted out \$1.80 here." Henry checked again.

"Good, you can have the tickets now," the man said, sliding the tickets to Henry.

The train came from the south. The man pulled the rope to sound a whistle, letting the people in the station know that the train would come in and stop for passengers. Mary heard the train whistle and looked through the window. She could see that the train had arrived. Shana looked out at the train, too.

"The train will go north won't it?" Shana asked the man in the booth.

"Yes, the train will leave here in fifteen minutes," the man said. "It will take you on the trip to Indiana today. All of you will be there in three days. Please go to the end of the cars. Those are the seats for coloreds only. There will be some food for you to eat during the long trip."

"OK. Thank you, we'll go right now," Henry said.

They went back to Mary, picked up their bags and then rushed outside. Mary and her grandmother kept walking with them to the end of the car where the colored people were allowed to sit.

"Sam, you better get the seats for us," Henry said.

Sam looked for available seats for three people. He found some and put the bags over the seats so that other people would not sit there. He came back out to talk with his sister and grandmother before the train would start to go.

Mary felt upset and uncomfortable that her father had told Sam to go and get in the train without even saying good-bye and hugging her and Betty. Henry looked at Mary's face and saw her anger. He was puzzled and wondered what was wrong.

"Mary, what is wrong with you?" Henry asked. "Are you

still upset about us leaving?"

"No, Daddy, I want to talk with Sam once more before he goes away on the train," Mary said, disappointed.

"Sam will come out and hug you and grandmamma. You can be sure of that, Mary," Henry sighed.

Mary felt better when she saw Sam coming back out of the car. He came out and hugged both Mary and his grandmother. He did not like having to leave them alone; they were too far away from where the others were going.

Sam looked at Mary and his grandmother with sad eyes.

"Grandmamma and Mary, I don't really want to leave here," Sam said sadly. "But I have to go with my parents. Maybe both of you can visit us there soon. Please, will you try to do that, Mary?"

Mary nodded and hugged Sam back.

"Sam, I will visit you when I have enough money to buy a ticket," Mary said, talking into Sam's ear. "Don't worry about us. We will be fine here. Maybe you can visit us when you get older and can afford to buy a ticket to come, OK?"

Sam understood what Mary said. Then he hugged his grandmother.

"Be a big boy. I will miss you," Betty said. "Your sister and I will visit you there, but when that will be I don't know yet."

Mary looked at Henry. He hugged her and almost felt like crying for some reason that he didn't quite understand. Shana did not say anything. She was just glad that she had been able to quit her old job.

"I will miss you, and I hope that you get to visit us there soon," Henry said.

"Yes, I'll try my best to save some money to buy a ticket for the trip to Indiana," Mary said. "Maybe I will bring my grandmamma with me to take a ride on the train."

Henry nodded and looked at Shana. He expected her to hug her daughter before leaving. He pulled at Shana's arm to move her closer to Mary. Shana looked at Henry. He couldn't have thought that she wasn't going to hug Mary. She looked back at Mary and had a hard time thinking of something to say.

"Mary, I am sorry that we have to leave for now," Shana sighed. "You can work with Mrs. Rhodes like you wanted to do. I want to know about it when you get to where you can come and visit us at Indiana with our cousins, OK?"

"Yes, I will do that," Mary said sadly. "I know that you and Mrs. Rhodes haven't been getting along for a long time. I will work with her in her house after you leave. Don't worry about it."

"I knew that you could tell that there was something wrong," Shana said. "Anyway, I do need to hug you and my mammy right now."

Shana hugged Mary and then Betty just a little bit. They knew that Shana did not get along perfectly with them either.

A man with a long blue jacket and hat came out to the train station helping people to get on or off of the trains. He pulled out a gold watch on a chain, held it across his vest and looked at it. The time was almost two o'clock in the afternoon. He put it back in his pocket and announced that it was time to get on board.

"Five minutes to two o'clock and you better get on before the train leaves without you," he called out. "All aboard!" like the notes of a song.

People heard him and rushed into the train. Then they waved from the windows at the people still outside. Henry told Sam and Shana to go in right away. Mary didn't want to stand still. She would have liked to follow them into the train and go right through it to the passenger car and then to their seats. Betty rushed to catch Mary before she could do that. Sam opened the window and put his head out. Mary laughed to see that he was waving and they could still call out to each other.

"Good-bye to you and grandmamma!" Sam yelled at them. "I will miss you and I'll miss my old home, too!"

"Yes, we will miss and love you too," Mary called. "We

will visit you soon if we can do it, I promise."

Henry and Shana's heads came out of the window too and they waved to Mary and Betty standing outside. The engineer pulled the whistle. He made it very loud to show that the train was really about to leave the station. The train began to move very slowly. People kept on waving to other people inside the train. Betty came over to Mary and held her hand, but Mary didn't want to stay with her grandmother; she kept walking alongside the train. Betty sighed and slowly followed Mary. People stood and kept on waving as the train moved out of the station; Mary was following her family and Betty kept on walking with her. At the end of the sidewalk, Mary stopped by the fence. She could not get past it to walk any farther along the tracks. The train finally faded away and was gone.

Mary cried out loud. Betty came over and hugged her to calm her down. At that moment the rain started to come, one drop splashing on Mary's cheek.

"I think we better leave now," Betty said. "The rain will come down and maybe it will be heavy later on this afternoon."

Mary nodded and wiped her eyes. They went inside and walked through the building to the wagon at the front of the station. Mary helped Betty up into the wagon, and then Mary untied the rope from the pole, climbed up into the wagon and left the station. They were on the way home.

The rain started to come down very hard. It hit their heads like little rocks. Mary had a hard time seeing the road to find the right way home. The horse seemed to know how to do it. Betty held a coat over her head to keep from getting wet. Finally they arrived at the house and kept straight on and back into the barn. Betty took the coat off and looked around the barn to see if the rain was going to come through the roof.

"Ahh! I hate it that my clothes got wet from the rain!" Betty complained. She shook the coat. "I would hang my coat up, but I have to use it again to get to in the house."

Mary jumped off the wagon and unhitched the horse. She walked around the wagon to her grandmother.

"Grandmamma, are you ready to come down now?" Mary asked. Betty stood up and started to put her foot on the wheel. "Be careful, I will help you get down."

Betty came down to the ground carefully and looked at Mary with a smile. Mary was wondering why she was looking so cheerful.

"Are you ready to work with Mrs. Rhodes?" Betty asked Mary.

Now Mary knew what her grandmother was saying, remembering that she had said she would like to become a servant when she was a little girl.

"I think that Mrs. Rhodes will ask me about that," Mary believed. "I think we had better go over to the house. Mrs. Rhodes might be worrying about us."

"Yes, we better go right away," Betty said.

Betty put her coat over both of their heads and they walked through the rain until they could go in the back door. Betty opened it and let Mary go in the kitchen first. They saw Margaret and Eloise sitting at the table. They had been waiting for them to come back from the station. Margaret stood up from the chair and came over to Mary. Mary knew that Margaret would ask her if she would begin to work for her now that Shana had left the house.

"Mary, has your family already left for up north on the train today?" Margaret asked.

"Yes, ma'am, my family just left a little while ago," Mary answered.

Margaret nodded her head. She was feeling sad that Shana was gone, finding it hard it to believe that this had happened so fast. She came close to Mary again to ask her the important question.

"Do you want to work with me today?" Margaret asked.

"Yes, ma'am, I have wanted to work for you since I was a

little girl," Mary said, and she looked at her grandmother. "When you came into the house with my mammy and grandmamma in the kitchen, I forget why, I think you brought something over for them, but you were going leave the house and I ran and asked you if I could work for you when I grew up. Now I can be your maid if you want to have me."

Betty and Margaret were surprised that Mary had never forgotten what she had told Margaret when she was a little girl.

"Umm? It's good to hear that, and I am glad that you want to work with me now." Margaret smiled and took her hand. "Thank you for saying yes, you can start to work with us right away."

Mrs. Rhodes told Eloise to come with her and they left the kitchen for the office upstairs. Betty came around and looked at Mary's face. She felt a little bit shocked that Mary still wanted to work for Margaret.

"What is the matter with you, grandmamma?" Mary asked.

"I can't believe that you still do want to work with her?" Betty said.

"Yes, what I want to be is a maidservant, like you and my mother." Mary smiled calmly and walked out of the kitchen to go upstairs.

Betty looked at Mary as she walked through the door to the dining room. Betty came to the kitchen table and pulled out a chair and sat down. She was wondering why Mary only wanted to become a servant, just the way she and Mary's mother had done, here in this house with Mrs. Rhodes.

Chapter 10

Much later, about twenty-five years or so, Mary was married and had three children of her own. They were all raised in the small house in the yard behind the home of Mrs. Rhodes. When they were old enough to go, all her children moved to Indiana. She lost her husband, Neil, after he fell asleep while working at the factory and his body was mangled. She had a broken heart and refused to ever remarry.

Mary's grandmother had passed away by natural causes. She had been working hard in the house without her grandmother for several months now. Margaret thought that Mary should have another person to help her, so she decided to hire a new maid named Dorothy Datson. She was shorter than Mary and enjoyed being playful while they worked. Sometimes they argued about little things, like the right way to fix a bed, or not cleaning a missed spot on the floor, or pouring out the wrong measure in cooking.

There was a bar called The Blue that was for colored people. Most of them went to The Blue every Friday and Saturday evening after finishing their work for the week. People would dance and talk and drink around the bar. Jazz singers would appear on the small stage, singing many different numbers every weekend. Dorothy was involved in the singing, too. She had a good voice and could also dance well.

Mary was sitting on a chair at a small, round table with a vase of flowers on it. She drank a cherry coke from a long glass and listened to Dorothy singing on the stage.

Dorothy came off the stage and went over to Mary's table.

Mary was surprised that Dorothy had come to her. Mary looked around at the people beside her. They were smiling and waving. She felt shy, so she hid her face with her hand and kept on drinking from the glass. Dorothy noticed Mary's behavior, hiding from the people around her, and rolled her eyes. She pulled Mary's hand down from her face and kept on singing to Mary.

"Mary is my favorite coworker at the big house," Dorothy sang as she pointed at Mary. "We always be arguing after stupid things, but we are still good friends! I do not understand why we are still good friends even though sometimes we are enemies!"

People were shocked and looked at each other. They couldn't understand how Dorothy and Mary were getting along so well. Dorothy kept on singing a song about Mary.

"Mary is working for a freak lady in a big old awful house," Dorothy sang. "I am so scared to death if Mrs. Rhodes gets mad at me or something like that! Oh what a freaking thing! I am going to die sometime when I can see her eyes are blue, but if she's mad they can become as red as fire!"

Dorothy was pretending to choke herself; she was fighting to get an evil spirit out of her body. People had many emotions, like shock, laughter and tears, while listening to Dorothy. After a while, Mary got mad, stood up and came over to stand right behind Dorothy. People saw Mary and tried to warn Dorothy to look behind her. She was puzzled and did look back at Mary. From the look in her eyes, Dorothy knew that Mary did not like it that she was making fun of Mrs. Rhodes. She wanted her to control her behavior instead of yelling out this bad song.

"Yes, Mary, what do you want from me?" Dorothy asked.

"Why did you make fun of Mrs. Rhodes?" Mary asked seriously.

"Oh, I was just singing about Mrs. Rhodes. That's all that I said." Dorothy smiled and looked around at the people. They were turning their heads back in another direction. They did not want to be involved in the problem with Dorothy. "Oh, excuse me; do you think that I am being rude to Mrs. Rhodes?"

"Yes, you are very rude!" Mary was really upset. She turned around and went back to her table to sit down. She did not look at Dorothy at all.

Dorothy was embarrassed that people thought she was insulting Mrs. Rhodes. She went back to the stage and thought of what she could do to sing a different song for Mary. Finally, she did think of a good song and started to announce it to the people. She wanted to apologize to Mary for seeming to insult her boss.

"I'd like to tell all of you about how sorry I am about Mary," Dorothy announced. People heard Dorothy's voice and then looked back at her up on the stage. Mary wouldn't look at Dorothy, but she did listen to her. "Mary, you can look at me or just listen to my voice. That's fine with me."

Mary could hear Dorothy and still did not care that she wanted to say something to her. Dorothy knew Mary very well. She would look back at Dorothy pretty soon. Dorothy was nervous and held her breath. People were waiting for her to sing. Mary was beginning to laugh inside herself that Dorothy wasn't starting to sing. She must be feeling kind of foolish up on the stage by herself. Dorothy looked at Mary across the floor and was finally ready to sing.

"Oh, my dearest Mary, I would like to tell you something," Dorothy began to sing smoothly and sweetly. "That I was such a bad little mean old woman. I was insulting your and my mistress. So, I would like to tell you that I am so sorry! Mary, is that OK?"

People started to clap for Dorothy. Mary was silent, a little bit unhappy that they were so ready to hear Dorothy apologizing. She looked at the people, and they told her that everything was OK and she should try to forget about the past.

"Thank you, I accept you saying you are sorry for insulting Mrs. Rhodes," Mary called out.

"Oh! Mary! I love you so much, and I won't ever do that again!" Dorothy was surprised and ran over to Mary and hugged her. People started to cry and cheered for both of them. "You are making me cry. Oh, boy! I don't want to mess up my makeup for the stage tonight!" Dorothy said.

"OK, Dorothy, that's fine. You better go back on the stage and begin to sing again, but just not that song," Mary said. "You better stop crying. Be brave now and go on back up on the stage and let people hear more from your beautiful voice tonight."

"OK, I will calm down now. Thanks, Mary," Dorothy answered. "I will go back on the stage and start all over with the singing for tonight."

"It's good to hear that. You better go right back up there now," Mary said.

"Well, I have been trying to think about the next song for tonight," Dorothy announced. People were laughing at her, thinking that she was joking.

"I am not joking with you; I meant what I said. Now, I have already thought of my favorite song for you tonight," Dorothy said excitedly. "I am ready to sing for everybody here, but I need to drink a glass of wine right now."

People were laughing and clapping for Dorothy. Mary understood that Dorothy wanted to play around with the people. A man gave Dorothy a glass of wine. She was laughing and took it from the man. She slurped down the wine, handed the glass back to him and walked to the middle of the stage.

Mary looked at Dorothy and then at the people on the other side. She could see that they probably believed that Dorothy would have to get drunk to be able to keep on singing. Mary did not say anything about what she was thinking. She needed to watch Dorothy to see if she would need more wine either after or before her other songs.

"I am so ready to sing for everybody tonight," Dorothy said with a smile. "This song is called 'My Lover.' That is my favorite song. Now, are you ready to hear me sing tonight?"

"Yes, we want to hear that right now, Dorothy!" People

were excited.

"Thank all of you so very much!" Dorothy smiled. "I am ready to begin to sing right now."

Everyone was cheering for Dorothy. They wanted to hear more of her voice. Mary was surprised that Dorothy wanted to share the next number with them, a sad and plaintive song.

"A man is my lover, he cannot leave me alone." Dorothy was singing softy now. "I can't leave him because I know he is my lover. So damn, I did not understand what he was doing when he was trying to steal my heart. My heart belongs to him now. I can't remove it. I don't know how I can get it back at all."

Dorothy walked toward the piano and leaned on it. She looked at the man playing the piano slowly and softly behind her improvised words. He looked at the glass on top of the piano. Dorothy followed his eyes and knew it was there for her. She grabbed it, drank all of the wine, and then put it back. She looked out at the people and breathed out more of the song.

"I will become like him; I'm going to steal his heart, too," Dorothy began again. "But he should not run away from me, because he was the one that started to put the medicine of love into my heart. Why did he give me a love potion? I don't know why or what he is doing with me. Never knew that he was making lots of women belong to him. Now I guess I'm just one of them, too."

People were starting to fall in love with her voice. Mary was watching her. She could see that many men would want to buy a glass of wine for her.

"I am chasing after that man, wherever he may be going," Dorothy sang. "I caught him in the bar, I mean this one right here where we are now! But I did not know then that he was the one who was trying to steal my heart. Who? Who? Who? That man who's trying to steal MY HEART!"

People stood up and clapped and cheered for Dorothy. They came up and crowded onto the stage. Mary was worrying and standing up. She was afraid somebody might hurt Dorothy in the center of the crowd. They all wanted Dorothy to come and join them. They brought her over to the counter and the men ordered still another glass of wine for Dorothy. Mary knew that Dorothy would like to drink lots of wine and would be drunk before long. The bartender gave the new glass to Dorothy and again she drank the whole glassful before putting the glass down on the counter.

"I want to have some more wine, please!" Dorothy was begging now. "I want to be really drunk tonight. I haven't done this for a long time, not since I was a very young girl!"

People were laughing at what Dorothy was saying. They thought that she was such a funny lady.

Mary worried. She knew that she would have to take care of a drunk tonight. She didn't really want to take care of Dorothy while she was out of control with alcohol.

Chapter 11

The people danced and talked in The Blue throughout the night. Some people were so tired they slept on their tables, others danced slowly on the floor. The bartender collected glasses and ashtrays and cleaned up. The owner of The Blue was in his office counting the money and putting it in a small box. He put the box in the safe, closed the heavy door, and looked at his watch. It was past 4 a.m.

He knew the people were going to be angry with him because they wanted to stay in the bar all the night, so he sighed before leaving his office for the bar. He stood and looked at the people around the smoke-filled room. "I want all of you to leave here now," he said as loudly as he could. The people looked at him. "The bar closes at 4 a.m.; you need to leave here now. You can come back later this afternoon. Get some sleep and we'll see you later."

The people heard the owner's voice and started to leave the bar slowly. Dorothy slept on the table with about six or seven empty glasses of wine that men had bought for her.

Mary did not drink alcohol at all. She tried to help Dorothy get out of the bar, but she knew Dorothy would not let her. She had to pull Dorothy off the table. At that moment, Dorothy awoke and looked at Mary, her face becoming cruel.

"You better leave me alone," Dorothy snarled. "I need to stay here and have more fun. I want to drink more wine and I want to sleep here in the bar. You better go to your own bed!"

Dorothy went back to sleep, putting her head down on her arms on the table.

Mary rolled her eyes up and shook her head. She really hated to see Dorothy act like this toward her when she got drunk. "No, I will not leave you alone in the bar," Mary said in frustration. "We need to leave right away. The owner wants us to leave here now! We did not have enough time to sleep."

"Why?" Dorothy yawed.

"It's four o'clock in the morning," Mary sighed. "So, we were supposed to be home by midnight, but you did not want go back because the men gave you free glasses of wine. That's why you got drunk!"

Dorothy opened her wide eyes, picked her head up from the table and stood up. However, her body would not stay balanced.

"Oh, that's right. We are supposed to leave here now," Dorothy muttered. "Now I am on the way to my home."

She started to walk, cruelly hitting people on her way. A fat man sitting on a short chair saw Dorothy. She was on the way to him. He tried to move out of her way, but he was too slow.

"Watch out and do not walk over me!" he yelled at Dorothy.

Dorothy heard the fat man's voice and looked at him, but it was too late. She fell over his legs to the floor.

The people were shocked and laughed at her because she did not see the fat man. Mary rolled her eyes and felt embarrassed. Dorothy got pissed off at the fat man and stood up, wiping off the dirt from the floor.

"Why did you sit there," Dorothy complained. "You might move it before I get there! Damn you fat, lazy man!"

"I am sorry about that," the fat man explained. "You are drinking and out of control!"

The fat man stood up and came close to Dorothy. She did not realize that he was about five foot nine. She was less than four foot nine. She looked him in the eyes and pushed his stomach.

"You are an idiot, fat man," Dorothy insulted. "No wonder you do not have a girlfriend because you're too fat to get ..."

The fat man got angry and planned to hit Dorothy. The people were shocked that Dorothy had the guts to speak out to the fat man. Mary blocked the fat man from Dorothy.

"Please do not hurt Dorothy," Mary begged. "You know that she got drunk and did not mean to say something like that. I am sorry that she got mean and hurt your feelings. I know that was not your fault. Please, God, don't hurt her, OK?"

Mary rushed to get out of the bar with Dorothy. She was shocked and wondered why Dorothy would insult him like that. She could not imagine what would have happened if she did not protect her from the fat man.

They were outside waiting for someone to take them home. The people walked out of the bar and got rides to their homes. Some walked home by themselves without a flash of light on the street.

Mary saw her friend in the car; it was still there. Her friend's boyfriend got out of the car and opened the hood. Mary wondered what was wrong. She wanted to talk to her friend, but she preferred not to take Dorothy with her. Dorothy wondered where Mary was going.

"Where are you going?" Dorothy asked. "I can't walk to my home with my high-heel shoes. It will kill my feet!"

"No, we are not going to walk home," Mary said, pointing to her friend in the car. "Something's wrong with her boyfriend's car. He can tell us what's wrong with the engine."

"Oh, that is your friend Helen from the church," Dorothy said. "Please don't take long. My shoes are going to kill my feet. I can't wait to get my shoes off and get into bed."

Mary heard and nodded at Dorothy. She walked over to her friend's car. Helen sat in the front of the car and looked at Mary when she came over with Dorothy. Helen rolled the window down.

"Mary, I don't know what's wrong with the engine," Helen said. "Earl will check it and find out. I am very tired and need to get home to bed very badly!"

"Oh, the poor car," Mary said. "I hope that Earl will find out and fix it so you can go home soon. My eyes are burning and I need to get to bed soon, but I will be getting up two hours later."

"What are you talking about?" Helen asked, puzzled. "It is supposed to be about midnight."

Dorothy heard Helen say it was midnight, not four o'clock in the morning, and thought that Mary had just wanted to get her out of the bar.

"Midnight is still good," Dorothy said, pissed at Mary. "I think that your watch is dead! You have to buy a new watch!"

She laughed and leaned back on the fender. Mary ignored her and showed her watch to Helen. It was 4:11 a.m.

"Oh no, it is already past 4 a.m." She was shocked and looked at Dorothy. "Her watch works. We might want to get home and rest for a few hours before we get up for work. I don't want my boss to be disappointed with me for getting to work late this morning!"

Helen opened the door and got out of the car. She called to Earl that it was past four o'clock. Earl dropped the hood and closed it.

"Are you giving up on the car?" Mary asked. "You can't go home without your car. What about Helen, she needs a ride home tonight."

"Yes, you are right," Earl nodded. "My car is dead now and I have to ride a horse for work tomorrow. Helen, I can pick you up and you can ride with me to work on my horse, darling."

Mary and Dorothy were shocked and looked at Helen. She rolled her eyes and walked close to Earl's face.

"You better stop that," Helen said. "I am sorry, I can't ride with you on your horse! I do not want my uniform to get dirty or my damn butt to hurt! I will meet my friend a few blocks away from my house and we can go there for work tomorrow morning."

Helen pushed Earl away from her and left him alone. Mary

and Dorothy looked at each other, then toward Earl, and then back to Helen. They needed to find a ride home. Helen looked for her friends, but no luck. Just then, she saw her friend's pickup truck behind the tree. She knew that they had not left yet and looked back to the people leaving the bar.

"Mary and Dorothy," Helen said, "my friend Kara and her boyfriend Shan are still here, but I do not know where they are going now."

"Can I and Dorothy ride with you?" Mary asked. "We need a ride home please."

"Of course, you should know them from church," Helen said. "Perhaps you will remember them, but you have not had a chance to talk with them after church because you are always in a rush to get home and clean Mrs. Rhodes' house with Dorothy."

"I guess so," Mary figured. "I did not have a chance to talk with them. Now I can talk with them tonight before we get to my home."

"Yes, Mary," Helen giggled. "You will have a good chance to talk with them on the way to your home tonight. It is a perfect time for you, but I might not find them very soon."

Helen looked for Shan and Kara somewhere around the bar's parking lot. It was hard to see them because the bar had only one light in front of the building and it was not bright enough to see the parking lot.

People were leaving and the parking lot was almost empty. She saw her friends; they were talking and smoking cigarettes with other people in front of the bar. She waved at them, but they did not notice her.

"I found my friends," Helen said. "Both of you can come with me and meet Shan and Kara there."

Mary nodded and followed Helen to her friends, but she did not take Dorothy with her. Dorothy stood alone, her head still dizzy from wine. Mary hoped that they would agree to take them home. She planned to talk with Dorothy, but she saw that

Dorothy had not come with them. Mary walked back and pulled Dorothy's hand to follow her to Helen's friends.

Kara laughed and talked with her friend. She noticed Helen on the way to see her.

"Shan," Kara whispered. "Is something wrong with Helen?"

Helen came to Kara and held her coat like a beggar. "I need a ride to home," Helen said. "Kara, do you know Mary and Dorothy? They need a ride home, too, if Shan doesn't mind."

"Yes, I know them from my church," Kara said. "How is your day? We will take both of you to your home soon after we finish talking with my friends, OK?"

"Oh, thank you very much, Kara," Mary said. "I am doing fine and had fun with Dorothy at the bar tonight. Oh, did you see her sing on the stage?"

"Yes, I saw her on the stage," Kara said. "She has a beautiful voice! I already love it."

Kara shook Dorothy's hand, but Dorothy didn't respond to what had Kara said. She was still drunk. Kara looked at Mary.

"I think it's better for us to leave now," Kara said. "Dorothy needs to go home to bed. I bet she will be hung over, poor Dorothy."

"Oh, shut up, Kara," Dorothy clucked. "I caught your face. I know what you are talking about it."

Kara was surprised that Dorothy had heard what she told Mary. Mary looked at Dorothy.

"Dorothy," Mary said, slapping Dorothy's shoulder. "Watch your mouth. Kara did not mean to insult you!"

Dorothy moved her head around to Mary and looked at her shoulder.

"Why did you do that to me?" Dorothy asked. "You are not my mother!"

Dorothy turned her body around to face another way, but her legs were stuck and twisted. She fell down to the ground. Kara tried to control her laughter. Mary was shocked when she saw that Dorothy had fallen. Mary and Kara rushed to Dorothy, picked her up and wiped the dirt off her dress. Dorothy was still dizzy from drinking lots of wine.

"Leave me alone. I need to get a ride for home now!" Dorothy complained.

Helen told Shan to get his pick-up truck and come over to get them. Shan agreed and went to get his truck.

Kara told Helen, Mary and Dorothy to get in the back of the truck and sit on the hay. They pushed Dorothy up on the truck and she fell asleep on the hay.

Kara climbed in the front of the truck and told them to sit down before Shan started to drive on the way to their home. They sat down, and they left the bar.

Eloise woke up a little late because she did not smell the coffee from the kitchen—because no one had set up the coffee for her. She wondered what they were doing. She decided to check the kitchen downstairs. When she arrived, she saw no one there to make breakfast. She felt something was wrong with the color women, so she ran upstairs to Margaret's bedroom.

Eloise told Margaret that Mary and Dorothy had not shown up to cook breakfast. Margaret was puzzled and rushed downstairs. She pushed the kitchen door open and looked around. There was no one there. This had never happened before.

They went to Mary's house and knocked on the door, but no one answered. They went back to the house and looked around. Eloise knew that Margaret was very worried about the two color women. She did not want to lose them because they were very good to her.

Mary sat back on the truck's gate and looked to the sunrise. She knew that Margaret would be angry because they did not make her breakfast this morning. She looked at Helen and Dorothy. They were quietly sleeping. She thought that she should also take a nap, but she couldn't because it would make her more tired when she woke up.

Shan stopped on the road near Margaret's house.

"Mary, here is your home," Shan called to her. "You can get off the truck and walk home with Dorothy."

Mary stood up on the truck and stretched her back. She looked at Dorothy asleep on the hay. Mary tried to wake Dorothy up, but her eyes did not open. She sighed and pulled Dorothy up. Her legs started to move, and they walked off the truck together.

Dorothy stood and moved her body an inch, her head still heavy and dizzied from being drunk. Mary told her to stand up, then went to see Shan in the front of the truck. "Thank you for taking us home," she told him.

Shan gave her a wave and started to leave. Mary waved to them as they drove away.

Dorothy tried to stand up, but her body began to weaken and started to fall to the ground. Mary heard the rocks moving under Dorothy's feet and knew that she could not stand any longer. She looked back and saw Dorothy on the ground asleep. Mary sighed and came over to her. She pulled her up and walked with her in the driveway of Margaret's house.

Eloise went to the office, sat on her chair and moved closer to the desk. She was looking at some paperwork when she spotted two people at the road outside. She went to the window and could see that it was Mary and Dorothy. Eloise was glad they had arrived home safely and yelled to Margaret in the other room.

"Margaret," Eloise said, "I saw Mary and Dorothy walking together outside. They are on the way here from the road."

Margaret heard that Eloise had found the colored women somewhere outside. She felt relieved and ran to the office from the hall.

"Where did you find Mary and Dorothy?" Margaret asked.

Eloise pointed to the colored women outside the window. Margaret followed Eloise's finger to the women outside. She saw them; they were on the way to their home. Margaret unlocked the knob and opened the French doors that led outside. Eloise followed her.

"Mary, why are you getting home so late?" Margaret asked, concerned. "What has happened with Dorothy? Did something hit her?"

Mary looked at Margaret on the porch with Eloise. She did not answer her question about Dorothy.

Dorothy woke up and looked at Margaret, whose gray hair made her look like a freak to her.

"Hey, you are a freaky witch!" Dorothy chuckled, still drunk.

Margaret and Eloise were shocked by what Dorothy had said to them. Mary held Dorothy's mouth with her hand to shut her up and kept moving toward her home.

"Why did Dorothy say that to me?" Margaret asked Eloise, confused.

"She probably got drunk at the bar last night," Eloise said.

Margaret nodded, thinking that it was not like Dorothy to say bad things to people for no reason. They went inside, sat down, and started to work on their paperwork without eating breakfast.

Mary carried Dorothy upstairs to her bedroom. She dropped Dorothy onto her bed without changing her clothes or putting her PJs on her. Mary left Dorothy's bedroom, closed the door, and went to her own bedroom.

She took her dress off and noticed it smelled from all the smoking at the bar. She went to the window, opened it, and hung her dress outside. She went to her bed and slept for a few hours before cooking breakfast for Margaret and Eloise later that morning.

Chapter 12

A long black dress was hanging out the window, flapping in the wind. Mary woke up, pulled the bedclothes off the bed and went to the window. She opened it, grabbed the dress, and put it over the back of a chair. She felt like going back to bed, but she was supposed go over to the house and cook breakfast for Margaret and Eloise. She had slept only two hours.

She went to the dressing table and poured some water into the bowl to wash her face and comb her hair. Then she put a small white cap on her head. She put on her uniform and went downstairs to the kitchen, where she ate a piece of bread for her breakfast. She knew that Margaret and Eloise were hungry and waiting for her to cook their breakfast. She went to the hall, took her coat from the hanger on the wall, and put it on.

She didn't hear a sound from Dorothy. It was very quiet. Mary was disappointed that Dorothy would be showing bad manners to Margaret by not getting up.

Margaret was trying to do some paperwork with Eloise, but she didn't feel like it because her stomach was empty. Margaret gave up on doing the work and left the office. Eloise was confused and called after her.

"What are you doing now?" Eloise asked.

"I can't think about work," Margaret complained. "My stomach is bothering me. I guess I'll just have to go to the kitchen and grab some food."

Eloise thought that she should go with Margaret downstairs to the kitchen and get something to eat for both of them. She followed Margaret to the dining room and looked at the table. It was empty, not even with a plate or a glass for breakfast. She knew that the maids must still be asleep in their beds.

Margaret came into the kitchen and looked around. No one had been in the kitchen that morning at all. She sighed and went to the thirty-year-old, brown, wooden refrigerator. She opened it and looked inside to get a glass of milk.

Mary rushed to the house, opened the door and saw Margaret and Eloise standing there. She was scared. She took her coat off and went to hang it up. Margaret put the glass on the table and came over to Mary.

Mary put her head down and looked at Margaret's white shoes on the floor. Margaret knew that Mary was ashamed and was worried that Margaret would be mad at her for not showing up on time. Margaret lifted Mary's chin and looked at her eyes. Mary shut her eyelids, not daring to look at Margaret's face.

"Mary, I would like to talk with you," Margaret spoke. "I want to know what is happening this morning."

"I am sorry, ma'am," Mary muttered. "Dorothy and I went to the bar last night. We had a good time. She got drunk, though, because the men all liked her and gave her two or three glasses of wine. I'm sure she did not mean to insult you."

Mary looked back down at Margaret's shoes again. Margaret understood that she was frustrated with Dorothy, who must have been drunk and out of control.

"That was not your fault, Mary," Margaret said. "That has happened before with Dorothy. She's always liked to get drunk a lot, and does not care what it does to other people. I think it would be better to let her sleep for now. You don't have to worry about what happened, Mary."

"Are you going to give us a punishment?" Mary asked.

Margaret did not say a word in answer to what Mary had asked. She pointed to a large iron pan on the stove. Mary knew that Margaret was hungry and still expected her to cook the breakfast. Mary nodded and went to the refrigerator. Eloise pulled the door open and took a basket of eggs and a brown bag of bacon to Mary, who was surprised. She was not used to seeing white women helping colored women at all in her life.

"Thank you," Mary said.

She put the food on the table. Margaret knew that Mary had never seen anything like that happening before. She told Eloise that they should go away from the kitchen and let Mary cook the breakfast by herself. They left and went to the dining room.

Margaret came over to the 100-year-old shelves that held English plates and cups. She took out two plates and cups and put them on the table. Eloise brought two each of the knives, forks and spoons. She set them out on the table without waiting for Mary. That was their first time setting things out for themselves, so many years after the Civil War was over.

Dorothy's stomach was full of cramps. She felt as if she might vomit at any time. She woke up alone and it seemed to her that her stomach was pushing to escape from her body. She got out of bed and ran to the window, opened it, and put her head out. She could feel it coming at any moment. She began to scream and vomit out over the grass. She looked at the people outside to see if anyone had noticed at her. She did not mean to scream like that. She brought her head back into the house.

Mary was in the kitchen cutting a pepper into a big pan of soup. She could hear somebody screaming outside. She put the knife and pepper on the table, walked to the window and looked outside. She thought maybe somebody was trying to call for help, but no one was there. Was someone trying to play a game with her for some reason? She pushed the window down and went back to work cutting the peppers.

Dorothy had a hangover and her stomach felt bad. She went back to bed and slept for a while. A few hours later, she started to wake up slowly and looked at the window. The sun was on a different side. That did not seem right to her. She was confused about where was the sun could have gone. She would have to get up and begin dressing.

She poured a pitcher of lukewarm water into the bowl and washed her face. Then she wrapped her face in a towel to dry it. She put the towel on the chair and put on her uniform. She went outside to the wooden shed with the crescent moon at the top of the door. She came out of the shed, went to the pump, and drew out some water to wash her dirty hands. She dried her hands by wiping them on her dress, then went to the big house.

Mary was in the kitchen cooking a big pot of soup. She looked at Dorothy but did not say anything to her. Then she looked back at the pot and continued to stir it.

Dorothy noticed that Mary did not welcome her when she came into the kitchen. She went over to Mary, trying to be nice to her.

"Good morning, Mary," Dorothy said with a smile.

Mary heard Dorothy's voice, but she did not respond to her. Dorothy was surprised that she really wasn't going to say anything to her.

"Mary, good morning," Dorothy said. "Did you hear me?"

"It was a bad morning. Now it is a bad afternoon, Dorothy," Mary said, and kept on stirring the pot.

"Excuse me, Mary," Dorothy said. "Why are you saying that to me? Please say, 'good morning, Dorothy?'"

"No, it isn't morning anymore," Mary said. "Now it's the afternoon. So, what do I say? Bad afternoon!"

Dorothy was angry. She had tried to be nice. She came over closer to Mary. Mary stopped stirring and looked at Dorothy.

"Excuse me, do you have a problem, Dorothy?" Mary asked.

"Yes, I would like to know why you said that to me," Dorothy said seriously.

"Well, it is the afternoon already," Mary said. She pointed to the clock on the wall above the door. Dorothy followed Mary's finger and looked at the clock. She was surprised that it was fifteen minutes past five o'clock in the afternoon. "The time is past five in the afternoon. So, I said, 'Bad afternoon!'"

Dorothy still disagreed with Mary's way of putting it. She looked at Mary and came close to her again.

"OK! Let it be that I said, 'good afternoon!'" Dorothy shouted right in Mary's ear.

"No! I said, 'bad afternoon,' for you, and that's what I meant!" Mary said. "Do you know why I told you that? Because you were drunk and showed bad manners to Mrs. Rhodes this morning. Do you remember that?"

Dorothy had not realized that she was really drunk at the bar the night before and had overslept that morning.

"OK, you are right that I was insulting to her," Dorothy admitted. "You know that I was drunk and did not even think about what I was saying to her."

Mary was stirring the soup and listening to Dorothy. She looked on the other side of counter for something that she needed, but it was not there. She stopped stirring, put the spoon down on the stove and went to the cabinets to try to find what she was looking for.

Dorothy kept on talking until she noticed that Mary had left her alone. Dorothy was puzzled. She wondered if Mary was trying to ignore her while she was trying to explain things to her. She did not care about what Dorothy was trying to say. Dorothy was disappointed in her. She could see some hot sauce on the small shelves up on the wall, and she thought that it would be a good revenge on Mary to pour some hot sauce into the soup.

Dorothy looked carefully to see if Mary was still looking in the cabinets. Dorothy started to move very quietly so that Mary would not hear her footsteps. She came to the small shelves, grabbed the hot sauce, then went back to the stove where the large pot of soup was. She poured the sauce into the soup.

Mary had found a small jar of basil for the soup. She turned back to the stove and saw Dorothy standing there. She wondered what Dorothy was doing with the soup. Mary went to check on Dorothy and saw the hot sauce bottle in her hand.

"Don't pour the hot sauce into the soup!" Mary shouted as loud as she could.

Dorothy was frightened by Mary's voice. She stopped pouring it into the soup and looked back at Mary.

Mary came over to Dorothy and took the hot sauce away from her. She took the spoon from the stove and picked up a little soup and tasted it. Mary was shocked that the soup had lots of spice, and she knew that Margaret would not like it that way.

"Dorothy! Why did you do that to Mrs. Rhodes' dinner today?" Mary was really upset.

"Oh no, I had an accident and spilled too much hot sauce into the soup," Dorothy tried to explain to Mary.

Mary looked at the soup and could see some of the sauce there at the top. She tried to remove it and then tasted it. She was very angry and looked at Dorothy with an unforgiving face. She dropped the spoon beside the soup pot and made a grab for Dorothy's neck.

"How dare you!" Mary screamed as she choked Dorothy. "Why did you pour the hot sauce in the soup for Mrs. Rhodes? She doesn't like any spices on any foods. What is she going to eat for her dinner today?"

Mary kept on trying to choke Dorothy, who moved her legs to kick at Mary.

"Mary! Please don't kill me! Please!" Dorothy said, begging her to forgive her for causing this accident.

Margaret was in the dining room reading the newspaper. She heard the screams from the kitchen and could not read anymore because the noise was bothering her.

"Mary and Dorothy! Please will you stop screaming at each other out there in the kitchen?" Margaret called to them.

Mary could hear Mrs. Rhodes' voice, so she stopped trying to choke Dorothy.

Dorothy could finally breathe. She looked at Mary. "Why were you trying to kill me?" Dorothy whispered. "God damn you!"

Dorothy had tried to avoid Mary's attempt to choke her. She went to the table and pulled the chair out and sat down, trying to get her breath back to normal. Mary was still mad at Dorothy for pouring the hot sauce in the soup that was supposed to be Mrs. Rhodes' dinner that day.

"You are evil and you are giving me a big problem with that damn spicy sauce in the soup!" Mary said seriously.

Margaret could tell the kitchen had become quiet for now, but her stomach was still empty.

"Mary, when you finish the soup, will you please bring me a bowl in here," Margaret ordered. "I am almost starved now, so please hurry up and finish the soup up soon."

Mary was mad at Dorothy because she would have to give the soup to Margaret. Dorothy was giggling by then. She wanted to hear Mrs. Rhodes scream after she tasted the soup with so much spice in it.

Mary knew that Dorothy liked to play games with her. Mary came over to the stove, took the spoon out of the pot and put it back on the stove. Then she took another long spoon and put two big spoonfuls into a bowl. She put the bowl on the tray and then brought it with her from the kitchen.

Dorothy followed Mary to the dining room. Mary put the bowl on the table in front of Margaret.

Margaret put her spoon into the soup, then tasted it, not realizing that the flavoring was too hot. She almost choked on the spicy taste. Mary had almost poisoned her. Dorothy seemed to be laughing about it. Margaret dropped the spoon and looked at Mary, who was staring back with frightened eyes.

"Why did you put hot sauce into the soup? Margaret asked Mary. "I don't like that. It's much too spicy! I want you to replace that with another soup. But I really hate having to wait for such a long time for you to cook some more."

Margaret felt as if she had burned her tongue. She drank some water to calm down the burning sensation. She looked at the plate of bread, took some and ate it. She put the bread into the bowl and stirred it into the soup, hoping to make it less spicy. Then she tasted it again to see if it was less spicy. It was not really all that bad, and she decided that whe would be willing to eat it.

"This is not so very bad and you won't have to make another soup today," Margaret said. "Mary, you have to be careful when you cook with spices in the food. I don't want my tongue to get burned again, OK?"

Mary nodded and looked at Dorothy. She was surprised that Margaret was so very clever that she could find a way to solve the problem. Mary went to the kitchen by herself for a few seconds. Dorothy had been planning to come back into the kitchen. She opened the door to the kitchen and looked around the room but she could not find Mary. She stood there and wondered where Mary had gone. At that moment, she was scared again by Mary, who had been hiding behind the door until Dorothy came in. Mary grabbed Dorothy and tried to choke her again.

"Don't do that again! I am going to die this time!" Dorothy screamed. "You had better get off of me right now! Please don't ever do that again!"

Mary stopped choking Dorothy and let her to go. Dorothy ran behind the table to keep Mary out of her reach. Mary came over to the table and pointed at Dorothy.

"I am glad that Mrs. Rhodes is not going to punish me!" Mary said. "You are so damn foolish!

"Yes, you are right that I was foolish!" Dorothy admitted. She walked to the door and opened it. "I am going home and going back to bed now! Bad-bye!"

Dorothy went outside, closed the door and walked to her small house. Mary was laughing by now thinking about how foolish Dorothy had been. She came to the stove and looked at the pot to see if she could find any more sauce that might be floating on the soup.

Chapter 13

The birds were flying around in the sky. They came to sit on the porch rail next to Margaret's window. There was an opening about five inches deep that let air come in her bedroom. The birds were singing and playing around a large pot that was full of water from the rain the night before. Margaret's bedroom had dull, peach-colored paper on the wall that she had never changed since her mother passed away. She did not want to change to new wallpaper because she liked this color. Her fifty-year-old brass bed frame was still in good shape. The birds kept on singing and playing, making a cheerful noise.

Margaret had given up on sleeping since the birds awakened her. She was thinking about making a plan for the day. She changed her mind and decided to try to sleep a little bit more. She pulled the flat sheet up over her head to ignore the birds, but she could still hear them outside. She gave up again, and removed the sheet from her head. She could smell something dank in the sheets. They seemed to be dirty. She thought that they should be changed.

She stood up and went into her bathroom. It had dark yellow wallpaper with many small floral pictures. She could see in her oval mirror that her hair looked uncombed and messy. She felt miserable. She should take time to wash her hair this morning so it would look less wild.

Margaret came over to a white tub that stood on four legs near the window and turned the water on. She looked at the window and opened it a little more to let some fresh air into the room. She sat on a stool and looked outside while she waited for the tub to fill. When it had filled, she turned the faucets off. She took her nightgown off and put it on the chair. She checked the water to see if it was warm enough. She stepped into the tub slowly and carefully.

She felt so relaxed, looking up at a glass lamp which hung from the ceiling. She let her head come down into the water a little, then raised it back up. She looked at the shampoo over on the small, round table nearby and poured some into her palm, deciding to wash her hair first and then her body. A half hour later, she got out of the tub and took a towel to wrap herself dry. Then she put her clean clothes on and went downstairs to look for Mary and Dorothy in the kitchen. She could already see them in the hall before she reached the lowest level of the stairs.

"Mary and Dorothy, I would like you to put fresh sheets on my bed today," Margaret said. "The sheets smelled awful this morning."

"Yes, we will do that for you this morning, ma'am," Mary said, smiling a little bit. Then she looked at Dorothy. "Will you come with me to change the bed sheets after we cook breakfast?"

"Yes, I certainly will," Dorothy said.

"Great. Then let's go into the kitchen and cook the breakfast right away." Margaret smiled and walked into the dining room. "I would like something to drink now and then both of you can go ahead and cook."

Mary went to the cabinets and took out a skillet to cook some eggs and bacon. Dorothy went to another cabinet to grab two plates, glasses and silverware. She went back to the dining room and put them on the table for Margaret and Eloise. Margaret went to the refrigerator and got out a pitcher of lemonade.

After Margaret and Eloise had finished with their breakfast, they left the dining room. Mary and Dorothy went to the table and collected the dishes and glasses on a tray, then brought them to the kitchen. Mary put the dishes into a large sink and washed them with soap. She gave some of the dishes to Dorothy, who wrapped cloth around them to dry. They finished cleaning up the kitchen and the dining room.

Mary and Dorothy walked upstairs to Mrs. Rhodes' bedroom. Dorothy went into the bathroom and opened a white cabinet full of linens. Mary went to the mattress, pulled the dirty sheets off and put them on the floor. Dorothy brought clean sheets to the bedroom and put them on the chair. She carefully tucked a bottom sheet around the corners of the mattress, then threw a top sheet widely open in the air and let Mary catch it to pull it smooth. Dorothy picked up the heavy quilt and laid it out evenly over the tight, smooth sheets.

"Dorothy, I would like to talk with you about something," Mary said.

"Yes, what do you want to tell me?" Dorothy asked.

"I heard something at church," Mary said. "But I am not sure if it could be true. Were you doing something with another man somewhere?"

Dorothy was surprised and confused by what Mary was saying she had heard.

"Mary, where did you get this story from?" Dorothy asked. "I want to know what you heard."

Mary rolled her eyes. She was finding it hard to decide if she should tell Dorothy the truth about what she had heard. Then Dorothy would be mad at her for no reason. Dorothy kept staring at Mary, waiting for an answer to her question.

"Dorothy, I hope I won't see you behaving badly and showing your temper after I tell you what the women at church said," Mary finally replied.

"No, I won't do that, but can you tell me about them, please?" Dorothy said.

"OK. They said that you were having an affair with a married man last week." Mary spoke softly, trying not to scold her friend.

Dorothy was feeling shocked and angry about what the women had said. She knew that they were making up this story about her. She jumped and stomped on the mattress.

"Dorothy! You better get off the bed now!" Mary yelled.

"I know those women! They are gossiping all the time!" Dorothy was furious. "I feel like killing them! I'm going to their house and I'm going to kill them!"

Dorothy jumped off the bed and started to rush out of the bedroom, but Mary brought her back and pushed her down on the mattress again. Dorothy looked wildly back at Mary.

"Why do you think you must push me down on this damn mattress? Dorothy hissed. "I want to kill those two gossiping women! I don't care if the police put me in jail for a lifetime!

"You better stop right now. I don't want you to get in a big problem for no murder!" Mary yelled. "God will not forgive you for a murder! When you die, then you will not meet me in heaven! Because you will be going to hell!"

What Mary said made Dorothy feel shocked. She stood up and came over closer to Mary's face.

"Oh! How can you possibly say that? I want you to come with me to hell!" Dorothy said. "I don't care at all about what you are talking about!"

Mary pushed Dorothy back onto the mattress once again. "What is the matter with your mind?" Mary asked. She slapped Dorothy's face as hard as she could.

Dorothy was even angrier than Mary had expected. She stood up again and yelled in her face even more rigorously than before.

In the office, Margaret and Eloise were working on paperwork for the factory. They could hear down the hall that the maids were arguing and being noisy. Margaret could not stand to hear any more of whatever the maids were doing in her bedroom.

"I have to go over to my bedroom and tell them to stop that arguing and keep quiet," Margaret sighed. "Otherwise, they will just have to go to the kitchen downstairs or back home. It's really a bother to us. We need to focus on this work."

"Yes, that is true, Mrs. Rhodes," Eloise agreed. "I think it's a good idea for you to go over and tell them to stop right now. We can finish our paperwork this afternoon."

"Indeed, I suppose so," Margaret said. She stood up and left her desk to go into the hall. "I will be right back in a moment, Mrs. Taylor."

"Yes, Mrs. Rhodes," Eloise said. She went back to work at some of the other accounts on her desk.

Margaret went down the hall to her bedroom and looked at the maids. They were still arguing over by the bed. Margaret rolled her eyes. There was nothing new about seeing them do things like that. She stamped her foot and both of the maids stopped arguing.

"What is the matter with both of you?" Margaret felt frustrated. She didn't know what else to ask.

"Oh, nothing, we are arguing about some stupid things about our personal lives. You probably know what I am talking about?" Dorothy answered softly.

Mary was puzzled and could not say anything. Margaret could see Mary's face. She suspected that something was wrong with her.

"Mary Waters, what is wrong with you?" Margaret asked.

Mary was surprised that Margaret was calling her by her whole name. "Oh, nothing, we are both fine. This just happened this minute, Mrs. Rhodes," Mary muttered.

Margaret still did not understand why they were making so much noise.

"Well, I want both of you to keep quiet and go back to work and fix my bed," Margaret ordered. "Please, will you stop making so much noise? Mrs. Taylor and I need to finish our paperwork so we can send some cotton to New Orleans this afternoon. You better listen to me now."

"Yes, we won't start to argue again, Mrs. Rhodes," Mary

said, and Dorothy nodded her head.

"Next time both of you want to argue, please don't argue here," Margaret warned them. "It would be better for you to go to the kitchen downstairs or back over to your house or something like that."

Mary and Dorothy obeyed Margaret's orders. They went back to work and fixed up the bed. Margaret sighed and went back to her office. Mary and Dorothy looked back at Margaret and watched her go. Then they looked at each other and would have liked to laugh, but they didn't dare.

The government announced by mail to the residents of Providence that the town's name would be changed to Lake Providence on September 4, 1923, because two other states had towns with the same name. Rhode Island's capital was named Providence, and the mail was often sent incorrectly.

When Margaret received her letter, she was surprised and talked with Eloise about the town adding the word "Lake" to its name. She called Mary and Dorothy to come up to her office.

"Mrs. Rhodes, did you want to talk with us?" Dorothy asked.

Margaret looked at them. "Yes, I want to tell you there is going to be a new name for our town," she said. "On September fourth, the town will become Lake Providence, not just Providence. When you write a letter to mail to anyone, you need to put your address as Lake Providence, Louisiana."

Mary did not understand why the town had changed its name. She looked at Dorothy. "Why are they going to call our town Lake Providence?" Mary wondered.

Margaret decided it would be too hard to explain it to Mary, so she let Dorothy try to tell her why it had happened.

"Mary, the reason they are going to change the name of our town," Dorothy explained, "is because another state has a city with the same name as this town, and people can't tell which is which."

"Which state is it that keeps getting mixed up with ours?" Mary asked Dorothy doubtfully.

"Oh, that is the town of Providence in Rhode Island," Dorothy answered.

"I see. The next time I might want to write it, the town name is Lake Providence, right?" Mary also wanted to know, "Where did they get the idea to call it that?"

"They made it up because the Mississippi River runs by here. It's water, too, you know." Eloise was pointing to the river outside. "That's the reason why we all are living in this town."

Mary could understand her point and came over to look out the window and see the Mississippi River there. She looked back at Eloise.

"It does make sense that they can call that water over there a lake for our town," Mary said. "Now I know that we are living near a lake."

Margaret smiled. "Yes, that's why they chose the name,"

Mary nodded and smiled at Margaret, then looked over at the river and wondered why they had named the town after it, but then called it a lake.

Chapter 14

Mary was reorganizing things for supper when she heard Margaret's footsteps as she came into the kitchen and grabbed a red apple from the bowl on the table. Mary watched Margaret closely, waiting to hear what she had come to say.

"Mrs. Rhodes, do you need anything this morning?" Mary finally asked.

"No, thank you, Mary; I just came to get this apple," Margaret said, showing the apple as proof. "I like to eat apples in the morning."

Margaret left the kitchen. Mary didn't say anything more to her, even though she knew that Margaret had already eaten her breakfast.

Mary collected the dishes from the dining room table, put them on a tray and brought them into the kitchen. She put the dishes into the sink and began to wash them. When she was finished, she went back to the dining room and moved the chairs away from the table. She took a white lace cloth from the table, brought it back to the kitchen and put it on a tall stool. She looked at Dorothy, who was still cleaning up the counter. Mary kept watching Dorothy until she finished her work.

Dorothy looked at Mary and wondered why she was standing there looking at her while she was cleaning the counter. "Do you want to say something to me?" Dorothy asked.

Mary nodded and pointed at the clock. Dorothy turned and looked at it too. She was surprised that the time was almost eight o'clock in the morning. She was supposed to go home and change into a nice dress to go to church at nine.

"Oh, it's time for church." Dorothy was surprised. "I think I'd better finish cleaning up here this morning. I have to go!"

Dorothy threw the cloth at the bucket and left the kitchen. Mary laughed and followed Dorothy back to their house.

Mary went to her bedroom upstairs and changed into a white dress with flowers printed on it. She put her hat on and looked in the mirror to see if it was set right on her head. She took her purse and walked out of her bedroom to the hall. At the same time Dorothy came out of her bedroom.

"Dorothy, do you want to wear that navy blue dress for church?" Mary wondered.

"Yes, I like it," Dorothy said, and she went downstairs.

Mary followed Dorothy down the steps and outside to Margaret's house. They came into the kitchen and saw Mrs. Rhodes there, wearing a nice white dress and a few artificial flowers on her hat.

"Can we do something for you, ma'am?" Mary asked.

"Yes, I would like to inform you," Margaret announced, "that I will not be back until late this evening. My friend and I will be having dinner together at her house, so you won't have to cook dinner for me. You have a nice day now, good-bye."

"Oh, yes, ma'am." Dorothy was smiling broadly. "Thank you for letting us know that you won't be here for dinner tonight. We'll be here for you early tomorrow morning."

"Yes, I will see both of you tomorrow first thing in the morning for breakfast," Margaret said before leaving the kitchen.

"So, we can save what we have already fixed for the next dinner," Mary said. "We are supposed to go. Our friends are waiting for us outside."

"Yes, we better leave right now," Dorothy said.

They rushed out to the front of the house and saw their friend's car parked on the dirt road. The man who had been waiting for them got out of the car.

"Hey, ladies, are you ready to go to church now?" he asked them.

"Oh, yes, we sure are!" Dorothy said. "I am sorry we had to keep you waiting so long, Mr. Nolan."

"Nah, this isn't so long," Mr. Nolan said. "We just arrived here a few minutes ago."

They climbed into the back seat. Mr. Nolan's wife was sitting in front. She looked back at them with a smile.

"Good morning, Mrs. Waters and Mrs. Datson," Mrs. Nolan greeted them. "How has your day been so far?"

"Yes, thank you. We're fine, and good morning to you," they both answered, more or less together.

Mr. Nolan pulled out on the road and began the five-mile trip to the church.

When they arrived, they saw the preacher standing in front of the church by the open doorway. Mr. Nolan found a place to park his car. Mary and Dorothy got out of the car and walked to the front of the church together with the Nolans.

The church was a small building made completely of wooden siding. There were four side windows, each one full of bright-colored panes of glass. At the rear of the building, there was a single, larger window with Jesus and two angels, one on each side.

"Good morning to all of you," the preacher greeted them. "How are you all, and what's doing in your lives?"

"Good morning, Reverend!" they answered as they walked through the wide doorway. Some of them told him, "We are doing fine and our health is great, glory to God."

"That's good to hear. All of you come on in." The preacher smiled and followed along behind the last few people to enter.

The room was very small, only about sixteen feet wide and not quite twenty feet in length. There was bare wood behind the studs and no drywall had ever been installed to cover it. During cold weather, people wore thick coats to keep warm. There was a small heating stove that was very little help. In the summer people wore light clothes and most of them used cardboard fans on little sticks to try to keep cool. One woman was sitting on a stool at the small, brown, upright piano. The Nolan family and Mary and Dorothy sat on the back bench. The preacher walked past the congregation to the pulpit. He opened his Bible and looked up.

"Good morning, I am glad to see that so many people have come here this morning." The preacher smiled.

"Good morning, Reverend!" the congregation called out together. "We are here for the glory of God!"

"Good to hear from you!" the preacher shouted. "God loves you! Jesus is living in your heart! I know all of you are in sin anyway, but God will always forgive you!"

"Yes, we have sinned and God is going to forgive us!" the congregation responded.

They went on reading the Bible and singing with the preacher for an hour. Dorothy was sitting next to the window and feeling bored. She looked at the window but could not see through it because of the paint that covered the glass. She thought that she should make a hole so she could see out. Dorothy started to scratch the paint off.

Mary was sitting next to Dorothy and could hear the little noise at the window. She looked and saw what Dorothy was doing. Mary knew that they were not supposed to destroy the paint on the windows, so she thought she had better stop Dorothy. She slapped at her hand. Dorothy looked at Mary with a shocked face.

"What is that matter with you?" she spoke out loud. "You are not my mother!"

The preacher could hear Dorothy's voice from the back bench near the window.

"Dorothy, you should know better than to do that to the church!" Mary whispered. "Please keep your voice down. Other people can hear you."

People did hear and they looked at Mary and Dorothy on the back bench. They were arguing and not looking at the preacher at all.

"Excuse me, you are not my mother," Dorothy said again, and she stood up.

Mary was really surprised that she would dare to stand up with all those other people there. "Please, will you stop acting like that in church?"

Mary did not like what Dorothy was doing, so she stood up too and came closer to Dorothy. "Dorothy, you better be grown up and sit down, now!" Mary ordered. "I mean, I really am your second mother!"

People in the congregation were starting to laugh at them. The preacher rolled his eyes. He thought this kind of thing would drive him crazy.

"Oh, you better not say that to me." Dorothy was really annoyed. "You are not my second mother, period!"

They were still arguing. The preacher was calling their names but they were not listening to him at all. He gave up and yelled out loud. Mary and Dorothy finally heard him and were quiet.

"Thank you, ladies; I need you to stop arguing here," the preacher said. "If you feel like you want to leave, that is certainly fine!"

Mary and Dorothy looked at each other and sat down without saying anything else. The preacher nodded and went back to the Bible.

After the church service was done at noon, the preacher walked through the congregation. He looked at Mary and Dorothy on their bench, showing a little disappointment at the way they had behaved in church that morning. He pulled the door open to permit people to leave. Mary and Dorothy came over to the preacher when they got outside.

"I am very sorry we were so rude at your church this morning." Mary was embarrassed. "We will not do that again right there in front of you. Please, will you forgive me and Dorothy?"

"Yes, we made a mistake to do that in your church," Dorothy interrupted. "Can you forgive me for what happened this morning?"

The preacher was surprised that they were so willing to tell the truth to him about having had a problem. He thought that it was important to forgive them.

"OK, I am going to forgive you for arguing in our church," he said. "Please, next time, will you promise not to begin an argument in church? OK?"

"Yes, we will not do that again at your church," Mary and Dorothy each told him. "God bless you, and we'll be here to see you next Sunday."

"Yes, see you next Sunday, and you have a nice day today." The preacher smiled. "God bless you, too. Good-bye."

They left and waited for their friends to talk with the preacher a little bit, then they all came back to the car and left the parking lot. They stayed over at their friends' house for the day and only went back home late that night.

Margaret arrived home at about the same time.

Chapter 15

Nancy and Billy were sitting on the dock and had a good view of the Mississippi River. They were having a good time talking and smoking. Billy was learning more from Nancy about her grandmother's life. He still wondered how Nancy had gotten so much information from her grandmother before she passed away.

Nancy felt comfortable talking with Billy, but she was becoming hungry. She thought that they should put off any more stories about her grandmother until they had lunch.

"Billy, I am very hungry," Nancy said. "I think we'd better stop for a while now. We could go to a restaurant and get something to eat. After that we can continue talking about my grandmother."

"Sure," Billy agreed. "What would you like to eat for lunch? I can take you downtown and we can look for a restaurant there."

"Yes, please let's do that. Thanks!" Nancy smiled, stood up and shook some dust off her coat. "You can choose where we eat. I have not visited the downtown area for a few years."

Billy stood up and rapped some dust off his pants. "Let's go. We will talk more in the restaurant."

"That sounds good. I'd like a softer chair to sit on for a little bit," Nancy laughed.

They arrived at Billy's car and he unlocked the door and opened it for Nancy. He got in the car and turned it around to go downtown.

Nancy saw a spot on the street and pointed it out. Billy

parked his car near the hardware store. They looked for a restaurant that Nancy had not eaten in before. She noticed a small restaurant across the street. It was called A Small Eatery. She told Billy that she would like to eat there. Billy did not mind.

They went across the street and into the restaurant. The hostess came over to Billy. "Hello, how many people will be at your table today?" the hostess asked before she noticed Nancy behind Billy. "Excuse me, is that colored woman with you?"

"Yes, she is with me. How long is the wait for a table please?" Billy said.

"I am sorry, but we do not allow colored people to sit at the tables for whites," the hostess said. "If you want to eat with her, then both of you can eat in the back of the building. There are a few tables out there with chairs. It is still quite a nice area for colored people."

"Excuse me, she comes from Indiana," Billy tried to explain to the hostess.

Nancy pulled at Billy's arm to stop him from asking the hostess to let them sit in the white area.

"Mr. Vangslia, you don't have to worry about begging her to allow us to eat in this restaurant," Nancy said. The hostess was surprised that Nancy's voice sounded like a white person from up north.

"Thank you, and you have a nice day," Nancy said. "Mr. Vangslia, we can go somewhere else and buy a deli sandwich, and then we can eat outside somewhere, OK?"

"Um? Sure. You have the right idea that we should not beg to eat here," Billy agreed. He looked back at the hostess. "Never mind. Thanks anyway."

The hostess did not say anything more as Billy and Nancy left the restaurant. Billy told Nancy that he knew where there was a food shop a few blocks away. They walked there slowly, talking about other items in their personal lives until Billy noticed the food shop was across the street.

"Here it is," Billy said. "My wife and I have been here often."

"Good! Let's go for it!" Nancy laughed and ran across the street with Billy. "I am hungry! I need to eat something very bad!"

"Yeah, me too!" Billy laughed and pulled the door open to let Nancy in. "I will show you where the deli sandwiches are."

They went to the long glass counter. People could look in it and see every kind of cheese and meat displayed inside, being kept cold and fresh. The sales clerk came over to them.

"Can I help you?" He spoke to Billy.

"We'd like some sandwiches," Billy said.

"I guess you would like a Swiss cheese and ham with rye bread?" the man asked Billy to make sure he had his usual order right. "Miss, do you want something different for your sandwich?"

"Yes, sir, I would like roast beef and American cheese on wheat bread," Nancy said. "And I'd also like to have mayonnaise, please. Thank you."

"I will make the sandwiches for you right now," the clerk said with a smile. He made the two sandwiches, put them in a bag and gave it to Billy. "Thank you, and come back again. Bye."

They went to the cashier, paid for their lunches, then left the food shop. Billy knew where there were tables nearby.

"Nancy, will you please come with me?" Billy asked. "The tables are right over there near the hardware store."

"OK, I will just follow you there," Nancy said.

Nancy followed Billy to the table. They could see cars passing by on the street.

"This is not bad here," Nancy commented. "Now we can finally sit down and eat the sandwiches!"

"Yes, sure! Go for it!" Billy laughed. "Here's your sandwich."

"Thank you very much for buying me lunch today," Nancy said. She smiled and began to eat the sandwich. "I will pay you back later."

"You don't have to pay me anything," Billy said.

After they had eaten their lunch they started to smoke cigarettes again. Billy looked at the hardware store. He noticed that there were bags in high piles near the door, but he did not know why they were there. He stood up and walked over to the store. Nancy was puzzled and went to follow him.

"What are you looking for?" Nancy asked.

Billy kept on walking and looked at the bags. He thought they each would probably hold about ten pounds or so.

"Nancy, do you know what these bags are for?" Billy asked. "If you don't know, then don't worry about it. I'll ask the manager what they are."

"Yes, I know what the bags are for. They are used to kill boll weevils and thrips," Nancy answered. "This is the stuff that goes in the crop duster plane. Then it flies over cotton plantations and sprays them."

"What are boll weevils and thrips?" Billy asked.

"I am not really an expert. I can remember what my grandmother told me," she said. "A boll weevil is a kind of bug that came from Mexico in 1890. They had gotten to Louisiana by 1904. But I am not sure if that is the right name for them."

"I see, and what about thrips?" Billy asked again.

"Well, I forget exactly what they are, but I think it's a problem that comes from too much moisture in the plants." Nancy was really trying to answer his question. "I'm trying my best, but I'm not sure if I can explain to you more clearly. I do remember that my grandmother told me about what happened with the beehive. I think that was just another name for the boll weevil bug. Whatever it was, it came into Mrs. Rhodes' cotton plants a long time ago."

Billy thought he understood what Nancy was talking about. The beehive, if that was it's right name, had been trying to eat the cotton crop.

Nancy thought that she would like to stay right there in town a little longer.

"I want to look around the town," Nancy said. "The last time I visited here was two summers ago. Billy, if you don't mind, I'd like to stay here for a while, then we can go back to the park later this afternoon?"

"Yes, Nancy, you can look around the town today." Billy smiled and started to smoke another cigarette. "Do you want one?"

"Yes, thanks," Nancy said. She pulled the cigarette out of the box and started to smoke.

They went down the street to the City Hall. Nancy told Billy that her grandmother had always talked about this downtown area where she had gone shopping with Dorothy and other friends many times before her death.

Chapter 16

During lunch break, the colored workers were eating on a long table inside the barn. One of them had finished his lunch, so he walked outside and looked at the trees. He found a tree with some shade near the cotton field. He went over and sat on the ground. He started to smoke cigarette, wanting to relax for a while before going back to work picking the cotton. He noticed that there were a few insects flying over the plants. He wondered what they were. He went over to the plants and looked at the bugs. He decided that this was the kind of bug called "beehive," and that it could be killing all of the cotton plants. He had to inform Mrs. Rhodes, so he ran back to the house.

Dorothy came into the hall and noticed that the long rug had some dirt on it. She could tell that the workers had not checked their shoes before coming into the house. Dorothy sighed, rolled up the long rug and took it outside to shake the dirt out. She saw the worker running toward her. She stopped shaking the rug and listened to what he was telling her.

"Please, will you tell Mrs. Rhodes," he shouted, "beehives are all over the plants. She needs to call for the sprayer right away!"

"OK, I will let Mrs. Rhodes know what you saw," Dorothy said. "I am on the way to her office right now."

Dorothy took the rug back into the house, dropped it on the floor and ran to the office. Margaret and Eloise were working with the records on the desk as usual. Dorothy came in and waited for them to stop and look at her.

Margaret could hear Dorothy's heavy breathing and figured

that she must have been running. She looked at Dorothy, who was standing near the door and looking scared. "What is the matter, Dorothy?" Margaret wondered. "Can you tell me what the problem is?"

Dorothy nodded and came over to Margaret's desk. "Yes, ma'am," she panted. "A worker told me that the beehives are coming to the cotton plants and eating them. He wants you to call the man that has an airplane and can fly over cotton fields with the sprayer that will kill all the beehives."

Margaret was shocked by what Dorothy was telling her. She looked at Eloise.

"We shouldn't have to do this again. We just did it a few years ago," Margaret sighed. "I really hate that! I have to call Mr. Williams right now. Dorothy, thank you very much for letting me know. Please, will you tell all of the workers to go away from the fields before Mr. Williams flies over them and sprays them today."

"Yes, ma'am, I will let them know that you are planning to call him right away," Dorothy said. She left the office and saw Mary coming upstairs as she was going down. She just said, "Mary, I have to go outside right now."

Mary nodded and let Dorothy go do what she had been told. Dorothy ran through the kitchen and out the back door. She kept on running until she got to the barn, where some the workers were still eating their lunch. She came into the barn and breathed heavily. The workers saw Dorothy and wondered what might be wrong with her.

"Did you come to tell us something?" one of the workers asked.

"Yes, I want to tell everybody that Mrs. Rhodes has to call the plane," Dorothy finally said.

"What for?" another worker puzzled.

"I haven't finished telling you," Dorothy said. She put her head down to keep from being so dizzy, then picked it back up again. "The plane will have to spray over the cotton fields to kill the beehives today."

"Oh my God! She's not going to do that again!" another worker said, horrified. "We have to get out of here and wait for the plane to come and fly over the whole plantation."

The workers stopped eating and put their food into bags to clear everything off the table. They left the barn and walked over to the fence by the fields to watch for the plane, which could be coming over at any minute.

Dorothy was on the way back to the house and could see Mary, who was coming to find her. Mary stopped walking and stood, waiting for Dorothy to come over to her. She walked past Mary and kept on going to the house. Mary did not like that Dorothy just ignored her.

"Dorothy! Please stop acting like that with me!" Mary complained. "I want you to come over here right away! Please, Dorothy! I want to know what is going on."

Dorothy stopped walking and rolled her eyes. She went back to Mary and looked her straight in the eye.

"What do you want to tell me?" Dorothy asked nicely.

"Will you please tell me what that is?" Mary was pointing to the plants.

"Oh, somebody told me that beehives were coming into the cotton plants," Dorothy explained. "I had to inform Mrs. Rhodes that they had seen them. Then she called the man to fly over the plants and kill them by spraying them with poison."

"Do you mean the boll weevil?" Mary wondered. "They can't work there while the plane comes over."

"Yes, you know that they have had a lot of problems for many years," Dorothy agreed. "There isn't any other way but to kill them. You can't let them make more babies and have them come over and eat the plants."

"Yes, that's what happens," Mary said. "Let's go back into the kitchen to get ready for suppertime."

"Yes, you're right." Dorothy said, and she slowly followed Mary back.

They went back to the house. Mary went to the cabinets and looked for the skillet to cook up some ham and cheese.

Dorothy had forgotten about the rug. She felt so tired since she had to run all the way to the barn. She sighed and started to leave.

Mary looked at Dorothy. "Where are you going to?" Mary was puzzled. "You are still supposed to help me cook for Mrs. Rhodes' dinner for tonight."

"I have to put the rug back properly in the upstairs hall," Dorothy said. "I will be right back in a minute, OK?"

Dorothy left the kitchen to go upstairs. Mary went to the refrigerator and took out the bags of ham and cheese to slice them up together.

Dorothy started upstairs, then sat down on one of the steps for a while. Eloise came out to go downstairs and saw Dorothy sitting there.

"Are you all right, Dorothy?" Eloise was concerned. "I know that you had lots of running to do today."

"Yes, you are right that I did do that, Mrs. Taylor," Dorothy sighed. "You know that I am too old to run around like that!"

She went the rest of the way upstairs. Eloise thought that Dorothy was trying to be comical about it.

"You are very funny!" Eloise laughed. "I like it that you said that you are too old to do that!"

Dorothy heard Eloise say that she thought what Dorothy had said to her was funny. She laughed too, then picked up the rug and put it on the floor properly. Then she went downstairs to the kitchen and helped Mary get things ready for Mrs. Rhodes' dinner later that evening.

Chapter 17

Nancy had a good time walking around town with Billy for an hour or so. They went back to Billy's car and got in. Nancy saw children playing and running over the top of a little hill. Billy started the engine and tried to talk with her, but she wasn't listening to what he was saying. He could see the children on the hill, too.

"The children always love to play on top of that hill," Billy said. "When parents come to the park with their children, after a while they always run up the hill so they can look out at the Mississippi River."

"Really? I did not know that the children liked going up there just to have a nice view of the river." Nancy laughed. "Do you know what they do that for?"

"I don't really know why they are playing over there." Billy thought about it for a minute. "I am not sure what your point is?"

"OK, let me explain it to you more clearly," Nancy said. "My grandmother told me that workmen created that hill to block off flooding from the Mississippi River."

"Oh, so that's why it's there" Billy said. "I am really learning something from you today."

"Yes, that's right," Nancy said with a smile. She started to laugh, and then Billy laughed at the tone of her voice.

"I don't mean to make fun of you," Nancy said, trying to quiet her laughter. "But when I was a little girl, my grandmother told me the story about the hill because she saw them building it herself."

Dorothy finished washing and folding Mrs. Rhodes' clothes, then put them into the drawer in the bedroom. She wanted to go downtown with Mary, but she had to ask permission to see if Mrs. Rhodes would permit both of them to be out of the house on the same afternoon.

Dorothy went to the office to talk with Mrs. Rhodes, but she was very busy. Dorothy thought that she should not ask right then, so she started to leave the office. Margaret knew that Dorothy wanted to ask her something but had been afraid to say anything.

"Dorothy, were you planning to ask me something?" Margaret asked. Dorothy heard her voice and stopped retreating. She hurried back to the desk.

"Yes, ma'am!" Dorothy was excited. "Can Mary and I go downtown this afternoon?"

"Did you finish washing the clothes today?" Margaret asked. "If you finished your job, then you may go downtown with Mary this afternoon."

"Yes, ma'am, I did finish washing and folding your clothes, and I put them into the dresser this morning." Dorothy said. She started to leave the office, but she remembered that she had forgotten to tell Margaret something, so she came back. "Thank you very much for letting me goes with Mary this afternoon. We will be back here in time to start cooking your dinner this evening. That's for sure. We'll see you later, ma'am, and good-bye."

Dorothy was feeling very good. She rushed downstairs to the kitchen and looked for Mary, but she was not there. She wondered what Mary was doing. Dorothy thought maybe she could find Mary at their house. She went to the house and called up the stairs, but no one answered. Dorothy tried to figure out where Mary could have gone? She guessed that Mary might be talking with the workers over at the plantation. She would have to go see if she could find Mary there.

Dorothy went outside again and walked past the house to the fields. She looked for Mary for a while more, and then she spotted her. She was talking with some of the field-workers. Dorothy called out to her, "Mary, come over here!" But Mary did not hear her and kept on talking. Dorothy started to walk toward Mary very slowly. At last, when she had almost arrived, one of the workers saw Dorothy.

"Mrs. Datson is coming here." The worker pointed.

Mary saw Dorothy and came over to talk to her. "Hey, Dorothy! Do you want something from me?" Mary asked in a friendly way.

"Yes, Mary, let me rest for a second, please." Dorothy was tired. "I spoke to Mrs. Rhodes about us going downtown today, if you feel like coming out with me for the afternoon."

"We could get back home by about five o'clock," Mary agreed. "OK, I will ask my friend if he can take us downtown for a few hours then pick us up to come back home."

"Yes, that would be a big help and save a lot of time. It's a long trip to walk downtown like we did once before," Dorothy agreed. "I need to go back to the house and change into a nice dress for downtown. Thanks!"

"OK, I'll go over to his home right now to see if he is willing to take us there," Mary said. "I will be right back, and then I can come in to change my dress too. See you soon. Bye."

Mary left Dorothy and went to her friend's house. Dorothy sighed and turned to walk to their house about three quarters of a mile away.

Mary went to her friend's front door. She knocked, but there was no answer, so she walked around to look behind the house. She heard a noise and followed it. She walked through the forest until she found him chopping a piece of wood to use in the fireplace.

"Eddie, please stop for a minute," Mary asked him. He looked at her. "I want to talk with you, OK?"

Eddie put the ax down on the ground and looked at Mary. "What do you want, Mary?"

"Mrs. Datson and I are planning to go downtown today.

We would just stay there for a few hours, and then we'd have to be back by five o'clock," Mary said. "Can you give us a ride there in a little while? Do you mind taking us there? You could go somewhere too and do what you need to do while we are there?"

"That is a good idea. I was thinking about going to the hardware store," Eddie agreed. "Yes, I will take you ladies downtown right away. I just need to change to nicer clothes, and then I will meet you at your house, OK?"

"Yes, thank you very much!" Mary answered. "See you later."

Eddie went into his house and looked for a bottle of beer that he had left somewhere around the living room. He knew he had put it there before he went outside.

Mary walked through the cotton field back to her little house. At last, she arrived and went inside. She looked upstairs to where her bedroom was. She didn't feel like going up because she had done lots of walking all morning. She had started up the stairs when she heard Dorothy's door opening.

"Did you ask Eddie for the ride to downtown?" Dorothy looked down at Mary and asked.

"Yes, I did ask him to take us," Mary said. "It's a good thing that he already had a plan to go to the hardware store, too."

"Oh, that's a perfect plan then!" Dorothy laughed.

"Yes, that's true!" Mary agreed.

"I'm going to get some food to eat before we go," Dorothy said. She went downstairs. "I'll wait for you to change your clothes and then Eddie will be stopping by."

Mary walked over to the old gray closet and opened it, looking for something nice. She picked out a dark gray dress that was printed with flowers. She put the dress on the bed, took her uniform off, and tried the dress on. She looked in the mirror and decided that the dress looked good on her. She put her downtown shoes on and then went downstairs. Dorothy could hear Mary coming and came out into the hall. Mary showed Dorothy what she was wearing and asked if she thought it would do.

"That looks good on you, Mary." Dorothy smiled. "Are you ready to go now? Eddie is in front of our house waiting for us to get ready."

"Oh, that was certainly fast!" Mary was surprised. "Yes, I am ready to go now."

"Great, then let's go right away!" Dorothy said as she opened the door.

Eddie got out of his car and came around to open the door to let the women in. "Good afternoon ladies, you are getting a ride in a fancy car today," he greeted them. "You can tell me where you want to go."

Dorothy thought that Eddie was a funny guy and his humor made sense. She looked at Mary, who was already laughing at what Eddie had said. Dorothy looked back at Eddie again and pretended to act like an old woman.

"You are so funny! We don't act like that!" Dorothy was joking.

"We are very poor, but still we are happy with our life!"

"I agree with her!" Mary was laughing. "We are poor, but we are still happy, and we can pray to God to keep on giving us joy and happiness in this life."

"I understand that. Both of you are leading a good life, and mine is good, too." Eddie smiled. "Are you ready to go?"

"Yes, we sure are," Mary said.

Eddie closed the door and went back to the other side. He got in the car and closed the door. He looked in the rear mirror at the women in the back seat.

"I am ready to leave now," Eddie said. He started the engine. "Let's go!"

Dorothy and Mary looked at each other and laughed. He left the house and headed down the dirt road. He drove very slowly and watched the other cars very carefully. Mary was thinking about what store she might choose to buy something for her bedroom.

Eddie drove past the hardware store on the right. He would have liked to stop there, but he had to drop the women off at Main Street downtown first. Then he would come back. He drove through the town and stopped at Main Street.

"We are in town now," Eddie said. "We can meet here when you are ready to leave for home, OK?

"Yes, we will meet here when it's time to go back home later," Mary said. She pointed at the place on the sidewalk where they were supposed to meet. "We'll see you in a few hours. Thank you. See you then."

Mary opened the door and stepped outside.

"Thank you for dropping us off here. We will meet you later," Dorothy said as she got out of the car. "See you later this afternoon. Bye!"

"You have a nice day, ladies. Bye!" Eddie waved to the women.

Eddie turned around and drove back to the hardware store. Mary was still thinking which store she might want to go to first. She was trying to make up her mind about what she wanted to buy.

"Dorothy, I want buy a little bottle of perfume first, and then go to the other store to buy a small frame for the flower that I have in my bedroom," Mary said. "After that, we can just take a walk around town until Eddie comes back and picks us up. Then we can go back home to get ready to cook for Mrs. Rhodes' dinner this evening."

"Yes, sure. We can go to Leeze's Perfume over there on the corner," Dorothy said, pointing in that direction. "Let's go across the street right now."

Dorothy and Mary walked across the street and into the store. Mary was looking for a perfume that smelled like wild roses, but she could not find the one that she wanted. A salesperson was at the counter and noticed her. She wondered how Mary could expect to find any perfume that she would be able to buy. The sales lady did not want to help Mary because she was colored, but she decided she would have to come over to ask if she needed any help. Dorothy saw the salesperson and came over to stand with Mary.

"Can I help you to find a perfume?" the sales lady asked.

"Yes," Mary replied.

"Mary, what kind of perfume are you expecting to find?" Dorothy asked.

"Oh, I forget what the name of the perfume is," Mary answered. "I am sorry that I can't remember the name."

"That's all right. Can you tell me what it smells like?" the sales lady asked.

"Yes, I do remember that it used to smell like a wild rose," Mary said.

"It seems familiar to me, too. I think that one of our customers bought that same kind of perfume yesterday afternoon just before our store closed." She went to another counter where the flower perfumes were. "I will look for that perfume, and then I'll be able to remember the name of the wild rose one that you want to buy."

Mary and Dorothy followed her to the other counter. Mary was looking at the shapes of the bottles to see if she could remember what the shape looked like when she used it before. Mary saw a small, dull, dark blue bottle with no label on it. It had a gold cap that was hidden behind a longer bottle next to it.

"I found the perfume right there!" Mary said, pointing at the perfume bottle inside the counter.

"Where did you find the perfume, in this counter?" the salesperson asked.

"Right there. You can see the small blue bottle that is behind the long bottle." Mary pointed.

The salesperson looked for the blue bottle and finally saw it.

"Yes, I have it." She smiled, came around the counter and unlocked the door of the showcase. She took the blue bottle out of the counter and showed it to Mary. "Now you have it. It's a lucky thing. That is the last one."

Mary was very happy that she had found the last one that was left. The sales lady opened the cap and let her smell it to see if it was the right perfume. Mary smelled the perfume, then looked at Dorothy, smiling.

"That is the kind of perfume that you are looking for?" Dorothy asked.

"Yes, of course, that is exactly the right one. I want it!" Mary was excited. She told the sales lady, "I want to buy this right away."

"Yes, that will cost you ninety-eight cents," the sales lady answered.

"Sure, I will check my wallet," Mary said. She looked in her purse. "I am afraid I don't have enough. I will get my paycheck next week, and then I will come back here again. Do you mind holding the perfume for me?"

"Yes, I can hold it for you until you get your pay, and then you can come back here," the sales lady said.

Mary pulled her wallet out of the purse and counted the coins once again. It turned out that she did have ninety-eight cents. She gave the coins to the sales lady.

"Wait! I do have ninety-eight cents here." Mary showed her the money in her hand.

The sales lady counted the coins. There really were ninety-eight cents.

"Yes, you can have the perfume now," she said, and she handed it to Mary.

"Oh, thank you very much, ma'am!" Mary smiled and put the perfume in her purse. "You have a nice day, good-bye!"

"You too, bye-bye." The sales lady smiled and waved to Mary and Dorothy as they were leaving.

Mary and Dorothy left the perfume store and walked to

another store. At that moment, they saw a group of men building a large pile of dirt and rocks, making it as a high as a hill.

"Dorothy, what are they doing with that?" Mary wondered.

"I don't know what they are building that for?" Dorothy said. She looked at the men and noticed that one of them was taking a break to have something to eat. "I know that man. He is a member of our church."

"Where do you see him?" Mary was looking for the man.

"Right over there near the cars." Dorothy pointed. "Why don't we talk to him and ask him if he knows what the pile of stuff is for?"

"Yes, that is a good idea," Mary agreed. "Let's go over there now."

They walked across the street to the man. He was leaning against the car. He noticed them walking toward him and recognized them from church.

"I know both of you from church," he said. "I am sorry, but I don't know your names."

"We don't know yours either," Dorothy said. "I am Dorothy Datson and this is Mary Waters."

"Hello, Mrs. Datson and Mrs. Waters, I am Tony Forde." He shook hands with them. "It is nice to meet both of you. What are you doing in town today?"

"We were wondering what they are going to build with all that dirt?" Mary asked.

"All right, Mrs. Waters, I will explain it to you in a moment," Tony said. He put his sandwich back into his lunch box. "We are building this to block against flooding from the Mississippi River. I forget what they call this thing, but I will ask one of my coworkers. He knows the right name from the meeting we had about it last week."

Tony looked for his coworker but he could not find him, so he asked another of the men.

"Sir, do you remember what they told us this is named?" he asked the coworker.

"It is a levee system," the man explained. "Do you remember when we had the flood last year? They decided to build a levee system to hold off these floods that come every year."

"I understand now. What they are doing is building a, uh, levee system," Mary figured.

"Yes, that is it, a levee system," Tony said.

"All right, thank you very much, Mr. Forde," Mary said. "I hope it will work. We don't want any floods here anymore."

"Yes, me too!" Dorothy agreed. "I really hate to see the stores get so wet by floodwater every year! I hope that this will be successful to stop it!"

"Yes, we all hope so! Only God knows about the future, but at least we can try to be successful in this town," Tony said. "Thank you for stopping by to see me today. I hope to see you at church next Sunday morning."

"Yes, we will see you next Sunday at church," Dorothy said. "I think we better go back up the street and wait for my friend to pick us up. We have to get back to Mrs. Rhodes' house to cook dinner for her this evening."

"Thank you very much for telling us about the levee system," Mary said. "We will talk with you about it again when you are finished with the work here. Good-bye."

"Yes, but both of you can stop and see me anytime I am here." Tony smiled. "I guess we will be done within a year or so. See you next Sunday. Good-bye."

Mary and Dorothy waved to Tony and rushed back across the street.

"Eddie is supposed to be waiting for us to show up," Dorothy said. "I hope that he hasn't left us here alone. We would have to take a long walk home and would be late to cook for Mrs. Rhodes this evening."

"I hope that hasn't happened. I am sure he will be waiting for us," Mary said.

They kept on walking and finally saw that Eddie's car was parked near the store on the right side, not on the left side where they were supposed to be meeting him. They had to walk across the street.

Eddie was in the car and he noticed in the rear view mirror that Mary and Dorothy were on the way to his car. He got out of the car and opened the door for them.

"Good Lord, you got here earlier than I thought you would." Mary smiled.

"I was just waiting for both of you so you could have a good afternoon downtown," Eddie said.

"We had better hurry and leave here for home right away!" Dorothy rushed into the car. "Mary, please come in right now! And let Eddie drive as fast as he can. Mrs. Rhodes could be getting home before we do."

Mary rolled her eyes and stepped into the car. Eddie laughed and pushed the door closed. Then he got into the car and started to drive back to their houses.

Chapter 18

Downtown, people were walking on the sidewalks and looking in the store windows. Billy thought that what Nancy had told him about the levee system was really interesting. He unlocked the car door for Nancy, then went to the other side and got in. Nancy wanted to go back to the park near the river.

"Billy, do you mind if we go back to that park again?" Nancy asked. "I would like to sit on the deck and smell the fresh breezes from the Mississippi River."

"Yes, sure, we can go back to the park if you want to," Billy agreed, and he turned on the engine. "Let's go right away."

They left downtown and drove to the park in a few minutes. Billy parked his car on the street and they walked to the park. They found a place to sit, lit two more cigarettes, and then began to talk about Nancy's grandmother.

The weather was turning a little bit cooler. Nancy pointed to the sun, which was slowly setting. Billy put his cigarette down and stood up so they could leave the park before dusk.

Nancy wanted to invite Billy to join her cousins and her for dinner that night, but didn't because he was white. She stood up and shook a little dust off her dress.

"Nancy, are you all right?" Billy asked her.

"Hah, well?" Nancy mumbled. "Can we leave here and go back to my grandmother's house now?"

Billy wiped some dust off his pants, then looked at Nancy.

"Yes, sure, I can drop you off at your grandmother's house," he said. "Now, let's go back to my car and you can show me where her house is."

"Yes, I will show you how to get there from here," Nancy said as she stepped down off the deck.

Billy did not say anything more to her. He was supposed to have heard more information about her grandmother. He thought that there would be another day when he could talk with her again. He did not know when Nancy would be leaving for Indiana. Was it going to be this week or next week? They went to the car and he drove to the house, just a few blocks away from the park.

Nancy pointed to the house. She would be staying there for a few days more. Billy parked his car near the curb and turned the engine off. He looked at Nancy and smiled.

"That house looks to be in good shape and a nice place to live," Billy said.

Nancy nodded, looked at the house, and then turned back to Billy again. He wondered what was the matter with her.

"Is there something wrong with you?" Billy was concerned.

Nancy found it difficult to tell Billy that she really would have liked to have him join her relatives for dinner that night. She moved over and spoke closer to Billy's ear.

"Billy, I would like to invite you for dinner with my relatives tonight," Nancy said softly. "One thing that I am supposed to do is talk with Dorothy. She lives in this house. I hope that if she does not mind allowing you to do it, you can come into her house and have dinner with us tonight, OK, Billy?"

Billy felt hit in the head by what Nancy was telling him. He opened and closed his eyes. He wanted to tell her that he did not want to have dinner with her relatives if they didn't want any white people to come into their house. But he did want more information from Dorothy about the years when she had worked with Mary.

"Billy, will you please come in and eat with us tonight?" Nancy asked.

Billy certainly did want go in there with Nancy. At last, he decided that he should agree.

"Yes, I would like go with you for dinner with your relatives tonight." Billy nodded his head. "But what if they don't want me to come into the house?"

"That's great. You don't have to worry about it," Nancy said. "I will explain to Dorothy that it is your job to ask questions about my grandmother to write an article about the history of the South. So, I just want you to wait here until I go and talk with Dorothy for a minute. OK, Billy?"

Billy nodded again. Nancy opened the door and let herself out of the car. She rushed into the house.

Nancy saw her cousins sitting with Dorothy. They were reading books in the living room. Dorothy was sitting on a green chair. She looked at Nancy, who was standing right there beside her.

"How was your day with Mr. Vangslia?" Dorothy asked her sweetly.

"We had a good time together," Nancy said. She smiled and looked at her cousins. "Well, Dorothy, do you mind if I invite Mr. Vangslia to join us for dinner tonight? Please?"

Dorothy opened her eyes wide and looked around at the people on both sides of her. She wondered if they would be able to accept allowing the reporter to come into this house. The cousins looked at each other and did not say anything.

"What is the reason you want to ask him to eat with us tonight?" one of the cousins asked Nancy.

Nancy looked at Dorothy. "I think that you might really like to tell Mr. Vangslia the story about the days when you were working with my grandmother at Mrs. Rhodes' house so long ago. Are you willing to talk with him about yourself, Dorothy?"

Dorothy was shocked that Nancy wanted to ask Mr. Vangslia to have dinner with them. Nancy looked at her and held her breath.

"I would like to have Mr. Vangslia come into my house for dinner tonight," Dorothy decided. "I will tell him about Mary and me and the many years we worked together."

Nancy felt very good. She kissed Dorothy on the cheek.

"Thank you very much for letting him join us tonight." Nancy was excited. "Mr. Vangslia will enjoy hearing your stories directly from you."

Billy was in the car, smoking a cigarette and looking at the house. He saw Nancy open the door and gesture to him to come in. He felt nervous. He took his key out of the ignition and walked toward the house. Billy came up to Nancy and looked at her with some uneasiness on his face.

"I wonder if they will be comfortable talking with me." Billy was really concerned.

"Billy, you don't have to worry about my cousins," Nancy laughed. "There is only one person who will be able to tell you the whole story about herself and about my grandmother, and her name is Dorothy Datson. Don't worry about it at all, OK, Billy?"

Billy was surprised that Nancy wanted him to interview Dorothy about the times when she worked with Mary at the old plantation estate.

"Did you ask Mrs. Datson to tell me the story?" Billy asked. "Will she tell me the story about her job working with your grandmother?"

"Yes, I am definitely sure she will!" Nancy smiled and raised her arm to welcome Billy in. "Please, come and meet Mrs. Datson and my cousins in the living room."

"Thank you very much for letting me come in tonight." Billy smiled and followed her inside.

Nancy guided him into the living room.

Nancy's cousins and Dorothy watched as they entered the room. They looked at Billy as if from a great distance, but they did manage to keep control of themselves. Nancy could see that they were not really able to be comfortable with Billy. As soon as he came into the room, Nancy brought him over to Dorothy.

"This is Mr. Vangslia. He works as a reporter for the *Lake Providence Sentry* newspaper here in town," Nancy said. "This is Mrs. Dorothy Datson. I've told you about her. She worked with my grandmother for many years. Here are my cousins, Shash, William, Renee, Fred, Paulette and Johnny. All of them live right here in this area."

Dorothy got up and held out her hand to Billy.

"Nice to meet you, Mr. Vangslia," Dorothy said. "Our dinner will be ready in a few minutes. I will check to see if the chickens in the oven are done. If they are ready, then I will call all of you to come over to the dining room and sit there."

"Yes, thanks, I'm certainly glad to meet you, too," Billy said. "Sure, I can wait for your call for when the chickens will be ready for dinner tonight."

Dorothy smiled and walked away from Billy. "I will be right back in a moment, Mr. Vangslia."

She pushed the door open and went into the kitchen. Nancy poked at Billy's back. She wanted him to sit down and have a conversation with her cousins. Billy followed her silent suggestion. He sat down in a chair and put his hands together between his knees. Nancy looked at her cousins; they did not sit back down right away.

"Please, will you all just sit down and talk with Mr. Vangslia?" Nancy asked them seriously.

She looked at Billy and came over close to him.

"Billy, I have to go into the kitchen and help Dorothy out a little bit with dinner," Nancy said. "I will be right back in a minute, OK?"

"I will be fine, thank you, Nancy," Billy said.

"Good to hear that." Nancy smiled at him.

Nancy patted Billy's shoulder and left the living room. She pushed the door open and went into the kitchen.

Dorothy took the chickens out of the oven and put them on top of the stove. She looked at Nancy, then looked around to see if anyone had followed her into the kitchen.

"Did you come in by yourself?" Dorothy asked.

"Yes, why are you asking me that?" Nancy wondered.

"Um, never mind about that," Dorothy answered. She looked the chickens over carefully. "Yes, they are ready for dinner."

Nancy was not satisfied that Dorothy had told her the truth. She walked over closer to Dorothy and tried to stop her from taking the chickens out of the pot to put on a serving platter.

"Dorothy, can you tell me what you are thinking?" Nancy asked. "Do you wish I had not brought Mr. Vangslia into the house?"

Dorothy was silenced and turned back to the chickens. She went ahead and put them on the plate. Nancy was still not satisfied.

"Dorothy, why don't you tell me about this?" Nancy sighed.

"OK, Nancy," Dorothy admitted. "It's hard to believe, but what you did by bringing him into the house is the first time anything like that has happened since Mrs. Rhodes' son, Nelson, was here a long time ago. But I am sure that it is fine with me for Mr. Vangslia to write a report in the newspaper about your grandmother."

At last, Dorothy had told her the truth about what she was thinking. Nancy was satisfied.

"Thank you very much for telling me the truth," Nancy said.

"Now you are getting it straight from me. I am not going to say anything against him at all," Dorothy said. "I think we had better go ahead and get all the food into the dining room. Do you mind picking up some of the platters and bringing them to the table, please, Nancy?"

"Um, yes, sure, I will take some in for you." Nancy smiled and kissed Dorothy's cheek, then took the platter of chickens. "I will call everybody to come on in for dinner."

"Yes, you can call them in for me. Thanks, Nancy," Dorothy said.

Nancy smiled and took the platter along with a bowl full of

bacon mixed with collard greens and walked through the door. Dorothy brought some other bowls with potatoes and lentils. They put the plate and bowls on the dining room table, then Nancy came back out to the living room.

"Dinner is ready," Nancy told her cousins. Then she spoke to Billy. "You can sit next to me and Dorothy so we can talk with you, OK?"

They stood up and walked into the dining room, sat down on theirs chairs and put the cloth napkins on their laps. Nancy pointed to the chair where Billy was supposed to sit. Billy nodded and sat down.

"I will go get some more food in the kitchen and bring it in," Nancy said.

Dorothy sat at the end of the table. All the food smelled delicious.

"Mrs. Datson, did you cook all of this food?" Billy asked.

Dorothy smiled. "Yes, I did."

Nancy took a bowl of cinnamon apple sauce and some spoons with her and came back into the dining room. She put the bowl on the table and set out some spoons for each of the bowls.

"Oh, I forgot to bring serving spoons." Dorothy was ashamed of herself. "Thank you very much for bringing those in."

"That's all right." Nancy giggled and sat down. "You did lots of cooking for all of this food tonight. Just looking at it makes me feel hungry!"

Dorothy was hiding her mouth behind her hand. She wanted to control her laughter from being too loud.

"Thank you! You certainly are making me laugh!" Dorothy said. "Help yourself and enjoy your dinner with us. God bless you, and let's all pray for Nancy's grandmother up in heaven, too."

"Amen," they all said at the same time.

They passed the food around and put it on their plates.

Then they started to eat and began talking about the old time memories together.

Chapter 19

When they were done eating, they sat at the table and talked for a long time afterwards, then the cousins left the dining room and walked to the living room for a nap. Nancy, Dorothy and Billy stayed at the table.

"Billy, have you enjoyed eating with us this evening?" Nancy asked. "Dorothy can cook a good dinner."

"Yes, I like her cooking," Billy said. "The beans taste so good. I want the same thing for dinner with my wife tomorrow!"

"Oh, you can take some with you to your house," Dorothy said with a smile. "You put the beans into a pot and you turn the oven to 350 degrees. Let them cook for about fifteen minutes or more, until the beans get warm. Watch out to keep them from burning, OK, Billy?"

"Thanks. I will take some." Billy appreciated the offer. "My wife can probably do it since you've already cooked the beans."

"My stomach is so full," Nancy moaned. "Billy, Dorothy and I will collect all of the dishes and bring them to the kitchen. You don't have to help us because you are our guest tonight, OK?"

"OK. Thank you very much for inviting me to dinner with your relatives tonight," Billy said. "I appreciate that and I hope we can talk more about your grandmother if you have enough time tonight?"

"Oh, yes, we can stay here longer if Dorothy doesn't mind." Nancy asked Dorothy, "Can Billy stay here with me for to-night? Then I can talk with him about my grandmother. I guess that we haven't really finished the story."

"Yes, you can stay here and we can make coffee for later," Dorothy said. "Do you like to drink coffee?"

"Of course I do. Thanks for letting me stay here longer with Nancy tonight," Billy laughed.

"That's great, but we do need to get all of the food back to the kitchen right away," Nancy said, and she began to collect some of the plates. "We will be right back in a moment."

"If you are a smoker, then I will bring a clean ashtray for you, OK?" Dorothy said.

"Yes, he does smoke," Nancy responded quickly. "You can get one for both of us tonight. Thanks, Dorothy."

"OK, I will get them for you from the kitchen," Dorothy said.

They went into the kitchen and put the plates and bowls on the table, then Nancy moved them to the sink. Dorothy went to the cabinet and found the ashtray.

"I will give this to him," Dorothy said. "Then I'm going to wash the dirty dishes and glasses. You can wrap up some of the leftover food for Billy to take home after you talk with him."

Dorothy went to the dining room and put the ashtray on the table so that Billy could start smoking there.

"Thank you for bringing the ashtray," Billy said.

"Yes, you are welcome." Dorothy smiled. "We will talk with you pretty soon after we've finished cleaning the kitchen."

Dorothy went back to the kitchen and looked around to see if any of the plates had been left there, but she didn't see any. Then she went to the sink, put all of the dishes in, and turned on the hot water. She poured soap into the sink, then went to the closet to get a clean towel to dry them. The bubbles began to rise up close to the rim of the sink. She saw the bubbles almost coming over the edge and ran to shut off the water. She moved over to another sink to fill it up with the water for rinsing after washing the dirty dishes.

Nancy got a few clean bowls and put some food in each one. She covered them with foil and put them in the refrigerater.

Nancy came over to the sink and pulled the dishes out of the water to dry them. She put them on the table so Dorothy could put them away.

Dorothy was quiet while she washed the glasses. In a moment, she realized that she should be showing Billy pictures of Mary and Margaret. She rushed through the washing and put the glasses into the rinse water.

"Nancy, I have a good idea," Dorothy said. "I will get some pictures of Mary and Mrs. Rhodes to show Billy what they looked like before they went to heaven. Do you think it is a good idea for me to show them to Billy?"

Nancy had never thought about what Dorothy was suggesting. "Yes, that is a good idea, Dorothy." Nancy smiled. "You can get some pictures and show him my grandmother and Mrs. Rhodes. I guess I'll wash the rest of these while you are looking for the pictures"

"Thank you very much for your help in finishing up here," Dorothy said. "Let the things dry out and then leave them on the table. I will take care of them tonight or tomorrow in the morning so we can have time to spend with Billy tonight. I'll go right to my bedroom to get the boxes of pictures."

Dorothy left the kitchen and rushed to her bedroom. Nancy laughed to herself thinking that Dorothy was such a funny person.

Dorothy went to her bedroom and opened the closet. She could see a small brown box with a few old stamps inside on the top shelf. She took the box, brought it to the dresser, opened the top and looked through the pictures. The room was too dark and she could not see them very well. There was a small lamp on the other end, so she moved the box over there.

She looked through the pictures and found some of Mary and Margaret together.

In the kitchen, Nancy was done with the dishes. She pulled the stopper out of the sink and let the water level go down. She twisted the towel to wring the water out of it, then opened it and put it on the rim of the sink to dry. She turned the light off and left the kitchen to go back to the dining room. She sat down and began to smoke with Billy.

"Thank God everything is done for tonight," Nancy sighed. "Dorothy will show you some pictures of my grandmother and Mrs. Rhodes. I want you to get to know what they looked like, OK, Billy?"

"Yes, that is a good idea," Billy agreed. "I would like to know who they were and what it was like when they worked in that house."

"That's good to hear." Nancy smiled. "Dorothy will be here in a minute."

Dorothy was still looking for more pictures, but there were too many to bring out. She thought that a few would be enough to show Billy for tonight. She turned the lamp off, came out of her bedroom and walked to the dining room.

"Here are some pictures," Dorothy said. "This is Mary and Mrs. Rhodes; they were working with me at the house for a Christmas party about ten or eleven years ago."

"Can I look through these pictures?" Billy asked.

"Yes, certainly, you can look at them," Dorothy said. "You can ask me if you have any questions."

Billy saw Mary with Dorothy in one picture and showed it to Nancy.

"Is that your grandmother Mary?" Billy asked.

"Yes, she is the one I've been telling you about," Nancy said.

Billy kept on looking through the pictures. Dorothy's legs began to weaken, so she sat down on the chair next to Billy and waited for his questions. Billy looked at the picture showing Mary standing beside the house. He showed it to Dorothy.

"Who was the owner of the house?" Billy asked.

"It was owned by Mrs. Rhodes. That was where I worked too for a long time," Dorothy said.

One of Nancy's cousins came into the dining room.

"Yes, do you want to tell me something?" Nancy asked.

"I think we had better go home right away," he said. "I would like to say good-bye and hope to see you again whenever you come."

"Yes, I will let you know. Thank you very much for coming here and remembering my grandmother." Nancy smiled and hugged him. "I want to thank all of the others too. I hope to see you again soon when I have enough money for a ticket to come back."

"Yes, that is all right, we understand that." Renee nodded and hugged Nancy. "It was a pleasure to see you again."

They did not say "good-bye" or "nice to meet you" to Billy. They left the dining room and walked to the front door, gave each of the two women a hug, then went outside. Dorothy closed the door and went back to the dining room with Nancy. It occurred to her that she should make coffee.

"Mr. Vangslia, do you want some coffee?" Dorothy asked.

"Yes, please, thank you for asking, Mrs. Datson," Billy said.

"All right, I will make a little coffee," Dorothy said. "I will be right back in a few minutes."

Billy lit a cigarette and then put it on the table. Nancy took it to light a cigarette for herself and then put it back. They were silent and looked at the smoke rising above their heads.

Dorothy heard the coffee pot whistling.

"Now the coffee is ready!" Dorothy smiled. "I guess I am serving maid."

"Oh, you are a silly old lady!" Nancy laughed and looked at Billy. "You know that she is a very funny person. I have known her since I was a little girl."

"Yes, I figured that out," Billy chuckled.

Dorothy put the tray on the table, poured the coffee into the cup and gave it to Billy. Then she poured another cup for Nancy. Nancy took the small jar of sugar and cream from the tray.

"Do you want some sugar and cream for your coffee?" she asked.

"No, thank you," Billy said. "I like black coffee."

Billy drank the coffee and thought that it tasted almost the same as what he drank every morning at work.

"All right, if you like it that way, then that's fine with me," Nancy said.

She poured cream into her cup, then took her spoon and dipped up some sugar, put it into the cup and stirred it. Dorothy sat down on her chair and took some sugar and cream from Nancy.

Billy still wanted to know about the Blackburns. He thought he might ask Nancy whether she had some more information from her grandmother on that subject before she died. He looked at Nancy as she drank her coffee.

"Nancy, can I ask you one question?" Billy asked.

"Yes, you may certainly ask me something."

"Can you tell me more detail about the Blackburns?" Billy said. "Probably your grandmother told you about the Blackburns when she grew up in the plantation?"

Dorothy was surprised. She looked at Nancy and then at Billy. "Who is the Blackburns?" Dorothy was confused. "Where did you get that name from?"

"The Blackburn name came from Mrs. Rhodes' father's side," Nancy said. "When my grandmother told me about her father, I asked her where the information had come from. She told me that her grandmother, Betty, had told her the story about the Blackburns."

"I see, I do remember about Mary's grandmother," Dorothy said. "They were working together at Mrs. Rhodes' house before I came in and began to work with Mary."

"Who was Betty?" Billy asked Nancy.

"Oh, I am sorry that I did not explain to you more clearly about Betty," Nancy replied. "Mary's grandmother was Betty; she was a servant for the Blackburn family in Greenwood Mississippi in the late 1850s. The two brothers were named Robert and Ron. They had been working together at cotton planting for a few years with their family before anybody from that family came here."

Billy nodded. He supposed it would be interesting if Nancy had more information about her great-great grandmother, Betty, during the time when she was working as a servant with the Blackburns. Dorothy was shocked that Mary had not told her about Margaret's family coming from Mississippi to Louisiana.

"When did she tell you the story? How long was it before she passed?" Dorothy wondered.

"You remember that I was visiting here for almost three months during the summer for a lot of years," Nancy said. She looked at Billy. "I can tell you about Betty's life and that she was working for Mrs. Rhodes' father. Would you like to hear more about Betty's story? I will be more than happy to tell you, OK?

"Umm, it sounds very interesting." Billy nodded. "I am ready to hear whatever you can tell me tonight."

Chapter 20

A year earlier, Nancy had been a sophomore at Butler College in Indianapolis. In literature class, she sat next to the window and listened to the teacher. She did not like him because he talked constantly and could bring the students to complete boredom. It was easy to fall a sleep if you didn't try hard to resist it. She looked out the window and thought that she could not wait to finish this class. There were almost four weeks left to the end of the semester. She was thinking about her plan to visit her grandmother in Lake Providence, Louisiana and stay there for three months during the summer. The class ended and the students left the room.

Nancy went outside and walked to her dorm. When she came into the lobby, she stopped by the desk. "Mrs. Rose, do you have a letter for me today?" she asked.

Mrs. Rose looked through the letters, but did not find one for Nancy.

"I am sorry, but you did not get a letter today, Miss William," she said.

"OK, thank you, Mrs. Rose," Nancy said. "I will check by tomorrow afternoon. Good-bye."

"You are welcome, Miss William," she said. "You have a good day and study hard."

"Yes, I will." Nancy smiled.

She rushed to her room and opened the door, dropped her books on her desk and opened the drawer to look for paper and an envelope. She found them and took them along with a book to her bed. She moved over against the wall to be more comfortable. She bent her legs and put the book on her lap, then started to write a letter to her grandmother. She wrote that she was planning to visit her for three months.

Nancy's mother had not told her as much as she wanted to know about the family from Louisiana. That was why she was visiting her grandmother. She knew her grandmother could be gone at any moment.

After Nancy completed her letter, she folded it and put it in the envelope. She got up from her bed and went to the desk to look in her purse; she found the stamp, then she left her room and ran downstairs to Mrs. Rose's desk in the lobby area.

"Mrs. Rose, can you mail this letter to my grandmother?" Nancy showed her the letter and gave it to her. "Will you drop it off at the post office today?"

"Yes, I will drop it off this evening. I'll be off duty at six o'clock today," Mrs. Rose said. "It will probably arrive in Louisiana within three or four days. It has a long way south to travel from here."

"Yeah, I know that is a long way." Nancy sighed. "Oh well, thank you very much, Mrs. Rose."

"You are welcome." Mrs. Rose smiled.

Nancy went back to her room and started on her homework.

A few weeks later, the mail carrier came into the dorm where Nancy lived. He came over to the desk and gave the letters to Mrs. Rose.

Nancy was in her room and could see from her window that the mail carrier was walking away from the building. She knew that a letter must have arrived from her grandmother. She ran downstairs to the lobby. Mrs. Rose saw Nancy hurrying to her desk.

"Did you get the letter from my grandmother today?" Nancy asked.

"You bet!" Mrs. Rose chuckled. "Your letter is right here."

"Thank God!" Nancy smiled.

Mrs. Rose found the letter and gave it to Nancy.

Nancy could see on the corner of the envelope that the letter was from her grandmother. She knew that her grandmother would be happy to see her again.

Nancy ran upstairs to her room. She closed the door, ripped the envelope open and read the letter. Her grandmother wrote that she would like Nancy to stay at her place for three months. She told her that this would be the first time she would be staying at her place for a good long visit since she was a little girl and her whole family had stayed at her house for three months at a time.

Nancy was so happy. She came over to her bed and lay on her back looking at the ceiling. She felt so good about having a chance to question her grandmother about the family stories.

After her final exams, Nancy rushed to pack her clothes. Her roommate helped her carry her cases to the car. She looked for Mrs. Rose at her desk, but no one was there. She went outside and saw that her friend's car was parked right there. He saw Nancy, walked to the back of his car and unlocked the trunk to put her cases in. She hugged her roommate and said good-bye. They left the campus and drove away to the train station.

Nancy took the ticket out of her purse and looked at her watch. The time was close; only ten minutes before the train would be leaving for Louisiana. She would have almost three days of travel. She did not want to miss the train and have to wait for the next day.

Her friend drove fast and they arrived at the train station just barely in time. She told him to drop her off in front of the station. He got out of the car, opened the trunk and took her cases out. She hugged him and rushed into the station, where she saw a large board of departures on the wall. She was departing from gate number five.

Nancy found her gate and ran to the door. She could hear the train whistle and knew that it was going to leave soon, but she managed to get into the train car and find her seat before the train pulled away from the station.

While traveling south, Nancy sat next to the window, read books and wrote letters to her family and friends. The train arrived at Memphis, Tennessee, where Nancy had to get off and transfer to another train for New Orleans. She had to sit in the last car because only those seats were for colored people, but it did not bother her at all because she was used to it from other trips.

She was not comfortable trying to sleep on the seat and could not wait to get off at the station in Vicksburg, Mississippi the next afternoon. She sat and talked with other people until the train stopped at Vicksburg.

Nancy felt so good knowing she would finally get some rest at her grandmother's house. She found her way off the train and managed to get her luggage from where it had been unloaded. She dragged her luggage across the station and to the outer door, then pushed the door open and looked for her grandmother in the parking lot.

Her grandmother and a friend were parked across the street waiting for Nancy to arrive. "My granddaughter is here!" Mary told her friend in the car. "Nancy, please come over to us!"

Nancy heard her grandmother's voice and could see her across the street. She saw her grandmother standing beside the car waving.

"Nancy, please come over here!" Mary called. "I want you to give me a hug!"

Nancy was glad they were there waiting right when she got off the train. She looked both ways on the road to make sure no cars were coming, then walked across the street and hugged her grandmother warmly.

"I am so happy to see you again." Mary was smiling.

"Thank you for coming here to pick me up," Nancy said. She couldn't help yawning.

Mary saw that Nancy's eyes looked tired.

"Aren't you tired? I bet you didn't get enough sleep sitting up on a seat all the way from Indiana for two days," Mary said.

"No, I did not sleep well enough," Nancy said. "I really need to go to sleep badly."

"Oh, you can sleep on the back seat while we drive to my house," Mary said as she took one of Nancy's cases.

Mary's friend came out of the car and opened the other door for Nancy. He went to the trunk and put her cases in it. They got back in the car. Mary looked back at Nancy, but she did not seem to be there. Mary was puzzled at first, then looked down and saw that Nancy was already asleep.

"Nancy is sleeping now," Mary whispered to her friend. "I think we should just leave her alone and take her right back home."

They left the station and kept on driving all the way back to Lake Providence, Louisiana.

The car's headlights reflected off the mirror right into Nancy's face. She moved her head to turn away from it and began to wake up. She could see a white curtain and a few vases on a window sill. She felt completely confused. Where was she? At last, she realized that she was in her grandmother's bedroom.

Nancy raised her head and looked around. She did not remember arriving at her grandmother's house at all. She sighed, got up from the bed and walked to the window. She looked outside to try to see who was in the car. She gave up and went out to the hall, where she heard her grandmother and Dorothy talking in the kitchen.

"Oh, Nancy," Dorothy said as she came over to Nancy. "How was your trip?"

"Not bad, thanks, Mrs. Datson." Nancy smiled.

"Are you all right? Mary wondered. "Were you comfortable in my bed?"

Dorothy knew that Mary was always worrying over little things.

"Yes, your bed is fine, but there is a car at the front of the house," Nancy said. "It has its headlights on."

"Oh, that is my son in law," Dorothy said. "He is supposed to wait for me until I am ready to leave. And Nancy can sleep in my bed if she wants to."

Dorothy went to her bedroom and got out her suitcase, then went back to the kitchen.

"I will come back next week," Dorothy said. "I am so happy to see you again and spend time together for three months. Welcome, and make yourself at home. I have to go now. Goodbye."

"You better be careful of yourself and have fun with your grandchildren!" Mary was laughing.

"Yeah, that is right!" Dorothy chuckled. "See you later, bye!"

"Thank you for letting me use your bed for a while," Nancy said.

"Yes, you are welcome." Dorothy smiled. "I need go now. Talk with you later. Bye!"

Dorothy left the kitchen. Nancy came over to the table, pulled the chair out and sat down. Mary noticed in Nancy's eyes that she had not slept enough again.

"Probably you will need to sleep more tonight," Mary sighed.

"Yeah, I know, last night was not really enough." Nancy nodded. "Well? I do need to eat because I am hungry."

"Did you eat in the train before you got here?" Mary asked.

"Yes, I did eat some, but not as much as I might have liked to eat. It is a very limited menu."

"Oh, I see," Mary said. "Oh well, I know that they don't bring enough food for people to eat during long trips."

"That's right," Nancy said. "What do you have in the way of food? I need to eat badly. Grandmother, can you make dinner for me, please?"

"Oh yes, I have plenty of food here." Mary was sure of that. "Would you like me to make you a sandwich with some turkey?"

"I don't mind eating that for now," Nancy said. "Thank you, grandmother!"

"Sure, I will make the turkey sandwich right away," Mary said. "Do you like it with mayonnaise or mustard?"

"I prefer to have mustard on the sandwich." Nancy yawned.

"Would you like me to add tomato and lettuce?" Mary replied.

"Oh, yes, please," Nancy said.

Mary opened the refrigerator and took out the mustard, turkey, lettuce and tomato. She put them on the table, then got a serving plate from the cabinet. She cut the bread and put it on the plate, then spread mustard on each slice. She pulled out some lettuce and put it on the bread, cut a slice of tomato and then opened the bag of turkey.

"How much meat do you like in a sandwich?" Mary asked.

"I guess there should be lots of turkey," Nancy said.

"OK, I will fix it for you," Mary said. She put some turkey on the sandwich, cut it in half and put it on the plate. She handed it to Nancy. "This is for your dinner tonight." Mary smiled. "What kind of drink would you like, Nancy?"

"I like to drink milk," Nancy said.

Mary went to the refrigerator, took out a jar of milk, then took a glass out of the cabinet. She poured the milk and gave it to Nancy.

"Thank you very much for everything, grandmother," Nancy said. She kissed her grandmother's cheek.

"You are welcome, anytime," Mary said. "You better eat now."

Mary was glad to have her granddaughter visiting her.

Nancy ate the sandwich and then drank milk. She was trying to think about the family tree and its history. She put the sandwich down on the plate and wiped her lips with the napkin.

"Grandmother, can I talk with you about something tonight?" Nancy asked softly.

"Yes, you can ask me anything you want. What do you want me to do for you?" Mary answered.

"Well, I would like to know about the history of our family," Nancy said. "If you know the family tree, can you tell me about it, please?"

Mary was surprised that Nancy wanted to know about the family tree. She stopped washing the knife and looked at Nancy. "Excuse me?" Mary said. "Are you asking me about my family history? Do you really want to know about all of that?"

"Yes, my mother hasn't told me about our family history," Nancy said. "I want to know about our blood relatives from the past, especially before and after the slaves were given their freedom after the Civil War."

Mary nodded and came over to the table. She pulled up a chair and sat down, trying to figure out what she should tell Nancy about her family and how she had grown up living with her own grandmother, Betty, after her parents and her brother had left for Indiana.

"Are you all right?" Nancy was concerned and reached over to hold Mary's hand.

"Oh, you don't have to worry about that!" Mary smiled. "I am just surprised that you went ahead and asked me about our family history before I could tell you. You asked me before I could get around to saying anything about it."

"Really, I did not know that." Nancy was surprised. "I did not know if you would tell me before I asked you."

"All right, that's fine," Mary said. "Your great-grandmother, Betty, told me about the family history before she died a long time ago. I was supposed to talk about it with your mother, but she doesn't come here very often. I thought probably that she was not so interested about the family history."

"Can you explain to me about Betty?" Nancy began by

asking. "She was your grandmother and worked like you did on the job with Mrs. Rhodes?"

"Yes, that is correct," Mary said. "Betty worked for Mrs. Rhodes' parents. They moved here from Mississippi before the Civil War happened."

"Mississippi?" Nancy wondered. "What part of Mississippi were they in before they moved here?"

"In Greenwood. It was about a hundred miles away from here," Mary guessed. "She was born and raised there, but your mother and I were born in the same house right at Mrs. Rhodes' place."

"Wow, that is interesting!" Nancy was shocked. "But I was born in a hospital in Indianapolis."

"Yes, I think that the hospital is the best place for people to be when babies are born," Mary said.

"What was different between being at a house and being in the hospital?" Nancy wondered.

"There, it's very clean and easy to take care of the babies," Mary explained. "In the house, there was more of a mess. You know what I am trying to explain to you?"

"Oh yes, I bet that there were some very nasty things like that!" Nancy said. "I would choose to be in hospital for my future newborn babies, if I ever have any."

"That is a good choice for the baby's sake," Mary said.

"Well? I still wonder why Betty moved here from Greenwood." Nancy wanted to know.

"Yes, her master, Ron, wanted to move here away from his brother Robert's place to plant cotton the way people do it here," Mary explained. "I do remember that my grandmother knew everything about all of that very well before they moved here."

"Can you tell me what your grandmother told you?" Nancy was excited and curious.

"Do you want me to tell you right away?" Mary wondered. "Don't you feel like going back to bed?"

"Nah, I will stay up and begin to hear your story." Nancy laughed and finished up the sandwich.

"All right, you can hear my grandmother's story tonight," Mary said with a laugh.

Early one spring, Betty was a servant for the Blackburn family in Greenwood, Mississippi. She was in the kitchen at night putting hot tea and two cups on a wooden tray for Robert and Ron. She left the kitchen and walked through the dining room in the direction of the office. She could hear Robert and Ron arguing in the office about something in relation to their business problems. Betty stood there listening to their voices.

Either Robert or Ron started to leave the office. Betty looked at the bottom of the door and could see the shadow of feet; she was sure that they were planning to come out. She backed away from the door. She did not want them to catch her listening to their conversation. She needed a place to hide. At that moment the door began to open, so she rushed into the living room and hid by the door. She could hear them leaving the office and walking to the back door.

Betty wondered what they were going to do outside. It had rained a lot that night. She thought that maybe she should go tell Rosemary and Lily that their husbands were having some kind of a problem and had gone outside. She had no idea why. She stood up, put the tray on the end table and went upstairs. She had to call both Rosemary and Lily, but she preferred to talk with Rosemary. She liked her better than Lily, who had not always treated her kindly.

Betty went to Rosemary's bedroom and opened the door quickly. Rosemary was in bed reading book. She looked up at Betty's eyes and saw that they were wide open. She seemed to be scared to death.

"What is wrong with you?" Rosemary was concerned.

"Ron and Robert are going outside," Betty said. "I don't know what they are doing out there with it raining so hard."

Rosemary did not understand what Betty was trying to tell her. "Please will you tell me," Rosemary asked seriously, "what did you hear them saying … before they went outside?"

"I brought the hot tea pot and cups to the office," Betty muttered. "I believe they were arguing about the business."

Rosemary was surprised at first at what Betty told her she heard from the men in the office. Rosemary had always trusted Betty.

"OK, you better keep quiet," Rosemary said, closing her book and putting it on the stand. "I will call Lily and we'll go downstairs."

Rosemary pulled the blanket off her legs, stood up and put on her robe.

"Which way did they go?" she asked.

"They went out the back door," Betty said, pointing the way.

"You better go back to the kitchen right away!" Rosemary said as she went to the hall. "Hurry up before I go over to Lily's bedroom."

Betty nodded and listened to Rosemary's advice. She went downstairs and directly to the kitchen.

Rosemary went to the door and took a breath to calm down before she opened it and looked at Lily on her bed. Lily looked up at Rosemary, a little bit sleepy still.

"Yes, Rosemary," Lily said. "Do you want to tell to me something?"

"Yes, I hear that Robert and Ron have gone outside," Rosemary said calmy. "I don't know what they are doing outside in all this rain."

"What? I don't understand why they are going outside if it's raining?" Lily was shocked. "What foolishness is this?"

"Yes, I think it's foolish too," Rosemary said.

"I think we better go and get them inside right away!" Lily decided. "I'll get my robe on and then we'll go downstairs and bring them in!"

Lily got up, put her robe on and went with Rosemary. They rushed downstairs to the back door and went outside, where they saw their husbands fighting each other without even noticing the heavy rain.

Chapter 21

"I already told this to Billy this morning," Nancy explained to Dorothy. "I am learning something about my great-grandmother, Betty. She was a very smart and wise woman, like my own grandmother."

"Wow, that is interesting to learn things about your family tree and its history." Dorothy was awed. "I wish that I knew something about mine, but there is nothing anybody knows about them."

"Yeah, that is why I came here last summer," Nancy said. "I wanted to know more about my family history before my grandmother passed. I knew she might go at any time."

"Oh, you did the right thing to try to get more information from her," Dorothy agreed. "You are very lucky that you could come here last summer."

"Nancy, I would like to know why Betty wanted to stay with Mrs. Blackburn," Billy asked. "She was supposed to leave the plantation after the slaves were given their freedom."

"He has a good point," Dorothy agreed with Billy. "What did Mrs. Blackburn do to convince Betty to stay there?"

"Okay, do you want me to tell you about her?" Nancy laughed. "I have been planning to tell both of you the story of what Betty was doing during that time."

"Yes, I would like to know what she was doing in the years with Mrs. Blackburn," Dorothy and Billy were both saying at the same time.

Nancy started to laugh because they sounded so comical.

"All right, I am going to tell you now," Nancy promised.

After her long travel to Louisiana from Indiana, Nancy enjoyed a long sleep in Dorothy's bedroom all night and into the late morning. She awakened slowly and wiped her eyes with her hands. She looked out the window for a few minutes, then went back to sleep again. After a while she began to feel a slight headache, probably because she had slept so long. She thought that would be enough for now and allowed herself to wake up again. She looked at the clock. It was past one o'clock in the afternoon. She stepped down off the bed and rushed to the bathroom for her shower.

After she was dressed, she went to the living room, but no one was there. She decided that her grandmother must be in the kitchen. Nancy went into the kitchen and saw her grandmother making a sandwich and wrapping it in waxed paper.

"Good afternoon, darling," Mary said. "How was your sleep?"

"It was good to have a bed instead of sitting up on a train seat for three days," Nancy answered. "Are you planning to go out for a panic today?"

"Oh, this is for our lunch," Mary told her. "I want to show you the old house where I grew up with your great-grandmamma, Betty.

"I think that it is a good idea for us to visit there today," Nancy agreed. "I hope you will tell me more about that house and explain what has happened to it since then."

"Of course I will tell you more about it." Mary wanted to be helpful. "My friend is supposed to be here, waiting outside. I think it would be a good idea for us to leave right away. Are you ready now, Nancy?"

"Yes, I am almost already," Nancy replied. "I just need to grab my sweater and my purse."

"All right, better hurry up, darling." Mary smiled. "I will go get my hat and purse too."

Nancy went to the bedroom, put her brush on the dresser and picked up her purse and sweater. Mary took the basket from the kitchen and put it on the dining room table, then went back to her bedroom. She looked over her hats in the closet and chose her favorite one. It had a tan bow on one side of the brim. She tried it on and looked in the mirror to see if it was still looking nice. She decided it was satisfactory. She went to the front door and opened it to see if her friend was there. He had arrived and was waiting for her to come out. Mary went back to the dining room, picked up the basket and called to Nancy, "My friend is waiting for us outside!"

"Okay, I am ready now!" Nancy answered and rushed out.

Mary closed the door and locked up before they got into the car and left for Mary's former home over near Mrs. Rhodes' house. Mary told her friend that she wanted him to drop both of them off at her grandmother's old house first. They passed by Mrs. Rhodes' place and then stopped at the old house. They got out of the car and Mary told Nancy to wait out in front of this house while she went to another house and looked for the man who would have a key for this old house. She found him and he came with her to the old house to unlock the door.

Nancy followed Mary inside. Nancy looked around the big front room. There was nothing left. It was empty except for a fireplace and lots of spider webs on the windows and dusty walls. No one had lived in this house since Mary and Dorothy had moved out. Mary walked through this front room by herself. Nancy did not want to follow her grandmother because she did not want to touch any of the spider webs or get them on her hair or dress. Mary looked at Nancy and wondered why she was standing beside the door and had not followed her to the kitchen.

"What is the matter with you, darling?" Mary wondered.

"Well, it's just that I don't want a spider to touch me," Nancy admitted. "Is this where you and Dorothy lived before you moved to the new house?"

Mary did not say anything about Nancy being fussy about the spider.

"Yes, we lived here for a great many years." Mary nodded. "You are very lucky that you did not have to. I'm sure you would have complained about having to go outside to use the restroom."

"What?" Nancy was shocked. "Where was the shower?"

"We did not have a shower or tub in this house," Mary said.

"How did you wash your body?" Nancy wondered.

"We got hot water from a kettle over the fireplace and then poured it into a big bowl and used a wash cloth," Mary explained. "You just wrapped it over your body with soap on it and then ringed it away."

Nancy found it hard to believe what Mary had been doing for so many years. She looked at the wall with what was probably the original paper on it.

"That wallpaper, was it something you put there?" Nancy said, pointing at the dusty walls.

"No, I have not changed anything since my grandmother has gone," Mary said as she wiped a little of the dust off. "The men did it before Betty moved in."

"When was it that Betty moved in?" Nancy asked.

"The Civil War was over, I know that much," Mary said. "I think it might be better for us to get out of here. I want to show you the place where I used to eat with Dorothy at lunch time."

"Wow, that would be neat," Nancy said softly. "Yes, we need to get some food and then we can talk about it some more, OK, grandmother?"

"Yes, I will tell you a lot more after we get settled and are having lunch."

They left the old house and carried the basket and blanket with them to a tree that must have been over a hundred years old. The branches were very long, and there was plenty of shadow to block out the sun. Nancy put the blanket on the ground and then Mary placed the basket on it. They sat down and ate their sandwiches and some apples. Then they each took a cat nap for a while. Nancy wasn't sleepy but she could see that Mary was. Nancy began to smoke a cigarette. The smoke was moving in different directions as the wind moved to the south from the north.

Mary woke up and looked at Nancy sitting beside the smoke. "Are you having a good nap?" Mary asked.

"Yes, I feel better, but I think that I ought not to sleep all day," Nancy answered. "Are you ready to tell me about your grandmother?"

"Yes, if you want to hear the whole story," Mary said. "Please come on over here and make yourself comfortable."

"All right," Nancy said. She threw the cigarette away before moving closer to her grandmother. "I am ready to hear whatever you want to tell me."

"It's good to hear that," Mary said. "I do remember a lot of what my grandmother told me was happening during the Civil War times."

In February 1863, the Union Army went to Providence, looking for the Confederates. They knew that the town was connected to the Mississippi River. Plantation owners had already freed their slaves and told them to leave. They knew that they no longer had any control over them because they got their freedom as an effect of the Emancipation Proclamation.

Betty was working in the big house and could hear the noise coming from outside. She went to the window and saw the cavalrymen. They came in and ran through the place. They were checking to see if the slaves were still there or had left. She wondered what they were doing looking around in this area. She heard someone come into the room and looked around at him. It was her husband, Eddie.

"We are free now!" Eddie yelled. "What are we doing here? Maybe we should just pack and take our children up north?"

Betty did not understand what he was trying to tell her.

"Should we leave this place just because the slaves are free?" Betty was confused. She pointed to the window where some of the cavalrymen were still standing outside. "What did they tell you? Are we supposed to just go to freedom without the mistress knowing about it?"

Eddie came over to Betty and put his hands around her shoulders.

"Yes, what they are here for is to tell us that we are free!" Eddie spoke slowly and carefully.

She pushed Eddie away from her and went to sit down on a chair. She felt confused about what he was telling her about "freedom."

"What does freedom mean?" Betty just couldn't understand. "How do you know?"

"They say we're allowed to have freedom!" Eddie was yelling at her.

The mistress, Rosemary, came into the room and saw them. Rosemary knew that they must be planning to leave the house, but Rosemary did not want Betty to go.

"Betty and Eddie," Rosemary said looking at each of them. "I think it might be better for you to leave here and have a new life. You could find a place and settle down somewhere and then decide what you want to do with your new life."

Betty was shocked that Rosemary was telling them that she would allow them to go away in freedom. Now Betty could understand what Eddie had told her before Rosemary came in. Betty looked at Eddie for a second and then looked at Rosemary. She stood up and came over to Rosemary, and she could see that Rosemary's eyes were filled with tears.

"Mistress, do you want us to leave this house?" Betty asked.

"Yes, you can go now." Rosemary nodded, she was plainly weeping now.

Betty saw that she could not choose just to stay on here. She decided to leave the house with her husband and the children. She began to leave the room with Eddie, but she could still hear Rosemary crying.

They went to their home. Betty saw the other slaves running away from the slave quarters with bags of their clothes. She still found it hard to believe that they were not slaves anymore. They began to pack their clothes and wrap them in a sheet to carry them. At that moment, Betty heard someone come in. She looked over in the other room and found that it was Rosemary. Betty wondered what she was doing here and called to Eddie to come over.

"What do you want to tell us?" Eddie said.

"If you did not find a place to live after leaving here," Rosemary said softly, "I am willing to pay a salary to both of you."

Betty did not understand what Rosemary said. She came over to Rosemary and looked at her eyes to see if they were still filled with water, but they were not.

"What are you talking about?" Betty asked.

"You can get some money for working for us," Rosemary said. "And Eddie will get some money, too."

"You would pay me to pick the cotton by myself, or would it be with other people?" Eddie asked. "I cannot do that whole job by myself. I would want some other people to help with it, not just me!"

"Yes, I would get help for you to pick the cotton," Rosemary promised. "Other people will want to work with us after this time is over."

"Would I have to work with you to pick the cotton?" Betty was shocked.

"No, you don't have to do that," Rosemary said. "You can go back to work doing what you did before, just the same way that you always used to work in the house. Only now you are not a slave anymore and you will get money. OK, Betty?"

"You will give me some money?" Betty asked, surprised. "What do you give me this money for?"

"You earn money for your support and you can buy a new

dress, or whatever you like," Rosemary explained. "And you can buy new clothes for your children."

"OK, I accept it, and thanks," Betty said. "But I did not really like this house because it was too cold during the night and it was a long walk to your house."

Rosemary had a hard time deciding what to do about Betty's wish for a new home.

"OK, Betty," Rosemary nodded. "I will find a place nearer my house so you can live closer. I will find someone to build a house for you soon."

"Yes, that would be great for us to live in a good house." Eddie smiled. "We need walls and windows to keep us warm, mistress."

"Yes, I will try my best to do whatever I can afford." Rosemary nodded and left to walk back down the road to her house.

Betty was shocked. "Wow, we are lucky that the mistress will make a new house for us," she said. "I am so happy that she will put a new wall and windows in the new house. It will be better than living here!"

After the Civil War was over, Rosemary hired some carpenters to remodel her house and then to build a new house. It was two stories high and had six rooms. After the house was completed a few months later, Rosemary brought Betty and Eddie to the house. She opened the front door and let them come in. They went to the kitchen first. Eddie walked to the fireplace and looked at the drywall that had been covered with nice wallpaper.

"These are nice paper walls." Eddie smiled. "I am glad to see that we have a real window here, too."

Betty was surprised that Rosemary had given them such a good home. She went upstairs and looked around at the three bedrooms. There was a good bed in each room, too. She saw Rosemary standing outside and realized that she was probably waiting for them to say something. She decided to open the window and called to Rosemary.

"I like this house much better than the old one over there." Betty was excited. "Thank you very much for giving us a good home."

"Yes, you are welcome, Betty." Rosemary smiled. "You can go back and forth from your old house to here when you want to."

"Yes, I will do that when I need to. Thank you!" Betty said, and she closed the window.

"No wonder why Nelson gave us this new house," Dorothy said, surprised. "This house where we are living right now!"

"When were you and my grandmother moved into this house?" Nancy asked.

"Well, so far as I remember, it was after Mrs. Rhodes had a stroke," Dorothy explained. "He paid for all of the furniture and for all of the kitchen stove and things too! I had a hard time believing that he could afford to pay for red brick walls around this house and for a full bathroom inside, instead of outside where we lived in that damn old cabin!"

"I did not know that Mrs. Rhodes had a stroke before you moved in here," Nancy said. "My grandmother did not tell me that had happened. Do you mind telling me how it happened? What was the cause of the stroke?"

"Really? I thought that she had told you that before she was gone." Dorothy was surprised. "Yes, I do remember what happened when Mrs. Rhodes had the stroke."

"Oh, Billy! I am sorry that I am still curious about Mrs. Rhodes," Nancy said and giggled. "Do you mind if I keep on asking about it? Is it all right with you?"

"Nah, that is OK with me. I would like to hear the whole story." Billy laughed too. "Don't worry about the time."

"That's great!" Nancy was pleased. "Dorothy, can you tell me about this now?"

Chapter 22

Dorothy would never forget the moment when Margaret had the stroke. During the middle of the Great Depression, they were still able to sell cotton in the Southeast. This section of the country was not suffering as much as the Midwest, which was so dry from drought that its fields were referred to as "dust bowls."

Mary was collecting dirty clothes and sheets from Margaret's bedroom. She brought a large basket downstairs to do the laundry beside the porch outside. Dorothy took some other sheets out of the washtub and brought them to the long clothesline to hang out to dry. Mary took the dirty clothes, put them into the tub, poured the powder in and stirred the tub with a stick.

Mary thought that she should help Dorothy hang the sheets up. She left the porch and went over to Dorothy to hold some while Dorothy tossed the others over the line.

"What nice weather this is today, Dorothy," Mary said as she looked up at the blue sky. "The sky is very clear and blue, and there are no white cotton clouds anywhere."

"What are you talking about clouds," Dorothy said, puzzled. "You are very funny and have a good sense of humor! I like what you said about that!"

Dorothy and Mary were laughing a lot. Dorothy took some clothes pins and pulled a large sheet over the line.

"I know that you were born and raised with the cotton family!" Dorothy said. She straightened the sheet over the line. "But I did not come from that ..."

At that moment, they heard the sound of Margaret's voice,

sounding strange. Dorothy was shocked and Mary looked at the house. They could hear Margaret, but could not make out what she might be saying.

"Do you hear something in Mrs. Rhodes' voice?" Dorothy asked. "She sounds like a child. Should we check with her to see if something is wrong with her?"

"Yes, I suppose so!" Mary agreed. "I think we better go upstairs and see her right away!"

Dorothy nodded and they both ran.

They went into the house and upstairs and saw Margaret in the hall. She was still wearing a nightgown and was arguing with her bookkeeper, Mrs. Taylor, and another coworker.

"Mary, she sounds like she is confused," Dorothy said.

"I have not seen anything like that before in my whole life!" Mary was astonished.

Margaret did not want to talk to the others anymore and left them alone. She moved, tottering along the hall.

"She is coming to us," Dorothy whispered. "What are we supposed to do to help her out?"

"I don't know what she is doing at all," Mary answered.

They kept their eye on Margaret. She was limping a little bit and did not pay any attention to a tall stand with a plant in it. She banged up against it and the plant fell to the floor. The bowl broke and the dirt sprayed in all directions. Mary and Dorothy held their arms in front of their faces to protect themselves from the dirt. Mrs. Taylor was not sure at all of what was wrong with Margaret.

"I think you had better call for Nelson right away!" Mrs. Taylor said.

"OK, I will call him now," a coworker said.

He went to the office, picked up the phone and dialed quickly.

Nelson was working in the company offices at Monroe. He heard the phone ring and picked it up. "Rhodes office, can I help you?"

"Mr. Rhodes, your mother has a problem at the house," the

coworker said calmly. "I think you had better come over here right away."

Nelson had a hard time understanding what the coworker was saying. His mother was having some problems? His mother did not seem to have any problems at all before that morning.

"I'm on the way to her house right now," Nelson said. "Thank you very much for the call. See you soon. Good-bye."

Nelson hung up the receiver and rubbed his face with his hands. His daughter Karen came into the office and could see by her father's face that something abnormal was happening. She wondered who had just called him.

"Dad, can you tell me what is happening?" Karen said, concerned.

"Someone just called me from my mother's house," Nelson sighed. He stood up. "He told me that my mother was having some kind of problem. I am not sure what he was trying to tell me on the phone, so I have to leave here right now to go to my mother's house."

"Oh, Grandmother!" Karen was surprised. "Probably I should go with you?"

"Yes, you can come with me. We can drive there in an hour." Nelson nodded and they left the office.

"I will get my purse from my office," Karen said. She rushed across the hall to her office. "I will meet you at your car outside in one second. Thanks, Dad."

"Better hurry up, Karen," Nelson said.

Nelson and Karen arrived at Margaret's house, parked the car out front and rushed inside. They found Mrs. Taylor in the dining room.

Mrs. Taylor saw them coming. She stood up and went to meet them. "Thank the Lord!" she said. "Thank you for coming here and helping with your mother."

"Can you tell me what is wrong with my mother?" Nelson asked.

"There is no way to explain it to you, Mr. Rhodes." Mrs. Taylor sighed. "Your mother is in the kitchen eating some food, but she is acting like a child. Or at least that is what I think about it."

"OK, I will check with my mother now." Nelson nodded. "Karen, come with me and see if she is all right."

"Yes, I'm coming," Karen answered. "Mrs. Taylor, we'll be right back, OK?"

"Yes, sure, thanks." Mrs. Taylor waited in the dining room to hear what was happening.

Nelson and Karen came into the kitchen and saw Margaret; she was sitting and eating some food. Mary and Dorothy were standing in the kitchen doorway watching her.

Nelson came over to his mother and took hold of her shoulder.

"Mother, are you all right today?" Nelson said softly.

Margaret looked at Nelson but did not say anything to him. She turned back to her food and kept on eating. Nelson felt so bad that she wasn't responding. He turned to his daughter; Karen knew something about what her father was feeling. It was so sad that Margaret's life had changed so radically.

"Dad, I think it would be best for us to take Grandmother to see her doctor today," Karen suggested.

"Yes, I think you're right." Nelson nodded. "But I think it would be better for us to wait until she finishes her lunch."

Karen agreed with her father. She walked out of the kitchen and began to smoke a cigarette while she waited.

Nelson and Karen were sitting at the dining room table waiting for Margaret to finish her lunch. Dorothy came to them.

"Your mother has finished her lunch," Dorothy said.

"That's fine. I am going to take her to see her doctor right away before it gets too late in the afternoon," Nelson explained.

"Can you find her coat somewhere upstairs?" Karen asked Dorothy. "We won't even take time to change her out of her nightgown. Just get a long bathrobe for her and we'll go right now."

"Yes, I will get her long coat." Dorothy knew just where it was. She went upstairs into Margaret's bedroom and opened the closet. She knew that Margaret used to wear this coat often over her other clothes. Dorothy found the coat, then went back downstairs to the kitchen. She placed the coat on Margaret's back and tried to help her get her arms into the sleeves. Margaret looked at her coat, then shrugged it off her shoulders to the floor.

"I don't want my coat on me!" Margaret yelled. "I don't want you doing that!"

She went back to her plate and tried to find something more to eat.

Dorothy was shocked and stepped away from Margaret. Dorothy could not understand Margaret's behavior.

Karen came over to Dorothy and tried to talk with her.

"Don't worry about her," Karen said. "We will take her to see the doctor right away. I know how bad you must feel about what's happening."

Karen picked the coat up and tried again to put it on Margaret, but she knew Margaret would take it off again. Karen decided just to hold the coat around her shoulders. Dorothy went to Mary and stood close to her.

"Dad, we'll have to take her right now," Karen said. "Grandmother, we are taking you to see your doctor today."

Margaret stopped trying to eat and turned to look back at Karen.

"Why are you taking me to see the doctor?" Margaret was puzzled. "What for? I do not have any problem!"

"Grandmother, I know what you are talking about," Karen said, gently trying to pull her away from the table. "Dad, will you please take her out of here right now?"

Nelson had a hard time understanding why his mother was having a problem with her behavior. He felt so sad for her.

"Mom, I am worried about you," Nelson said, looking at her sadly.

He had to pull his mother away from the table. Margaret was confused and looked at Nelson with anger in her face.

"You are very rude to interrupt my lunch!" Margaret was upset. "Be nice to your mother! I don't appreciate what you are doing! Shame on you, Nelson!"

Dorothy was frightened by the tone of Margaret's voice and moved to hide behind Mary's back. Karen tried to calm Margaret down.

"Shh, please do not yell at your son," Karen said as firmly and calmly as she could. "We are going to take you to see the doctor. Please, will you put your coat on for me, Grandmother?"

Margaret did listen to Karen. She let her take the coat and help her put it on. She even turned and walked over to the door.

"Dad, will you please open the door for your mother," Karen whispered. "We can go right out to your car now."

Nelson opened the door. "The weather is good outside, mother," he said.

Margaret stopped walking and looked at Nelson. Karen felt that she might be getting worse again and wished that her dad would not say anything at all to his mother. The coworker, Mary and Dorothy started to leave and go into the dining room quickly before Margaret began yelling at Nelson again. Nelson noticed the people trying to leave the room. He knew that they did not want more problems and looked at his mother.

"Mother, I am sorry. I did not mean to be so hard on you." Nelson sighed.

"No, you are right." Margaret nodded. "I think that I should go to see my doctor today. Thank you, my boy!"

She started to walk through the door all by herself. Karen was surprised that Margaret did not yell at her son. She was glad that her dad had figured out the right thing to do, to be nice to his mother. Karen looked at him.

"Dad, you are very lucky!" Karen sounded awed. "If you

hadn't handled it just right, she would have kept on yelling at you. It's a good thing she decided that she should accept help from us."

The coworker, Mary and Dorothy stopped walking away. They were relieved that Margaret had stopped yelling at Nelson.

"Did you hear what Mrs. Rhodes said?" Dorothy asked.

"Yes, I heard that," Mary replied.

Dorothy could see Margaret outside with Nelson and Karen. They got into the car and rode away. Dorothy and Mary walked to the door and watched as the car continued down the road.

Nelson and Karen were trying to talk each other, but they were still feeling sad about Margaret's problem. Karen looked back at Margaret in the back seat. She was looking out the window and was quiet. Karen wondered what could be wrong with her grandmother's mind.

They arrived and parked in front of the doctor's building. They got out of the car, walked into the building and went to speak to the nurse in the lobby. She was working on records and typing at her desk. She looked up at Margaret.

"Good afternoon, Mrs. Rhodes," the nurse said. "How can I help you today?"

Margaret did not answer the nurse. She was puzzled about something being wrong with her, but she wasn't sure what it was.

"We need to see her doctor, please," Nelson said urgently.

The nurse did not understand why Nelson had brought his mother to see the doctor without making an appointment.

"Can you tell me what is wrong with your mother?" the nurse asked Nelson. "Is it something that has to be seen to-day?"

She could see that Margaret was wearing a nightgown under the coat.

"She probably has something missing in her mind," Karen explained. "One of her coworkers called my father in the morning and told us she has been behaving very strangely, in a way that they have not seen her doing before today. Please, will you talk with the doctor about her right away?"

The nurse was willing to help. She could sense how urgent the situation was. She went into the doctor's office, but he was on the telephone. She indicated that she needed to talk with him. He looked up at her and asked the patient on the phone to wait a minute.

"Miss Massey, do you need to talk to me?" he asked.

"Yes, Dr. Farmer, I need you to see Mrs. Rhodes," she informed him. "She is here in the lobby with her son and grand-daughter. They are concerned about her acting very strangely this morning. I think that they will be able to explain what is happening more clearly than I can."

"OK, I will be right with them," Dr. Farmer said. "I need to go now. I will talk with you later. Good-bye."

He hung up the receiver and went out to the lobby with Miss Massey. Dr. Farmer saw Mrs. Rhodes. He wondered why she was not wearing her usual trim clothing as was her custom for a medical visit. He could tell that there was something strange going on.

"Mrs. Rhodes, can you come with me to my office?" he asked. He said to the others, "You can both come with us if you like."

Karen and Nelson looked at each other and of course agreed to come with them into the office. Dr. Farmer pointed to a chair for Margaret; she did understand his gesture and went over and sat down.

"You can sit over there and watch us," Dr. Farmer told Karen and Nelson. "Either of you can tell me what you have noticed about her while I am examining her, all right?"

Karen and Nelson obeyed Dr. Farmer and went to the other chairs and sat down. Dr. Farmer knew that he needed to ask Margaret some questions and see if she would be able to an-swer those questions appropriately.

"Mrs. Rhodes, can you tell me what you are doing this morning?" Dr. Farmer asked.

"I did not know what do I suppose …?" Margaret gave a confused answer.

"I see? Can you tell me where you are now?"

"I guess so, but I did not know where I am?" Margaret struggled to answer.

"That's right, Mrs. Rhodes," he nodded. "You are in my office."

He knew that she had lost some part of her memory and language functions. He looked at Nelson and disliked having to tell him his diagnosis.

"Dr. Farmer, can you tell me what it is that is wrong with my mother?" Nelson asked directly.

"Well, I am sorry to have to tell you that your mother has had a stroke," Dr. Farmer said.

"What could cause a stroke to come on like that?" Karen asked.

"I think that the stroke was probably caused by the stress from her job for so many years," Dr. Farmer said definitely. "I am sorry, and there is no way I can help her return to normal."

"Yes, I knew my mother was always under lots of stress even since I was a little boy," Nelson said, nodding.

"Yes, I agree with that," Karen said. "I can understand that all that hard work must have caused it."

"What am I supposed to do with my mother?" Nelson asked Dr. Farmer.

"My suggestion is that you take your mother to the nursing home at Monroe," Dr. Farmer advised. "I think that's best so that both of you can visit her more often instead of driving over an hour each way. Isn't that the most sensible thing for both of you?"

"Yes, I agree with him," Karen said. "I think it would be better for us to take her with us to the same town where we are living now."

Karen and Nelson stood up and shook hands with Dr. Farmer.

"Thank you very much for your help with my mother," Nelson said. "I find it hard to believe that she had a stroke today."

"Yes, you are welcome, Mr. Rhodes," Dr. Farmer said. "I am sorry about your mother."

"Yeah, this is very sad for my grandmother," Karen said. "She doesn't deserve to have this happen to her. Thank you very much, Dr. Farmer."

Karen told Margaret that they could leave the office. They went out through the lobby, where Miss Massey saw them. They did not say anything to her at all. She was puzzled about what might be wrong with Mrs. Rhodes and walked into the office to ask the doctor.

"Dr. Farmer, did you find something wrong with her today?" she asked him.

"Well, she has had a stroke, caused I suppose by all of the stress from her job for so many years," he answered.

"Oh! I am sorry to hear about that." The nurse really felt bad about their longtime patient.

Nelson opened the car door and let his mother in. Karen and Nelson came around to the front. They were going back to Margaret's house to pack her clothes. They were planning to travel back to Monroe with her that same night.

Chapter 23

Nelson and Karen were quiet. They were deciding how they could manage to take Margaret's clothing to the nursing home. Her doctor had called and referred her case to the physicians there. They would try whatever medicines were available, but he was sure she would need continued, full-time nursing care. Nelson knew he would have to take over her share of the family business. He would have to talk with the salesperson from the factory in New Orleans. It was possible that firm could take over the work she had been doing.

Nelson looked into the rear mirror. His mother was sitting in the back seat. She was quietly looking out the window while they traveled along on the road. He looked at Karen, who was also very silent.

"Are you all right, darling?" Nelson asked. "I know that was a rough time for you, trying to get my mother where she could be helped."

"Well, I feel sad for her." Karen sighed. "We have to do something about what Grandma will need. What about her business? I wonder if you can take over and run her part of the business for a little while."

"Now, you don't have to worry about the business," Nelson said. "I will take care of it myself for now. And I will talk with the manager at the New Orleans plant."

Karen was concerned. "You should probably talk with Mrs. Taylor. She will have more information that you might not know about what dealings your mother had with the factory. We don't know much about it, do we?"

"I will talk with her when we get there today," Nelson said. "We'll be getting back to the house pretty soon."

He turned left and went off the main road to a side road. He drove more slowly on the non-paved surface to avoid the rocks and uneven places. He noticed that some of the field hands were standing in front of the house. He knew that they had gathered to wait for them to come home from seeing Margaret's doctor downtown.

"Karen, do you see those people standing over there?" Nelson pointed them out to her.

"Yes, I see them. They are waiting for us," Karen said. She looked back to her grandmother in the back seat. "I am sure that they are concerned about Grandma, and about us, too."

They drove up to the house slowly and parked on the circle near the kitchen door. The cotton pickers were following along behind the car. They wanted a look at Margaret inside. Nelson got out of the car and found them all around him, wanting to be of some help.

"Please, will you move back?" Nelson told them. "Let's make room for my mother to walk through here into the house. I will make an announcement to you about her in a few minutes after I take her to her bedroom."

The coworkers followed Nelson's orders and moved back from the car. Karen got out and opened the back door to take Margaret out of the car. Keeping the coat wrapped around her, she guided her into the house.

Mary and Dorothy were in the kitchen. They had been waiting for Margaret to come home, but they did not see Nelson's car drive up to the front of the house.

"Mary, did you just see Mrs. Rhodes?" Dorothy asked.

"Yes, they are back. I can see her coming in with her granddaughter," Mary said, looking out the window.

She went down the hall to the door and opened it for them to come in the house. Karen pulled her grandmother into the kitchen slowly and looked at Mary.

"Thank you for opening the door for us," Karen said with a smile. "I will take her to her bedroom upstairs and we'll let her rest for a while."

Mary and Dorothy watched them as they walked through the kitchen and then upstairs. Nelson came into the kitchen and closed the outside door. Dorothy heard the door closing and came over to talk to him.

"Can you tell me what the doctor said?" Dorothy asked.

"OK, I will talk with you and Mary in a few minutes," Nelson said. "I need to help get my mother settled upstairs, and then I will be right back down."

Dorothy still wanted very much to know what was wrong with Margaret. She sat down on the chair and looked at Mary, who was still standing there waiting and looking at her.

"Do you feel something is really wrong with Mrs. Rhodes?" Mary was wondering.

"Well, we don't know yet," Dorothy pointed out. "We are supposed to wait for Nelson to come back down here. I'm sure he will tell us what the doctor said."

Mary nodded. She sat down and waited for Nelson to finish attending to his mother.

Nelson went upstairs, walked over to Margaret's bedroom and looked at his mother in the bed. She was lying on the bed and already fast asleep.

"Karen, how can she be asleep?" Nelson muttered in Karen's ear.

"Yes, Dad, she went right to sleep a few minutes ago, even before you could get up here," Karen told him quietly.

Nelson was relieved. "That is good. We should let her sleep for now."

They went back out to the hall. Karen closed the door softly and they walked over to the office. Nelson went to his mother's desk and sat at it. Karen looked at him and wondered what he might be feeling.

"Dad?"

"I feel bad for Mary and Dorothy," Nelson said. "They will not be able to keep their jobs here if my mother has to go and live in that nursing home. I think what I should do is let them live in one of the houses we have downtown right near the nursing home. They could be some help to Grandma and you could walk over there sometimes. Do you think that is a good idea, Karen?"

"Oh, that is so sweet of you!" Karen was surprised. "They have worked hard in this house for such a long time. I think that they certainly deserve our help. I think that the house should be thought of as a reward for their special gift to our family. They've served us all of their lives."

Karen came over and hugged her father.

"Yes, I do think that they deserve to have a new house," Nelson said. "Let's go downstairs and tell them that my mother had a stroke and that we will be giving them a new home."

Karen went to the door. "Dad, I am so proud of you! I love you so much!"

They went downstairs into the kitchen and looked at Mary and Dorothy, who had been sitting there waiting for them to come back.

"Thank you for waiting for us," Nelson said. "I am sorry to tell you that there is bad news about my mother. Her doctor has told us that she has had a stroke. I have to take my mother to live in the nursing home near my home at Monroe.

Dorothy was very shocked by what Nelson was telling them. "Oh no! I feel bad for her," Dorothy almost screamed. She looked at Mary to see what she would say.

"I don't understand what Mr. Rhodes is saying about his mother?" Mary said.

Dorothy calmed herself so she could explain to Mary what Nelson said. She looked at him for a second, then turned back to Mary again.

"Mary, Mrs. Rhodes has had a stroke," Dorothy explained.

"She is not to be the same as she used to be with all of us. Right now, she has lost her memory of a lot of the past and the things she was doing through the years. I guess we can probably expect she will know our faces sometimes, and sometimes she won't. I guess we can't be sure about that yet. We will find out if she will remember us."

Mary understood it now that Dorothy had explained it to her, but she did not like that Nelson wanted his mother to live near his home in Monroe. That would be too far away from Mary and Dorothy.

Karen moved closer to her dad and tried to whisper to him that he should go ahead and tell Mary and Dorothy that he was going to give them a new house. But Mary thought Karen was telling her father something about her. She stood up angrily.

"What are you saying? Is it something against me?" Mary shouted.

Karen and Nelson were both shocked at the tone of Mary's voice. Dorothy was unhappy too, and she came over to talk to Mary.

"Mary! You should not yell like that against them!" Dorothy calmed her down. "I'm sure they would let us visit Mrs. Rhodes in the nursing home."

Mary did not say any more to any of them. She sat down and was quiet. Dorothy was nervous about Mary and looked across the room at Nelson.

"I am sorry about this." Dorothy sighed. "I will try my best to see if I can help her understand. I know that it is hard for her to accept what you told her, that your mother has to live in a nursing home in a different place, not here."

"Yes, I know how she feels. She doesn't like having my grandmother living far away." Karen nodded and looked at her father. "Dad, please, will you tell them right away."

Dorothy and Mary looked at Nelson and wondered what else Karen expected him to tell them.

"I have a special gift for you today," Nelson said. "Karen

and I were talking about a different house for you. It would be near downtown. Both of you could live there and walk to the stores any time you want to go."

Dorothy was surprised that Mr. Rhodes was going to give them a new house. She looked at Mary, but she did not seem ready to thank them.

"Mary, did you hear what he just told us?" Dorothy asked.

Mary did not answer Dorothy's question. She rolled her eyes and looked at Nelson.

"Thank you very much for giving us a new place to live near downtown," Dorothy said. "But I want to make sure of something else. Would we still be able to work here without your mother living here?"

"Yes, you can work here until the business office in this house is moved or closed," Nelson said. "After that time, you and Mary will not need to work here anymore. By about that time you will be able to get something from our company's retirement funds. But you won't have to pay any money for the house."

"We will pay it all off for you, OK?" Karen added.

Dorothy was awed and surprised that the Rhodes family was going to be so nice and pay everything in full for them.

"Oh, thank you!" Dorothy gasped.

"You are welcome," Karen smiled. "We will take both of you to see my grandmother sometimes when we come over here to take care of the business, OK?"

"Yes, I appreciate your great kindness and help to us," Dorothy said with a smile.

"Sure, anytime!" Karen returned the smile. "We will let you know when the house is ready. It will probably be next year, or maybe even earlier."

"OK, I need to explain things to the coworkers outside right now," Nelson said. "You can go back to work and do whatever there is for you to do today."

"OK, I guess we will finish the laundry," Dorothy answered.

Nelson and Karen left the kitchen. Dorothy was still a little shocked and looked at Mary. She could tell from her face that Mary did not totally like what Nelson had told them about the new house.

"Mary, what do you think about this special gift?" Dorothy asked. "They are very nice to give us a new place to live in near downtown so we don't ever need to ask anybody for a ride anymore."

"I don't know!" Mary was still upset.

Dorothy did not say anything more to Mary. She thought maybe she should check on what Nelson was saying out on the porch. She left the kitchen and went upstairs. She could see Nelson outside. He had announced to the farm workers about Margaret's health. Dorothy closed the window again since Nelson had already finished. She left the window and rushed past the office. She could hear Nelson and Karen coming back into the house from the porch. They went into the office. Dorothy went past the closet and came over close to the door. Suddenly she could hear someone coming and walked back from the office door and stepped into the closet. She closed the door a little bit and looked at the person who was coming; it was Mrs. Taylor. She went into the office. Dorothy left the closet and closed the door. She peeked in and could see three people in the office.

Nelson was sitting on his mother's desk and Karen was leaning on the window sill and starting to smoke a cigarette. They were looking at Mrs. Taylor, who must have been wondering what she could expect to hear.

"Mrs. Taylor, you are doing fine and can continue to work with us for a while if you wish," Nelson said. "I know how you feel about your close friend. You worked together with my mother for many years."

"Yes, that is right." Mrs. Taylor nodded. "I find it hard to believe that you and Karen are giving Mary and Dorothy a house."

"Yes, Mary has live here for many years," Nelson said, "since her grandmother was the first person our family ever had as a servant with pay. She lived all her life in the house where they are living now."

"Yes, I do remember her grandmother, Betty." Mrs. Taylor nodded again. "But I still find it hard to believe myself ..."

"What can you tell us about them?" Karen wondered.

"Well, I will tell you something about her," Mrs. Taylor said. "Margaret's last servant was Mary."

They were all silent for a moment. Dorothy was surprised that she did not know about Mary's family history. She thought that she really should leave this business conference alone, but she was stuck because they might catch her walking past the door and realize she had been listening. Finally, she managed to walk very carefully back past the door, and no one saw her. She felt relieved and went back downstairs to the kitchen.

Dorothy came in and looked for Mary at the table, but she was not there. Dorothy knew that Mary was upset by what Nelson had said. She probably had gone to her bedroom in the other house. Dorothy sighed and went to her home. She checked Mary's bedroom, but she was not there. She decided to give up on looking for Mary. Then she looked out the window and glimpsed Mary's arm under the tree. She was sitting there all alone. Dorothy was glad to find her and hurried downstairs. She went back out and walked over to her.

"Dorothy, I can hear your footsteps," Mary said.

Dorothy stopped walking when she heard Mary's voice.

"Please, will you leave me alone, Dorothy?" Mary asked.

Dorothy turned around to go back into their house. "OK, I will leave you alone," Dorothy said respectfully.

"Thank you, Dorothy." Mary appreciated her understanding.

Dorothy went back into the house, closed the door, and leaned back against it. She could understand how Mary was feeling. She did not really want to leave this house. It had been her grandmother's first house, the first property their family had felt they could call a home since right after the Civil War ended.

Chapter 24

During the next year, Nelson continued working with his mother's business and dealing with the factory in New Orleans. He took Mary and Dorothy to visit Margaret at the nursing home in Monroe twice a month, and they were happy with the attention he was giving them. The work on bringing their house up-to-date took about eight months.

Nelson was in his mother's office working on the paperwork he needed to complete to ship some of the bales the plantation produced to other companies. The phone rang and he picked up the call.

"Can I help you?" Nelson answered.

"Mr. Rhodes, this is Bob Rusk, the contractor. The house reconstruction is finished as of today. I have the key with me now. When can I give it to you?"

"Good to hear that!" Nelson exclaimed. "The key is with you now? Can you come over here and give it to me today?"

"Yes, sir," Bob said certainly. "I will come over to your mother's place and give you the key right away."

"Thank you very much for the call," Nelson said. "See you later."

He hung the phone up and looked at Karen. She was at the next desk helping out with paperwork.

"Karen, I just now got the call," Nelson said. "The contractor told me that the house is ready for Mary and Dorothy to move in any time."

"Oh that is wonderful, Dad!" Karen was surprised. "I am so thrilled to hear that."

"I just have to wait for him to drop the key off over here," Nelson said, and he went back to his work.

"I will let Mary and Dorothy know," Karen said, "that the house is ready for them to move in any time, OK, Dad?"

"Yes, sure, you can tell them right away," Nelson agreed.

Karen left the office and went downstairs to look for Mary and Dorothy in the dining room but they were not there. She thought that they probably were in the kitchen. She went into the kitchen and found them.

"I have good news for you," Karen said, surprising them both. "Your new house is ready for you to move in today!"

Dorothy was excited and looked over at Mary. She knew that Mary still did not really want to leave her childhood house. Dorothy looked at Karen and rolled her eyes. Karen knew too that Mary did not really want to leave here for the new house.

"Thank you very much for letting us know," Dorothy said. "When can we see the house? Today?"

"Yes, we can go there today," Karen said. "But we have to wait for the contractor. He is bringing a key for the house. He'll be here sometime soon. Don't worry about that, OK, Dorothy?"

"Yes, we'll watch for him to come," Dorothy said. She walked with Karen to the hall. "Don't worry about Mary; she will get used to it when we have been in the house for a few months. I hope she will get to where she can forget about her old house."

"Yes, I hope so, too. Thanks anyway!" Karen agreed.

Karen went back to the office upstairs. Dorothy went back to the kitchen and helped Mary dry the dishes. She did not say anything to her about Karen's information.

Bob arrived at Margaret's house and knocked at the back door. Dorothy was cleaning the kitchen floor with a mop and could hear him from there. She put the mop into the bucket and went over to open the door.

"Can I help you, sir?" Dorothy asked.

"I am dropping off this key for Mr. Rhodes today," Bob said.

"Come in please, Mr. … sir?" Dorothy said.

"Bob Rusk," he said. "In the morning, I called Mr. Rhodes to tell him that the new house is all done today."

"Oh! That is great to hear!" Dorothy said. "I will get him for you, or do you want to go up to see him in his office upstairs, Mr. Rusk?"

"Yes, can you show me where Mr. Rhodes' office is?" Bob asked.

"Oh sure! I can go upstairs and find him for you," Dorothy said. "Please just follow me."

Bob went upstairs with Dorothy and followed her until they came into the office.

"Mr. Rhodes, Mr. Bob Rusk is here to see you," Dorothy said.

Nelson heard Dorothy's voice and looked up at her, and then at Bob. "Thank you for bringing Mr. Rusk up here," he said.

"Yes, you're welcome," Dorothy said before leaving the office.

Nelson stood up and came over to Bob.

"Thank you for stopping by here today," Nelson said. He shook hands with Bob.

"Here the key is for you," Bob said.

"Oh that's great!" Nelson said. "I will take the two colored women over to see their new home today."

At that moment, Bob was feeling a little bit uncomfortable about what Nelson had said. It was surprising to him that Mr. Rhodes had ordered him to do all the updating needed to make such a nice house for them.

"It is good to hear that," Bob said quietly.

Nelson could see that Bob did not really like his idea about giving a practically new house to Mary and Dorothy, but he did not really care what Bob thought about it. "Thank you for stopping by here today," Nelson said. "You have a nice day, goodbye."

"Yes, the same to you too, thanks," Bob said as he shook Nelson's hand. "Thank you for choosing our business. I hope your friends will enjoy their new home."

Bob left the office and went downstairs to the kitchen. He could see Dorothy in the dining room cleaning and mopping up the floor. Bob thought that maybe he ought to thank her again for bringing him to the office upstairs. He came into the dining room and tried to call her.

"Excuse me, miss," he said softly.

Dorothy could hear something strange in his voice. She turned her head and looked up at Bob. She stopped mopping the floor.

"Yes, may I help you?" Dorothy asked.

"Thank you very much for bringing me upstairs," Bob said softly.

"You are welcome, sir," Dorothy said and smiled.

"Congratulations to you on having a new house," Bob said.

Dorothy was surprised by what Bob said. She looked at Mary in the kitchen to see if she could also hear Bob's voice. Bob was suspicious as to what might be wrong with Dorothy.

"Excuse me, I don't mean to be rude to you, sir," Dorothy whispered. "I am not sure that Mary ought to hear this news yet. She really does not want to leave her childhood home next door to here."

"Oh, I did not know that," Bob said, trying to figure it out. "That small house out where I parked around the corner?"

"Yes, that's it," Dorothy said. "But I really hate that stupid old cabin!"

"I bet!" Bob laughed. "But she doesn't want to leave that house since it was her parents' or grandparents' first home after the Civil War was over?"

"Yes, definitely!" Dorothy nodded. "That is why Mary has

a hard time getting used to leaving. It was her home. I know it is hard for her to accept having to move."

"I am sorry to hear about that," Bob said. "Probably she will get used to it when she has lived in the new house for a while."

"Yes, I hope so!" Dorothy agreed with Bob. "I can't wait for Mary to forget about that nasty old house!"

Bob was laughing at Dorothy. He thought that Dorothy was a comical person. She looked back at the kitchen and gestured to Bob to laugh more quietly, but Mary had not heard Bob laughing.

"I think that you are such a funny person!" Bob was still chuckling. "I hope that both of you will get to love the new house. Probably it will be better than this creaky old mansion."

"Oh, is that really true?" Dorothy was surprised. "Thank you for telling me about the new house. I can't wait to see inside it myself."

"Yes, I am sure that's so," Bob said. "You will see it right away. Mr. Rhodes is going to take both of you to see the new house today. I think I'd better leave right now. It has been nice to talk with you. Good afternoon."

"Yes, thanks, the same to you." Dorothy smiled.

Bob left the dining room and walked through the kitchen to the back door. He looked at Dorothy and Mary and waved to both of them. Dorothy waved back, then went to the door and closed it behind him.

Dorothy knew that Mary did not want to see the new house. She sighed and walked over to get closer to Mary.

Mary looked at Dorothy slowly, puzzled that she seemed to be staring into her eyes. "Why are you staring at me?" Mary asked.

"That way I can read your mind ..." Dorothy suggested.

Mary was scared by what Dorothy was saying. She could hear somebody in the hallway that led to the kitchen. The door began to open and they both looked at it.

It was Nelson. He came over to them. Dorothy looked up at Nelson to see what he might want to tell them.

"Can I help you, Mr. Rhodes?" Dorothy asked.

Mary knew that Dorothy would always change her behavior and talk about another subject whenever somebody would come into the room.

"I would like to tell both of you something today," Nelson said. "Your house is ready and you can see inside it today before you move in."

"Yes, I want to see inside it!" Dorothy was excited. "Mary, why don't we change into nice dresses to go and see our first home today?"

"No, I will not go there!" Mary said. "I want to stay here, where I began."

Mary went back to her work. Dorothy rolled her eyes and looked at Nelson. He understood that Mary was feeling that she should not have to leave her childhood home.

Dorothy had a good idea. She tried to convince Mary to just come and visit with her at the new house.

"Mary, please come with me?" Dorothy begged. "I don't want to be alone when I am in the new house. You never know, I could get lost somewhere over there in that house. That's why I need you to come with me, please?"

"Why do you want me?" Mary acted as if she was puzzled. "You don't need me to hold you like a child! You are a big girl and you can go there by yourself!"

She went back to work again. Dorothy was failing to convince her and she rolled her eyes.

Nelson was shocked at Mary. He told Dorothy to try to find another way to convince her. Another idea turned up in Dorothy's mind. She bent her knees down on the floor and pulled Mary's uniform. Mary looked at Dorothy and saw that she was acting like a child. Mary didn't know what to do. She looked around at Nelson. He was surprised and almost had to laugh, but then he turned his head away instead. Mary saw him do that and thought that he was upset at her for not accepting his offer to give them the new house. She looked at Dorothy again. She was still reeling, silently begging Mary to come with her.

"Please will you come with me?" Dorothy said. "You never know what might happen? Nelson or Karen might decide to put me to death! I am afraid of them! That is why I need you to fight back against them with me! Please?"

Nelson heard what Dorothy was telling Mary about him and looked at Dorothy in surprise. He knew that she was putting on an act, trying to convince Mary to come with her.

"OK, you have won!" Mary sighed and rolled her eyes. "I will go home and change my dress and go with you today. But please, will you be nice to them, Dorothy?"

Dorothy stopped the begging act and stood up to act like a grown woman again. "Yes, I will be nice to them," she said.

Mary gave up on the work she was doing. She took off her white uniform and put it in the kitchen closet, then went to her house to change her dress.

Dorothy looked at Nelson and winked. Nelson was glad that Dorothy had done such a good job of convincing Mary to come with them to see the new house.

"Thank you very much for trying to convince Mary for me." Nelson smiled. "You had better go now. I will park my car out in front of your house and wait for you to get ready, OK?"

"You are welcome. Anytime," Dorothy said. "I will go home and change into a nicer dress. Yes, I am sure that we will be ready in a few minutes, Mr. Rhodes."

Dorothy went home and into her bedroom. She looked in a closet and selected one of her two nice dresses. It was a plain, light purple. She put it on her bed, then removed her uniform and put on the dress. She left her bedroom to go check on Mary, but she was not upstairs. She turned out to be standing in their small kitchen, looking at the fireplace, which had many small stones in a pattern around the opening.

Dorothy knew that Mary did not want to leave there at all. She looked through the window and could see Nelson's car already parked in front of the house. She looked back at Mary again and gently tried to speak to her.

"Mary, Mr. Rhodes is waiting for us outside," Dorothy said softly. "Can we leave here now?"

Mary nodded her head and left the kitchen. She made herself open the front door and go outside.

Dorothy sighed and followed Mary out, then closed the door behind them.

They went through the center of down and a little bit farther past it. After a few blocks, Nelson turned left and parked at a small private park next to the new house.

Mary and Dorothy looked at the house. It had only one story, but the walls around the house were white brick, and there was a new, shiny, red door. They looked at each other and were awed by what they saw. The house was really simple and plain, but it seemed very fancy to them.

Nelson and Karen got out of the car and opened the doors on both sides for Mary and Dorothy to come out. They got out of the car and then came back together again to go up the front walk. Nelson showed them the key.

"This is the key to your house," Nelson said. "You can take it and open the door and look inside all by yourselves."

Dorothy looked at the key and then at Mary. Then she looked at the house again. Dorothy took the key from Nelson and started to go into the house.

Mary was not feeling so sure. She still felt as if the house was not really their home. "Dorothy! Don't go over there!" Mary suddenly shouted at Dorothy, who stopped walking and looked back at her. "I want you to give the key back to Mr. Rhodes right now!"

Dorothy rolled her eyes. Nelson and Karen were surprised that something was still wrong with Mary.

"Why are you yelling at me?" Dorothy sighed.

"I don't know if that house is really going to be ours." Mary was still afraid to go ahead.

"You don't want me to go into the house all by myself?" Dorothy said, and she gave the key back. "Lets ask Nelson to open the door for us to come in. Will you please open it for us?"

"Yes, I will open the door for you," Nelson said.

He went to the house, unlocked the door and opened it; then he went back to Dorothy and gave her the key again.

"You can come in the house yourself," Nelson said, and he stood by the doorway to welcome them in. "We will stay out here and wait for you to come out and let us know if you are satisfied with everything about this house. If something needs fixing, we will do what we can to change it for you."

Dorothy looked at Mary and raised an eyebrow, then turned back to Nelson again. "Thank you, Mr. Rhodes," Dorothy said. "I will take Mary in with me and we'll both go in the house. Of course, I will be glad to tell you all the things we are going to like about it."

"That is great. Why don't you just go ahead in right now?" Nelson said.

Dorothy came over to Mary and pulled her by the hand toward the front door. Mary did not want to go in but she had to hold on to Dorothy's hand and follow her. They found a small foyer first, and then a living room. There was furniture in every room. Dorothy came into the living room and went over to touch each piece: a dark blue sofa and chair with a white lace headrest on top of each one. They looked very soft and comfortable.

Mary came into the living room slowly. She noticed a new, tall, brown, wooden radio next to the fireplace. "Look at the radio over there," Mary said. She pointed to it with her first smile of the day.

Dorothy looked at the radio, walked over to it and turned it on. She turned the dial and could hear that there was more than one station on the air.

"That is great to hear so many stations," Dorothy said. She turned it off. "We can go back to the radio again later. We need to look all around the house right away. I do not want the Rhodes to be waiting around for us any longer, OK, Mary?"

"OK, we can look at another room. Are there still more?" Mary asked.

"I think that there have to be more rooms," Dorothy said. She could see the dining room, and another room or a hallway must come after that. "Look, there is a nice dining room right there."

Mary looked at the dining room. There was a dining furniture set with a buffet that had glass doors and a full set of dishes inside. She looked back to Dorothy again.

"OH MY LORD!" Mary marveled. "This is so great!"

"I have a hard time believing it too!" Dorothy said as they walked into the dining room and looked around. "All of the dinner set is there, ready for us to eat here tonight. Can you move in with me tonight and make a good dinner for us, Mary?"

"I don't know about the kitchen," Mary said. "How are we supposed to cook dinner there tonight?"

"You do not have to worry about that ahead of time," Dorothy said. "We need to keep on looking at the other rooms."

"OK, I will follow you to find the kitchen," Mary said. She pushed at Dorothy to go ahead.

Dorothy looked at the other dining room door. It had a little round window in it. She believed it must lead to the kitchen. She went over to the door, opened it, and saw that it was the kitchen. She was surprised and looked at Mary quickly. "I found the kitchen right here!" Dorothy pulled Mary after her. "Does everybody have one like this?"

Mary was astonished as she looked around this room, there was much more than she could have expected.

Dorothy went to the stove and turned the gas on. It had a pilot light and didn't even need a match; she jumped when the flame came up.

Mary found a refrigerator on another side; she walked over and opened it. It was already full of food that they liked to eat and cook. That was the biggest surprise of all. Bob Ryan's housemaid had done the shopping for them, they found out later.

"Dorothy! Look in the refrigerator!" Mary called.

Dorothy looked at Mary and went over to see what she had found.

"They bought lots of foods for us."

"That is wonderful!" Dorothy said. She looked at the breakfast table set in the middle of the room. "Look at that table; it's so cute and small. It is just right for us to eat there if we want to."

"I like this kitchen." Mary was accepting things now. She saw a new homestead washing machine in another small room. "Look that! A washing machine is right there."

Dorothy could tell that Mary had finally decided she would like to move into this house. She followed as Mary pointed to the small room where the washing machine was. When she entered the room she could see the backyard. There was a fence around it and a tree with a few branches near the fence. She knew there must be something else inside this house.

Dorothy went back to the dining room. Mary was puzzled as to why Dorothy went back in there. She followed her and saw that Dorothy had moved on to a hallway that went down the middle of the house. She was pointing at a room that opened off the other side.

Mary followed Dorothy and was surprised that it was a bathroom with tile on the floor, and halfway up the walls, too. Dorothy came into the bathroom and looked at the toilet with a black lid on it.

"Now we have a toilet in our house!" Dorothy laughed out loud. "I am so happy that we have one now and I don't have to worry about splitting my butt on the wood out in the shed!"

Dorothy looked around for Mary, but she was not there. Dorothy went out of the bathroom to look for Mary. She found

Mary in one of the bedrooms, sitting on the mattress and looking around quietly.

Dorothy looked around. There was a full-size bed, two lamp stands, one on each side, a four-drawer chest and a chair next to the window. She knew that Mary might still not want to leave her old childhood house. It was so hard for her to accept that they had to live here because of Margaret's health problems.

"Mary, are you all right?" Dorothy asked.

"I don't know yet," Mary answered.

"If you want this room, then you can have it now," Dorothy said. She started to leave. "I'll let you alone and I'll go find another bedroom where I can stay, OK?"

Mary did not answer Dorothy, but laid her head down on the bare mattress.

Dorothy went to the other bedroom. She looked around this room, which was almost exactly the same as the one Mary was in. Dorothy liked this bedroom furniture better than what she had in her bedroom at the old house near Margaret's. Dorothy went to the mattress and sat on it. It felt good. She looked out the window at the front yard, then lay down on her bed and looked at the ceiling. She wondered how it could possibly have happened that they were so lucky that the Rhodes family had given them such a special gift.

Chapter 25

Dorothy had a hard time believing that Nancy had learned so much about her family from her grandmother. "Nancy, where did you get all that information?" she asked. "I suppose that you got most of it from your grandmother. It couldn't have been your mother, could it? Did your grandmother get some of the story from her grandmother, Betty?"

"Absolutely, yes," Nancy said. "I will explain to you what happened."

"Oh! I would like to hear about that," Dorothy said. "She didn't tell me anything about her parents. They had left here a long time before I was born."

When Mary was 18 years old, her mother had problems getting along with Margaret, so she decided to leave her at the house to go to Indiana with Mary's father and her younger brother. They all traveled together by train. Mary and her grandmother, Betty, stayed behind, and Betty kept on working for Margaret.

They came home from the train station downtown and went into the kitchen. They saw Margaret sitting at the table with Eloise. They were waiting for them to come home without the others. Margaret looked at them and asked them where the family had gone to in Indiana. Betty told Margaret that they had just left a little while before. Margaret was still a little bit surprised that they had already left for good. Then she asked Mary if she would like to work as a servant along with her grandmother.

Mary wanted to work as a servant. She had even when she was a little girl. She worked at Margaret's house for many years until Margaret had a stroke.

Betty was gradually becoming weaker and was afraid that she could die before much longer. She thought that she ought to make sure to tell Mary about the history of their family before it would be too late.

Betty was in her bed in the only room on the first floor at their little house and could not walk up the stairs anymore because her knees were getting weaker.

Mary helped her grandmother every evening after she finished working in Margaret's house. One afternoon, Mary brought some food from Margaret's lunch to give to her grandmother. She came into Betty's bedroom, put the food on the tap tray and gave it to her to eat while sitting up in bed.

"Do you want anything else from me?" Mary asked.

"No, I think this is fine, thanks," Betty said.

Mary was planning to go back to work and was leaving Betty's bedroom, but Betty's decided she wanted to tell Mary about the family tree.

"Mary, I need to talk with you!" Betty called.

Mary stopped walking and came back into the room.

"I thought you said you don't need anything else from me?" Mary said.

"You need something from me," Betty said. She patted on her bed where she wanted Mary to sit down. "I want you to sit right there for a while, please?"

Mary was puzzled because Betty had not done anything like that before. She came over and sat on her bed.

"I think I'd better talk with you about our family tree," Betty began. "But not whole the story. I will tell you a little piece at a time when you come here for a break or something like that, OK?"

"Yes, that is great. I really do want to know about my family tree," Mary said.

"Good, I'll start out by telling you about my family," Betty said. "Your grandfather and I were born in Greenwood, Mississippi."

"You were born in Greenwood, Mississippi?" Mary asked.

"Yes, that's where I come from …" Betty nodded. "Your mother was born in the same house where I was born, a little cabin in the slave quarters of a plantation there."

"Do you mean to tell me that my mother was born in Greenwood, Mississippi?" Mary asked. "But I was born in this house."

"Yes, you have that right," Betty said with a smile. "I can tell you more about our family, and Mrs. Rhodes' family too."

"Do you know lots about her family?" Mary was surprised.

"Yes, I do."

"Wow, I do want to hear about that," Mary said.

Every break time and every night, Mary sat and listened to more of Betty's stories. About a month after they began, Betty passed away. Mary had a full memory of what she had heard, but she didn't write anything down on paper. She had never written anything down with a pencil and paper in her life.

"Wow that is interesting to hear about her." Dorothy was awed. "And before your own grandmother died, you did the same thing with her."

"Yes, that is why I wanted to know all about our family history," Nancy said as she started to light a cigarette. "That is a strange thing about my mother. She didn't talk with her mother or write a letter or even call Mary on the phone. She could have called Mrs. Rhodes and asked to speak to one of them. Maybe they just didn't get along so well. Who knows?"

"I didn't ever think about that," Dorothy admitted. "But I don't know if your mother told you anything much about the family history, did she?"

"No, my mother didn't tell me anything about it," Nancy responded.

"I figured it out that the family skipped a generation somehow," Billy suggested. "Betty told her granddaughter, Mary, but not her daughter, Shana, because Shana had chosen to move away. I think that was the way it went. Nancy's grandmother, Mary, told you but she did not tell your mother. Didn't you notice that?"

"Yes, that is true!" Dorothy said definitely.

"Wow, I never thought about that." Nancy was surprised. "I am glad that you told me about them before you wrote it all up in your newspaper article. Thanks for stopping by for me this morning, Billy."

"You are welcome," Billy said. "Dorothy, can I ask you something about yourself?" Billy turned to talk to her. "When did you get a job as a servant to work along with Mary?"

"Yes, that's a good question!" Nancy said. She was curious about it too. "Can you tell us about you and my grandmother and working together at Margaret's house?"

"Oh no, I did not really want to do that!" Dorothy said and rolled her eyes.

"Please, can't you just tell us a short story?" Nancy begged.

"OK, I guess I can tell both of you," Dorothy admitted. "I won't ever forget what happened when I got my first job at Mrs. Rhodes' house to work along with Mary."

Chapter 26

Mary was sad after her grandmother passed away. She worked hard around the house all by herself. Margaret was concerned about her health because Mary was getting tired very easily. She would even fall asleep in the kitchen sometimes. Margaret decided to hire another servant to help Mary out and put less stress on her.

Margaret called the newspaper company downtown and put an advertisement in the help-wanted section asking for a servant to work as a housemaid.

A short, colored woman named Dorothy Datson applied. She was probably in her late twenties and could still be a little bit mischievous.

Dorothy had enjoyed playing games with her coworkers at the factory where she used to work. One quiet afternoon there, she was working with dirty sheets, soaking them in hot, boiling water to try to kill bacteria. She was bored and just threw the dirty sheets into the water from shoulder height. Suddenly, there was a large splash, and the water hit her in the face. It knocked her down and she had to rub her face with her dress to dry it off. She stood up and felt that she really needed a break from the work for a while. She began acting like a boss, just standing there looking at the coworkers as if she was watching what they were doing with their work.

The women were washing the sheets in the boiler, and they noticed that Dorothy was walking along by herself. They looked at each other and wondered why she wasn't working.

"Are you my new boss?" one woman asked.

They were laughing out loud. Dorothy looked at her co-workers from the other side of the line.

"Be quiet!" Dorothy said, giving the order like a soldier.

They stopped laughing and went back to their work. Dorothy was surprised that they really did listen to her. She rolled her eyes and stamped her foot on the floor.

"Don't go back to work," Dorothy said. "Now is the time for a play day. We are just going to play around and throw these stupid sheets over the top of that hot-as-hell boiler!"

They stopped their work and looked back at Dorothy. Then they looked at each other, and then back at Dorothy again.

"Are you trying to play a joke on us?" one of the women asked.

"I don't care what you think about me at all," Dorothy answered.

The woman began to laugh at Dorothy. She thought that Dorothy was just being funny. Other women were laughing, too. The manager in his office heard the noise and knew that what was happening was coming from Dorothy. He decided to give up on keeping her as an employee. He stood up and left the office.

One of the coworkers saw the manager and told another woman that he was on the way to the room. The coworkers looked at him, then went back to work.

Dorothy was puzzled at the way they went right back to work so suddenly. She felt that someone was standing there behind her back.She turned her head and caught sight of the manager.

Dorothy screamed and kicked him on the leg. He fell to the floor. The women could hear from the manager's voice that he was in pain. They looked at him on the floor and were shocked by what Dorothy had done, but then they just turned and went back to work again.

"Why did you kick my leg?" the manager yelled. "That hurt

me badly! I want you to get out of here right away!"

"Hell no! I don't think so!" Dorothy doubted if he meant it. "You can't do that to me because I am still working here, can't you see that?" She went back to her work. She took the sheets out of the boiler and put them into the bucket.

The manager was very angry. He stood up slowly and came over to Dorothy. He pulled her up to carry her out, draped across his back, holding her by one hand and one foot.

"Put me down now!" Dorothy was yelling. "You are a mean guy and I know that nobody likes you because you are such a jerk!"

He kept on walking through the work area to the back door. He pushed the door open and threw Dorothy out on the ground. She was furious and glared up at him.

"You are fired," he said, and he closed the door.

"That is fine with me!" Dorothy yelled. She picked up some rocks and threw them at the door. "You are a jerk and I am very happy that you fired me, that is for sure! Now I am as free as a bird!"

Dorothy was still mad as she stood up and wiped the dirt off her dress. She walked away from the factory, through an alley, and noticed a man at another factory. He was on a break and was reading the newspaper. After his break was finished, he threw the newspaper in the trash and went back to work. Dorothy looked both ways, then walked over to the trash can and took the newspaper out. She looked through the newspaper until she came to the help-wanted advertisements. She read that the owner of a house wanted to hire a servant.

Dorothy thought that she would like take that job right away, but she didn't have a phone where she lived. She knew where the phone was back where she had just been fired. She went back to the factory and walked in slowly, keeping an eye out for the manager.

The other women could see her walking back in it. She asked them to keep quiet, and they did. She found the phone in the hall and had the operator patch her through to Mrs. Rhodes' house. She kept watching for the manager.

In Margaret's office, the phone on her desk rang. She picked it up. "The Rhodes Company, can I help you?" Margaret answered.

"Hello, this is Dorothy Datson," Dorothy said. "I am looking for a job as a servant at your house."

"Well, I am glad to hear that!" Margaret exclaimed. "Can you come over here tomorrow in the morning?"

"Yes, I'll be glad to. Where can I find your place?" Dorothy asked.

"Just go across the river where the bridge is and make the first left. You will see a big house with a porch and lots of cotton fields around it," Margaret directed her.

"Yes, I got it," Dorothy said. "My husband and I will be there tomorrow about seven thirty or eight o'clock in the morning if that's OK?"

"Yes, that is fine. We will see you tomorrow morning at eight o'clock," Margaret said. "Thank you very much for calling. We will talk with you then. Good-bye."

"Yes, you are welcome." Dorothy was excited. "I'll see you tomorrow in the morning. Good-bye."

She hung up the phone and saw her manager on the other side. He caught her before she could run away and hide.

"Why did you come back here?" he asked.

"I was making a call to tell the police about you!" Dorothy told him, then she started to run away.

Dorothy kept on running through to the work area. The other women looked at Dorothy, and then at the manager on the other side of the line of boilers.

"Why did you call the police station?" the manager wanted to know.

"Because you don't pay the colored women anything," Dorothy answered. "You think that we are your slaves! We are not in the nineteenth century now. We are in the twentieth century!

What foolishness!"

The women were shocked and giggled at what Dorothy had told the manager. They new it was a made-up story that she had called the police station.

The manager was really upset that Dorothy had called the police station about him. "Why did you tell them such a lie?" he said. "I do pay all the other colored women, but not you! Now I guess I have to pay you something right away!"

"Yes, that is right!" Dorothy said. "I need the money that you owe me for all of the time that I worked here."

He was very annoyed, but he did take a few dollars out of his pocket and gave them to Dorothy. She took it and counted the money. It was about what she had earned in hourly wages.

"Thank you very much. I will call them again," Dorothy said, and she left right away.

The next day, Dorothy and her husband, Andy, arrived at Margaret's house. She jumped off the wagon, said good-bye to her husband and started walking around the house to look for a rear door. She could hear that the wagon wasn't leaving, so she went back to talk to Andy. He was standing up and staring in awe at the house.

"Andy? I think you better go now," Dorothy said.

Andy didn't answer her. She looked at the dirt road. There were lots of pebbles. She had a good idea. She picked up a large rock from the dirt road and threw it at the horse's rear end. He went out of control right away and began to run. Andy fell down into the wagon.

Dorothy had not realized that it would be so dangerous for her. She fell to the ground to protect herself from getting hurt by the horse.

Margaret and Eloise were in the office and could hear something going on outside. Margaret wondered if something was wrong with the horse. She went to the window and saw that the horse was running faster and faster down the road.

"There's nobody sitting on the front seat," Margaret said. "I don't know what's going wrong out there."

Andy tried to pull at the reins to calm the horse down, but it did not help. The horse kept going on and on. Andy saw another wagon coming the other way and tried to pull hard, but they still kept going until they knocked the other wagon off the road.

Dorothy stood there feeling really upset that her coat was dirty from the road.

"You are such a stupid horse!" Dorothy said as she shook her fist at them. Then she went around to the back door of the house and knocked twice.

"Oh, that must be Mrs. Dorothy Datson," Margaret said. "I told you about her yesterday afternoon."

"Yes, she should be here by about now," Eloise said.

They went downstairs to the back door. Margaret opened the door and looked at Dorothy, who was wiping dirt from her dress.

Margaret and Eloise looked each other, then looked back to Dorothy.

"Hello, are you Dorothy Datson?" Margaret asked.

Dorothy heard Margaret's voice and looked back to her quickly.

"Yes, that is me!" she answered.

"I am glad to meet you," Margaret said. "Please wipe the dirt off your face before coming in."

Dorothy had forgotten to clean her face before knocking on the door. She was very embarrassed. "I am sorry. Thank you for telling me about it," she said.

"That is all right. Will you please come in?" Margaret said.

Dorothy came in and Margaret closed the door.

"I would like to introduce you to Mrs. Taylor," Margaret said next. "She is my bookkeeper for the business. We sell the cotton that you saw on the plants outside before you came in."

"Yes, it is nice to meet you, Mrs. Taylor," Dorothy said.

"Yes, Mrs. Rhodes, I did see the cotton. This is really a large plantation."

"Yes, thank you. I'm glad to meet you, too," Mrs. Taylor said.

"Will you please follow me to my office upstairs?" Margaret said. "I'll show you around the house later today, but first I want to ask you some questions, Dorothy."

"Yes, ma'am, that is fine with me," Dorothy said. "I can't wait to jump right in working here today."

"It's good to hear that!" Margaret laughed.

They went upstairs and came into the office. Margaret and Eloise went to their own desks and sat down. Dorothy wasn't sure if she was supposed to sit down or just wait to be told what to do.

Margaret looked for a paper on her desk, the one with the note about the call from Dorothy the day before.

Dorothy stood there and waited for Margaret's questions. She spotted someone outside in the hall, listening beside the door. She tried to keep an eye on that person, who seemed to be trying to peek at her.

Eloise noticed that Dorothy was acting like a cat trying to catch a mouse. Margaret found the paper and was going to ask Dorothy something, but she was puzzled by what she seemed to be doing. She was looking out at the hall. Margaret sighed and called out her name.

"Dorothy, may I ask you some questions?" Margaret spoke to get her attention.

Dorothy looked at Margaret directly.

"Yes, Mrs. Rhodes," she answered.

"How old are you now?" Margaret asked.

"I am 28 years old," Dorothy answered, then looked out at the hall again.

Margaret suspected somebody was out in the hall, but had not seen anything herself.

"Dorothy, are you all right?" Margaret asked.

"Yes, ma'am, I am doing fine. Do you have any more questions for me?" Dorothy said. Her eyes moved back toward her future employer, then to the door again.

Margaret did not understand at first what Dorothy was trying to tell her, but in a moment she got the message and knew that somebody was outside the door. Margaret thought that she ought to check out in the hall to see who was trying to hide from Dorothy. She stood up and walked over to the door, where she found Mary and pulled her into the office.

"I would like to introduce you two. This is Mrs. Dorothy Datson," Margaret said. "And this is Mrs. Mary Waters. She is our servant. I want you each to know the other person before you start to work together. I'd like that to be as soon as possible."

"It is nice to meet you, Mrs. Waters," Dorothy said. She tried to shake hands with Mary. "I will be glad to work with you."

"No! You are a devil!" Mary said as she pointed at Dorothy.

Dorothy was shocked that Mary was insulting her for no reason. Margaret rolled her eyes and pulled Mary's hand down.

"Behave yourself," Margaret said. "I want you to go back to work now. Please do that, Mary."

Mary did not say anything more to them. She just stared at Dorothy for a few seconds, and then she left the office. Margaret was overwhelmed by Mary's behavior and looked back at Dorothy.

"Dorothy, I am very sorry about the way she is behaving." Margaret sighed and walked back to her desk. "Since her grandmother passed away a few weeks ago, it has been hard for her to accept that she is gone. She had been working with her for such a long time. Now she is alone and the work is too hard for her to do by herself. That is why I need you to help her. You will clean up the house and prepare and serve meals together, but you don't really have to worry about her, I feel sure."

"Yes, that will be fine," Dorothy said. "If she doesn't want to talk with me then I'll just let her be. I can wait for her to come to me when she is ready to talk and be friends."

Margaret was surprised that Dorothy so understood about Mary's bad feelings and would want to help Mary forget about her loss. Margaret looked at Eloise, then looked back at Dorothy again.

"Well, it sounds to me as if things will be great," Margaret said. "I'm sure that if you will give Mary time to talk with you when she is ready, that will be fine."

"Yes, that is OK with me," Dorothy said. "I can just wait for her to get used to me by herself."

"That is a very good idea," Margaret said. "I would like to show you around this house before you begin working today."

"Yes, I am ready!" Dorothy was excited. "I'll get to know all of the rooms that I'll be supposed to keep clean."

"It's good to hear that," Margaret said. "Come on and just follow me as we go."

Dorothy followed Margaret around the house. The last room they went to was the kitchen. Margaret told Dorothy that she would order a new uniform for her to wear during the work day.

Chapter 27

"How did you and Mary get along so well after that rough beginning?" Nancy asked.

"I have never forgotten the way it happened." Dorothy laughed. "Mrs. Rhodes' granddaughter, Karen, was only a little girl. She needed us to get her kitten out of the pipe."

"The kitten was in a pipe?" Billy choked on the smoke from his cigarette.

"It came from the wood stove in the greenhouse," Dorothy said. "I will explain to both of you how we became very good friends."

Even after a year had passed, Mary and Dorothy were still not talking or helping each other at all. Mary would work by herself upstairs and Dorothy would work alone downstairs at the same time. When they met in the same room, they would begin to argue about which one had arrived there first. Margaret would hear them and would have to send them to separate rooms.

On an afternoon that had started out quietly, Dorothy was in the kitchen washing a dust pan in the sink. She wrapped it in a towel to dry it and put it in the closet. Mary came into the kitchen and saw Dorothy in the closet.

"What are you looking for?" Mary yelled at her.

Dorothy was scared because Mary's voice had come so loud and suddenly. She looked back to Mary.

"Why are you trying to yell at me?" Dorothy yelled back at Mary. "You nearly scared me at death!"

"What is your problem?" Mary was insulted.

"Well, I guess it is your problem, not mine!" Dorothy said, slamming the closet door hard.

"Excuse me?" Mary said. "Why did you shut the closet that way? You could break something."

"Who cares?" Dorothy said. She walked over to the table and picked up a bowl.

"You are a devil …" Mary insulted her again.

Karen came into the kitchen from outside and rushed over to them.

"Do you want me to do something for you?" Dorothy asked.

"I need you to help me get my kitten, please?" Karen said. Her eyes showed that she was ready to cry.

"Where is your kitten?" Mary asked. "Is he up in the tree and can't come down?"

"No, he is stuck in a pipe," Karen said. "Please come with me now!"

Mary and Dorothy looked at each other and wondered what Karen was talking about. What pipe? Karen ran to the door and opened it for them to come outside with her.

"What a minute, Karen," Mary puzzled. "I don't understand what you are talking about. What is this pipe that your kitten is in?"

"Yes, he is in the pipe right now!" Karen said.

"We don't know what kind of pipe your kitten is stuck in. Is it out there?" Dorothy asked.

"He was playing in the wood stove and he climbed up the pipe," Karen explained.

"Oh, is that in the greenhouse right beside the kitchen?" Mary asked.

"Yes, please come with me right away!" Karen begged.

Mary and Dorothy looked at each other and sighed, then they followed Karen to the greenhouse. They went into the greenhouse and Karen pointed to the pipe between the ceiling and the wood stove.

"That is where your kitten is, inside the pipe?" Mary asked.

"Yes, he is still inside and he can't get down to the top of the wood stove," Karen said.

They could hear the kitten inside the pipe. He was walking back and forth and meowing. Dorothy came over to the wood stove and opened the gate so she could see inside.

"The kitten will not come out," Dorothy said after looking up inside. "How did he get in there?"

"I guess that the top was open and the kitten climbed up and went into it," Karen said. She pointed to the top of the wood stove.

"That explains it!" Dorothy sighed. "You know that cats always want to sneak in somewhere if there is anyplace they can go."

"Probably the kitten won't come out," Mary said, pointing to the pipe. "Keeps going back and forth."

"I want the kitten out of the pipe, please?" Karen begged.

"All right, we will take care of the kitten for you, OK?" Mary calmed Karen. "I will find something to open the pipe and let the kitten out. Do you think that will work, Dorothy?"

"Yes, that is a good idea," Dorothy agreed. "But I am short and I can't do that by myself without help."

"Mary is taller than you and she can reach the pipe!" Karen was happier now. "You can catch my kitten when Mary opens the pipe."

"Yes, you are right!" Dorothy said and smiled. "I can hold the kitten when he comes out."

"I will open the pipe ," Mary said. "Are you ready to catch the kitten?"

"Yes, I am ready," Dorothy said. She held her hands together to form a kind of basket.

Mary looked for a space between the joints and tried to break them apart, but the kitten was scared by the noise and ran wildly back and forth inside the pipe.

Karen looked worried.

"Please don't hurt my kitten," Karen said, sounding really scared.

"OK, Karen, please, will you calm down?" Mary said. "We will take care of it for you."

Mary tried to open the pipe slowly, but it snapped apart and the kitten came out. The smoke started to spread around the room.

"I got the kitten!" Dorothy said, catching it before it could fall.

Karen heard Dorothy say she had the kitten, but she couldn't see anything because the room was full of smoke.

"Meow!" The kitten cried in Dorothy's hands.

"Toby! I am here for you!" Karen said. She found the kitten where Dorothy was holding him.

"Yes, you can have him now," Dorothy said with a cough. "I really hate getting all of this mess on my face!"

"Thank you very much for catching my kitten," Karen said. "And you too, Mary."

The smoke became a little less heavy and they could all see the room more clearly. Karen looked at Mary and Dorothy and laughed at them because their faces and uniforms were covered with soot.

"I got lots of smoke on my face and dress," Mary said.

"Yes, me too!" Dorothy sighed. "I need to wash myself."

"Yes, I believe you do," Mary said.

Dorothy wiped some dirt off her face with her hand and looked at Mary. A few seconds later they were both laughing and hugging each other.

Karen was surprised that they were getting along so well today. She knew that they had not talked to each other before they worked together to save the kitten.

Margaret had been looking for them in the kitchen but they were not there. She thought probably they had gone outside with Karen. Margaret sighed. She didn't like to see Karen asking them to come outside away from the house. She went outside and saw a wisp of smoke coming out of the greenhouse. She wondered what was happening and went to the door. She saw Karen coming out of the greenhouse with the kitten and went over to wipe some of the soot off her dress.

"Tell me what is happening," Margaret said. "Why have you been playing in the greenhouse?"

"My kitten was stuck in the pipe. He went into it from the top of the wood stove," Karen said. "I called Mary and Dorothy to get my kitten out of the pipe. But I am surprised that Mary and Dorothy are friends now."

"What are you talking about?" Margaret was puzzled.

She went into the greenhouse and saw Mary and Dorothy sitting on the floor and laughing together. Margaret was surprised that what the little girl had said was true. She thought she had better just leave them alone, so she went outside.

"Yes, you are right, they are getting along," Margaret said. "I am glad that what the kitten did made them decide to be friends. I think it's better for us go back inside. You should take a bath before your father comes to pick you up this evening."

They went back to the main house. Mary and Dorothy were still sitting in the greenhouse looking at each other and laughing.

"It is certainly neat to hear that story." Nancy was awed. "That was wonderful that Karen and her kitten made you and my grandmother became best friends!"

"Yes, it was wonderful!" Dorothy said. She smiled. "Now I really miss her a lot."

"I am glad that you and Mary decided to get along," Billy said. "How long did Margaret live after she had the stroke and went to live in the nursing home?"

"She lived in the nursing home for almost nine years," Dorothy said. "I have never forgotten the last time we visited her before she passed away."

"Oh! That must have been awful!" Nancy said sympathetically.

"I don't mean to ask you if you don't want to tell us," Billy said. "Is there anything you can say about your last visit before Mrs. Rhodes died?"

"Um, I don't mind telling you about what happened," Dorothy said.

Chapter 28

Dorothy went to the living room and took a book off the coffee table. She sat on a chair that had a lace doily on each of its arms. She felt relaxed and opened the book.

Mary rolled her hair up on the back of her head and put in a few clips to hold it in place. She took a small, round mirror and turned her back to another mirror on the wall so she could check to see if her hair would stay in place. She left the bathroom and walked toward the kitchen. The sink was half full of dirty dishes. She supposed she ought to finish them before Nelson stopped by to take them for a visit to Margaret at the nursing home.

Nelson drove to Mary and Dorothy's house from Monroe. He parked his car, got out, and looked around to make sure no one would see him get the two colored women and put them in his car. He hurried to the front door and knocked on it heavily.

Dorothy dropped her book on the floor. She was scared that someone meant to do them harm. She ran to Mary in the kitchen.

Mary looked at Dorothy in surprise. "What is the matter with you?" Mary was puzzled.

"Who is trying to damage our house?" Dorothy screamed. "You better check who is at the door right now! I am afraid because I am just a short, old woman. You are so tall and big. You can fight back if you have to!"

Mary rolled her eyes and thought that Dorothy was imagining too much. She dropped the dish into the sink and went to the front door.

"Dorothy, you better stop acting like a child," Mary sighed.

"I will go to the door and see what the problem is. You had better start behaving!"

Mary passed Dorothy and walked through the dining room to the front door. She looked through the small window in the door. It was Nelson standing outside. She laughed to think that Dorothy believed some strange person was trying to scare her to death.

Dorothy walked out to the dining room, and from behind the wall her head looked out at Mary just as if they were playing peek-a-boo.

"Dorothy, this is Nelson," Mary said. "Don't you know better than that? Today is the day we visit Mrs. Rhodes at the nursing home."

"Oh, that is right!" Dorothy said. "I forgot. I have to get my purse and my hat from my bedroom before we go with Mr. Rhodes."

"Yes, I need something else too," Mary said. "I will let him know that we will come out in a few minutes."

Mary opened the door.

"Good afternoon, Mary," Nelson said. "Are you ready to visit my mother at the nursing home today?"

"Good afternoon, Mr. Rhodes." Mary said. "No, we are not ready yet. Can you give us just a few minute please?"

"Yes, you can take your time," Nelson said pleasantly. "I will wait for you to get ready."

He went back to his car and got in it. Mary closed the door and rushed to the kitchen. She took a towel and dried the dishes very fast, put them on the table, then left the kitchen for her bedroom. She put her hat on, took her purse and came out. She met Dorothy at the hall.

"Are you ready to leave now?" Mary asked.

"Yes, I am ready," Dorothy answered.

"Good, let's go then," Mary said.

They left the house, Mary locked the door and they came to the car. Nelson got out of his car and opened the back door to make sure they were in and settled, then he closed it. He came back to his seat and drove away from their house.

They traveled on the road to Monroe for an hour. Nelson arrived at the nursing home and dropped Mary and Dorothy off at the front of the building. Dorothy got out of the car, then Mary moved over into her seat to talk with Nelson.

"We will call you at your office when we are ready to go home, if that is all right with you," she said.

"Yes, just let me know when you are ready to leave for home and I'll get back as soon as I can," Nelson answered.

Mary got out of the car and closed the door. She and Dorothy went into the lobby and spoke to the woman who worked at the desk.

"May I help you?" the woman asked. "I think that you are supposed to be visiting Mrs. Margaret Rhodes today?"

"Yes, that is right," Mary said.

"You can go upstairs now," the woman said. "You'll have a nice visit with her, I hope."

"Thank you," Mary said. "Dorothy, let's go upstairs."

Dorothy rolled her eyes. "You know she isn't my mother."

The woman was writing at the desk. She heard Dorothy's words and almost had to laugh. She thought that Dorothy was being pretty comical.

Mary and Dorothy went upstairs, walked to the end of the hall and came into Margaret's bedroom. They tried to speak to her, but she was looking out the window.

Mary came over to Margaret, who turned her head and noticed Mary on the way to her. She moved around to look at her.

"Good afternoon, Mrs. Rhodes," Mary said. "How has your day been today?"

"I am doing well, thank you," Margaret said. "What about you?"

"I am doing fine, and Dorothy is too," Mary said, pointing to Dorothy.

Dorothy rolled her eyes. Margaret looked at Dorothy and recognized her. She remembered that she had hired Dorothy as a servant to work along with Mary a long time ago. But Margaret really loved her a lot, and Mary too.

"Can you bring the chairs over here?" Margaret asked. "I would like to be close to both of you."

Mary and Dorothy brought the chairs nearer to Margaret's bed and sat down to visit with her.

"We are here with you now," Dorothy said. "You can tell us if there is anything we can help you with."

"Nah, you don't need to be doing anything to help me, thank you." Margaret smiled. "What are you both doing with your lives?"

"I am doing fine. I can sit and read a book in our living room," Dorothy said. "It is a long time since we have had to work. Of course, I do miss being on the job at your house. Mary does too."

"That is true," Mary agreed. "We always will miss working at your house. But we are retired now. We have a good time resting at home, and sometimes we can take a nice walk. It's just a few blocks to downtown."

"I am glad to hear that," Margaret said. She looked at Dorothy. "I will never forget one thing that happened to you."

Dorothy didn't understand what Margaret was talking about and looked over at Mary. She didn't know either. Dorothy moved a little closer to Margaret.

"What is it you want to tell us about me?" Dorothy asked.

"Yes, I remember what you did when you put hot sauce in my soup," Margaret said. "When I ate that soup, it was very spicy. But I know that it was you that did it and not Mary."

Dorothy's eyes opened wide and she moved back a little in her chair. Mary was surprised that Margaret had never forgotten what happened when Dorothy had poured hot sauce in Margaret's favorite soup for her lunch.

"Don't worry about that, Dorothy!" Margaret was laughing. "I really liked the taste of it, but it was too spicy for me."

Dorothy was relieved that Margaret wasn't going to get mad at her for something that had happened such a long time ago. She turned back to Margaret again and tried to tell her the truth.

"Yes, I did pour the hot sauce into the pot," Dorothy admitted. "I am very sorry about that, OK?"

"You didn't have to say that!" Margaret laughed. "I always had a good time with both of you since I've been here, and at my house, too."

"Yes, it is the same thing with us." Dorothy laughed and pointed at Mary. "I will never forget that first day when I met you and Mrs. Rhodes. You were insulting to me. You said that I was a devil!"

Mary did remember that she had been mad at Dorothy because she didn't want her to come and work there in that house.

"Yes, I do remember that!" Mary laughed. "Mrs. Rhodes told me to leave the office. I was surprised that you dared to stay on with me acting like that!"

"Yes, you made me so embarrassed in front of Dorothy!" Margaret laughed. "But I thought the whole thing was so funny!"

Margaret and Dorothy laughed along with Mary, and they had a good time talking back and forth.

"I feel sometimes that my feet get cold," Margaret said. "Please, will you get out an extra blanket for me?"

"Yes, I will look for a blanket for you," Mary said. She went to look in the closet.

Dorothy checked the weight of Mrs. Rhodes' blanket, and it was really thick. She wondered if it was too heavy. The room was pretty warm, and outside it was very hot.

"I can't find one here," Mary said. "I will ask the nurse to give us another blanket for you."

"Yes, you can ask the nurse," Margaret said.

Dorothy looked at the end of the bed and checked to see if

either blanket or sheet was out from the bottom of the mattress, but they were both still tight. Margaret's memory seemed to be better than ever today, but she looked and sounded very weak and frail. Dorothy had a definite feeling that Margaret could be going at any moment. Dorothy looked at Margaret slowly and came over to her.

"I would like to say something to you," Dorothy said. "I want to thank you very much for hiring me to work with you. I have certainly already missed being with you. I will see you in heaven, I know that. I love you Mrs. Rhodes."

"You are welcome, Dorothy," Margaret said and smiled. "I am pleased to have had you working for us. Yes, I will wait for you to come to see me in heaven. I love you, too."

Mary came back into the room with another blanket. She placed it gently over Margaret's body and tucked it around her feet.

Dorothy smoothed the blanket just under the mattress corners and then tried to tell Mary something quickly.

"Mary, you can talk with Mrs. Rhodes about when you will see her again." Dorothy was convinced that is would happen.

"What are you talking about?" Mary was puzzled.

"OK, Mrs. Rhodes needs to talk with you a minute, please?" Dorothy begged her to come closer and brought her over to Margaret.

Dorothy kissed Margaret's cheek and left the room quickly. She went out in the hall and sat on a chair beside the door, but she was still listening to hear what they might be saying. Mary did not understand why Dorothy had left the room. Margaret seemed to be trying to call her name.

"Yes, do you want something from me?" Mary asked.

"Yes, I need to talk with you," Margaret said in a whisper.

"I can't hear you. Will you please say it again?" Mary asked.

"Mary, I love you, and I will miss you," Margaret mumbled. "I am going to wait for you to see me in heaven."

"Yes, I will meet you in heaven," Mary said.

Dorothy was sitting out in the hall alone and kept listening to their conversation until Margaret stopped talking to Mary. Mary tried to say something more, but Margaret did not respond. Dorothy knew that Margaret would soon be passing away and she began to cry.

A week later, Margaret was gone and had been buried next to her husband. Mary and Dorothy were walking downtown and wondering how they would feel from now on. They were not used to being without Margaret since they had been visiting her twice a month for almost nine years. Mary looked at Dorothy.

"Dorothy, why didn't you tell me?" Mary asked. "How did you know that Mrs. Rhodes was about to die?"

"Well, you remember when she told us that her feet were cold?" Dorothy explained.

"Yes, she said she needed an extra blanket," Mary remembered. "But did you leave the room without saying good-bye?"

"No, I talked with her and I told her that I would see her in heaven," Dorothy said. "That was before you came back in, and then I wanted you to talk with her alone because I was sure she was going to die soon after that."

"Yes, I see," Mary said. "It's a good thing that I did tell her the right thing. I said that I loved her and that I would see her in heaven. The last words she said to me was, "I love you and I'll see you heaven, too."

Mary noticed that Dorothy didn't seem to be listening to her and was just looking somewhere else.

"Dorothy! Are you hearing my story?" Mary asked.

Dorothy looked at Mary quickly and pointed in another direction. She followed her pointing finger to see somebody else. Mrs. Taylor was on a bench with her face hidden in her hands.

"Why is Mrs. Taylor crying?" Mary wondered.

"I don't know," Dorothy said.

"I will go over and ask her if she is all right," Mary said.

"Yes, I will follow you," Dorothy agreed.

They went over to the park and called her name. Mrs. Taylor heard them coming and turned to look at them.

"Oh, thank God!" Mrs. Taylor cried. "I am so glad to see both of you here."

She came over to Mary and hugged her for the first time in their lives. Dorothy was shocked and looked around in both directions to see if anyone had seen them because they were colored. Mrs. Taylor hugged Dorothy too.

"Mrs. Taylor, are you all right?" Mary wondered.

"Yes, I am doing fine, but I just received a letter from the Army today." Mrs. Taylor sighed. "My grandson has been killed in the war in Europe."

"Oh, I am sorry to hear that." Dorothy was shocked.

"Now I understand why you were crying," Mary said. She hugged Mrs. Taylor. "Now he is safe in heaven."

"Yes, I thank both of you so very much for your sympathy," Mrs. Taylor said. She sat down on the bench and cried a little more.

Mary looked at Dorothy, then went and sat with Mrs. Taylor. Dorothy was still looking from side to side because Mary was not supposed to sit on the bench for white people.

"I know how you loved your grandson so much," Mary said, trying to help her out. "Our country should be very proud of him."

"Yes, thank you, Mary," Mrs. Taylor answered. "I appreciate that. I think I had better go now. I hope I'll see you around here sometime again."

"Yes, of course you can go if you want to," Mary said. "We will see you again somewhere around here. Good-bye, Mrs. Taylor."

"Yes, good-bye to both of you," Mrs. Taylor said as she waved to them.

She left the little park and walked across the street. Mary

and Dorothy were really sad about Mrs. Taylor's grandson being killed. They had known him well from when she had brought her little grandson to Margaret's house a few times while his parents were away on vacations. Now, he was grown up and lost to all of them.

Chapter 29

Billy was pretty tired. He looked at his watch. He had not realized that it was past midnight. He was trying to figure out what his last question for Nancy should be before he would leave for home that night.

"Nancy, can I ask you one more question before I leave for home?" Billy asked. "It is already past midnight, I suppose you've noticed that."

Nancy and Dorothy were surprised too that it had been such a long night.

"You don't have to worry about staying here until late," Dorothy laughed. "We are so pleased to be talking with you about all of this."

"Yes, thank you. I feel the same way about it." Billy smiled.

"Billy, did you want to ask me another question?" Nancy wanted to know.

"Yes, I have only one more question for you," Billy said. "How did you find out about it when your grandmother was dying?"

Dorothy raised her hand.

Billy thought this was a strange reaction. He wasn't a school-teacher. Why was she trying to raise her hand to get his attention?

"I got a call at my dormitory," Nancy said. "'When I came in from my last class that day, the woman at the desk called my name and gave me the message. Dorothy had called to say that my grandmother was dying."

A few days before Mary was to die peacefully in her own bedroom, she felt that her body was becoming weaker and that her time for going to heaven was about to come. She called to Dorothy.

Dorothy was in her bedroom and could hear Mary calling her name. She went over to Mary's bedroom and looked at Mary, who was laying in her bed.

"Mary?" Dorothy wasn't sure if Mary really had called her.

"Good, you're here. I need you to call Nancy at her dormitory," Mary said.

"I don't know her phone number up there," Dorothy said.

"You can look in my chest of drawers." Mary pointed at it.

"Where do you suppose I can find it?" Dorothy asked.

"Just look in the top one. You will see her name on a small piece of paper inside there," Mary directed her.

Dorothy went to the chest, pulled the drawer out and looked inside it. She could see the little piece of paper with Nancy's phone number on it. "I found it," Dorothy said, and she showed the paper to Mary. "I'll go over to the living room and make the call for Nancy right away."

"That is good. Please hurry up and do it, Dorothy," Mary said.

Dorothy went to the living room and picked up the phone. She dialed the number to call Nancy in Indiana. Mrs. Rose was working at the desk in the girl's dormitory and picked up the phone when it rang.

"Good afternoon, this is Seton Hall Dorm, may I help you?" she greeted the caller.

"Can you please give a message to Miss Nancy Williams?" Dorothy asked her.

"Yes, I'll be glad to pass a message along to her for you."

"Please tell Nancy that this is Dorothy Datson calling. I want to tell her that her grandmother wants her to come back home to Louisiana right away. When she can arrange to fly down here, will you please ask her to give me a call? Thank you very much for giving her the message."

"I'll give the message to Nancy as soon as she comes back to the dormitory. That should be in just a little while."

"OK, I'll wait for her call me back later today." Dorothy sighed. "Thanks again, and good-bye."

Dorothy hung the phone up. She went back to Mary's bedroom, put the note back in the drawer and closed it. Mary awakened again and looked at Dorothy.

"Did you call Nancy like I asked you to?" Mary asked.

"Yes, I did, and I gave the message to the woman that answers the phone," Dorothy said. "The woman will give Nancy the message when she comes back from her classes. I'm sure Nancy will call back as soon as she hears that you need her to come."

"It's good to hear that." Mary smiled. "Thank you for calling Nancy. I hope that she will be able to get here pretty soon."

"Yes, you are welcome, anytime." Dorothy nodded. "If you feel like you need my help with anything, please just yell out to me and I will be right in here, OK?"

"OK, I will call you if I think of anything that I might need. Thanks a lot …" Mary said, and she drifted off to sleep again.

Dorothy left the bedroom for the living room and sat on the chair to read the newspaper. She would look in and check on Mary in a little while again. She was hoping to hear from Nancy pretty soon.

After her last class, Nancy went back to the dormitory. She came into the lobby and started to go right upstairs. Mrs. Rose saw Nancy and called to her right away.

"Miss Williams, I have a message for you," she called.

Nancy was on the stairs already, but she turned back and looked at Mrs. Rose.

"Yes?" Nancy said as she walked over to the desk.

"I have a message for you from Dorothy Datson," Mrs. Rose said. "She called and wanted me to tell you something about your grandmother. She really wants you to fly down to Louisiana as soon as possible."

"Oh, thank you very much for the message." Nancy was surprised and shocked. "May I use this phone to call Dorothy?"

"Yes, you can call her right away," she said.

Nancy dialed the number to call Dorothy. Dorothy was in the living room doing some mending when the phone began to ring. She put the sewing basket down and hurried over to pick up the phone.

"Hello?" Dorothy answered.

"Hello, Dorothy, this is Nancy," Nancy said. "How is my grandmother's health?"

"She is doing fine, I think, but …" Dorothy sighed. "She does want you to come down here soon if you can find a way to do it?"

"Yes, I'll buy a ticket and fly south," Nancy said. "Probably I can leave here by tomorrow morning. I will let you know what time it will be and what airport is the closest to you. I'm not sure if it will be in Mississippi or Louisiana, OK?"

"Yes, please call me before you leave," Dorothy said. "My friend and I will be able to pick you up at the airport if you let us know where and when."

"Yes, I'll call you back when I get ready to fly," Nancy said. "Thank you for calling to let me know about my grandmother's health. I love you and good-bye!"

Nancy put the phone down.

"Thank you very much for letting me use this phone. Um, let me think about what to do right now," Nancy said. "I need to pack some clothes, and of course I have to try to get a ticket at the airport as soon as possible."

"You are welcome. I am sorry to hear that you need to go right away," Mrs. Rose said. "I hope that you will be able to get a ticket to fly south right away."

"Thanks. I need to go now, bye," Nancy said, and dashed up the stairs to her room.

She went upstairs to her room and told her roommate about her grandmother. Her roommate and her other friends wanted to help Nancy buy a ticket for the round trip. They went with her to the airport and bought the ticket at the counter there. The man told Nancy that she would to be able to leave at eight o'clock the next morning and would be arrive at Monroe, Louisiana at noon. Nancy went to the phone booth and made a call to Dorothy to let her know that she could meet Nancy at the airport in Monroe at noon.

The next morning, Nancy's roommate dropped her off at the airport. The airplane departed on time and flew for four hours. Nancy had not slept well the night before because she was worried about her grandmother's health. A few minutes after the plane took off, she began to feel drowsy, and soon was completely sleep.

The airplane arrived at Monroe at just past noon. Nancy didn't feel anything, not even the landing. The announcements had woken her up momentarily, but she went right back to sleep again. The passangers stood up and began to leave the airplane slowly. The stewardess noticed that Nancy was still asleep in her seat. She came over and gently awakened her.

Nancy was glad that she had arrived safely and was looking forward to seeing her grandmother. She stood up, took down her purse and coat from the shelf, then walked out of the plane and down the flight of steps. The airplane had stopped about a hundred feet from the airport building. Nancy sniffed the air. It was early spring here, but in her northern home the season was still winter. She went downstairs and kept walking through the building. She picked up her suitcase and went out to the street in front of the airport. People were standing alongside the parking area waiting for someone to come pick them up.

Nancy looked for Dorothy and her friend. She saw them parked across the street. Dorothy saw Nancy and rolled the car window down to wave to her.

"Nancy! We are over here!" Dorothy called to her.

Nancy heard Dorothy's voice across the street and saw her waving. She went across the street to meet them.

Dorothy got out of the car and hugged Nancy. Dorothy's friend, Aaron, took Nancy's suitcase and put it in the trunk.

"I am so glad that you have come," Dorothy said with a smile. "Your grandmother will be very happy to see you again."

"Yes, thanks, Dorothy." Nancy yawned. "I can't wait to see her."

"We'll leave right away," Dorothy said, and she opened the door. "You can come on in and sleep there a while. I will wake you up when we get to the house. OK, Nancy?"

"Yes, thanks again," Nancy said.

She hugged Dorothy again and then got into the car. She went to sleep in the seat almost immediately.

They left the airport and started out on the long trip back to the house. After an hour and half they finally arrived at Dorothy's house and parked in front.

"Nancy, we are home now," Dorothy said, touching her gently on the shoulder.

Nancy began to wake up slowly and stared at Dorothy for a second. Then she picked her head up and looked at the house where her grandmother lived.

"Thank God, we're here!" Nancy said. "I need to see her so badly."

"Yes, you can go ahead in and see her right away," Dorothy said. "She is in her bedroom waiting for you to come."

Nancy got out of the car, went into the house and headed straight for Mary's bedroom. Nancy saw her grandmother on her bed. She was fast asleep. Nancy sighed, walked over to the bed and sat next to Mary, holding her hand. It felt dry and warm.

"Grandmother, are you all right?" Nancy whispered. "I have come down to see you."

Mary heard Nancy's voice and began to wake up. She looked at Nancy's face. They were both in tears.

"I am so happy to see you again," Mary managed to say.

Nancy hugged her grandmother.

Dorothy came into the house and told Aaron to leave Nancy's suitcase in the living room. He put it on the floor by the fireplace and left the house. Dorothy went to Mary's bedroom to see if Nancy had been able to talk with her grandmother. They were together, and both were silent for the moment. Dorothy had a feeling that Mary would be in heaven before much longer. She decided to leave them alone and slowly closed the door.

"She was alive for a few hours that day," Nancy sighed. "And then she passed away at about 5:45 late that same afternoon. So, that's all that I can tell you from the beginning of the story right up to the morning when you met me at the funeral."

"Wow, now I have the whole story about your grandmother's side of the family just since this morning," Billy said. "I think that's it. I'd better get going now."

Billy stood up and put his pack of cigarettes and lighter in his coat pocket. Nancy and Dorothy stood up at the same time.

"Thank you again for taking so much of your time to talk with us this evening," Dorothy said. "You had better be careful driving home tonight. You must be tired."

"Yes, I'll take care of myself. Thanks," Billy said. "Nancy, I do appreciate your sharing all this time with me today. I hope you have a safe trip back to Indiana."

"Thank you," Nancy said. "I expect to be back in Indiana by about two days from now."

They went to the front door and opened it. Billy went out and started to light another cigarette. Nancy thought of what she should have told Billy about the Blackburn family. She came over to him. He looked at Nancy and held out the pack of cigarettes to her.

"Would you like a cigarette?" Billy asked.

"Well, yes, thanks." Nancy said, and she picked out a cigarette.

Billy lit Nancy's cigarette.

"I would like to tell you something else that ought to be in the article," Nancy said. "Maybe you could add the story of what happened in the Blackburn family along with my grandmother's story? Do you want to do that?"

Dorothy looked at Nancy and was puzzled as to why Nancy would want to offer to add the story about the Blackburns to what Billy already had for the article.

"Why are you suggesting that?" Dorothy wondered. "I don't see any reason we need to come up with that!"

"Wait a minute." Billy was confused. "Why did you suggest it?"

"Well, they were split apart," Nancy sighed, "since their uncles became enemies. Today their children have grown older and have children of their own. I mean, there are grandchildren and possibly great grandchildren who are cousins of Nelson and Karen in Mississippi. God knows who they are."

"I guess that they did not know each other at all growing up," Billy said. "I do think it would be interesting for people to hear about all of that."

"I want you to do it for their sake," Nancy said.

Dorothy rolled her eyes. "What about your side of the family from Mississippi?" Dorothy asked.

"I don't have much of an idea about that," Nancy said. She looked at Billy. "Do people from your family live in this area too?"

"What? I am sorry. I don't understand what you are talking about?" Billy was really confused.

"I am speaking of people living here in the South," Nancy said.

"No, my parents were Norwegian immigrants," Billy said. "I am the first child born here in America."

"Are you a Norwegian-American?" Nancy was awed.

"Yes, I am," Billy said with a nod. "And you are an Africa-American."

"Yes, you are right about that," Nancy said. She looked at Dorothy.

"Yes, that is true," Dorothy agreed.

"I can't wait to read you're article," Nancy said. "Will the newspaper come out tomorrow or the next day?"

"Probably it will be in the newspaper about two days or so from now," Billy said.

"Oh, by that time I will be going back to Indiana," Nancy said. She turned to Dorothy. "Can you send the newspaper to me later after you read it, please?"

"Sure, I'll send it to you," Dorothy promised.

"That will be great, thank you!" Nancy smiled.

She looked at Billy again and kissed his cheek. Dorothy looked up and down the street to see if somebody was looking at them, but there was no one around.

"How do you dare to do that?" Dorothy was really upset. "You do remember that we are in the South?"

"I know that." Nancy laughed. "I understand. Are you all right, Billy?"

"It's OK," Billy chuckled. "Thank you for your conversation, and I want to thank you, too, Dorothy. I think it's best for me to get going now. Good night and good-bye."

"Yes, the same to you! Good night and good-bye!" Nancy and Dorothy both told him.

Billy waved and went over to his car, then turned back suddenly. He had forgotten to ask them something. He came back over to the front steps.

"I forgot to ask you something," Billy said. "Who was it that said Margaret's last servant was Mary?"

"Mrs. Eloise Taylor," Dorothy answered. "She was Margaret's bookkeeper for a long time, up until the time that Margaret got the stroke."

"Ah! I got it." Billy said. "That's all that I needed to know before working on the story. Thanks again, and I really do have to go now. Good-bye."

"If something comes into your mind again," Nancy suggested, "you can give us a call and we can give you the right answer before you get ready to put it in the newspaper, OK?"

"Yes, I'll do that. Thanks and bye!" Billy was laughing.

As he drove back to his house, he was thinking how it had been a lucky day for him to catch up with Nancy before she left to go back to college.

Chapter 30

Billy arrived at his home and went into the house. He turned the light on in the dining room, where his desk and typewriter were. He put his notepad down and read through this notes a little, then began to work on the article, spending a good part of the night on the first draft.

Vicky was in bed and could hear Billy typing in the dining room. She turned the lamp on and looked at the clock; it was three o'clock in the morning. She wondered why Billy was still up so late at night. She got out of bed, put her robe on and left the bedroom to go downstairs.

Billy was typing busily, but he finally noticed Vicky's feet in the doorway and looked up at her face.

"Vicky, why are you awake?" Billy asked.

"I heard your typing," Vicky yawned. "I came down to see what was happening."

"I am sorry that I woke you up," Billy said.

"That's all right," Vicky said. She kissed him and sat down on a chair. "How was your interview with Miss Nancy Williams?"

"I had a good time interviewing her," Billy said. "She is a very nice person. We spent the whole day together until it got dark, then she invited me to her grandmother's roommate's house for dinner. We spent a long time there with Dorothy Datson. She worked with Nancy's grandmother in the main house at an old cotton plantation for a long time."

"Wow, it sounds as if you were pretty lucky!" Vicky was surprised. "Did you get more information from both of them?"

"Yes, that's why I am working on this article tonight," Billy said, showing her some of what he had already done. "There are lots of stories about her grandmother's life, and the family they worked for, too."

"Can I read these notes?" Vicky asked as she pointed to the pile of papers.

"Yes, sure, you can read anything you want," Billy said. He gave her most of the notes he had already gone over. "Let me know after you read some of this what you think about the story."

"Yes, I would be more than happy if it will help you out," Vicky said. "I'll get something to eat and drink before I start to read. Would you like some coffee?"

"Yes, please, that would be great, Vicky," Billy said.

Vicky went to the kitchen and took down the pot to fill it with water, then put it back on the stove and turned the gas on. She collected some cookies and cake and put them on a plate to keep them going for the rest of the night. Billy was typing over some items he had made mistakes on. Vicky read through the papers, and they drank the coffee and ate some of the cookies and cake.

The sun came in through the dining room window. Billy and Vicky were both asleep at the table with their heads down. Papers were spread around the table and floor.

Vicky was bothered by the light, so she turned her head to face the other way. She didn't feel comfortable with the light that way either. She reached for the switch and turned the lamp off, but the room still wasn't dark enough. She wondered why the lamp hadn't gone off. Then she looked out the window, rubbed her eyes, and looked out the window again. The light was coming from the sun and not from the lamp. She looked at the clock on the wall above the door. It was past nine in the morning. Only then did she realize that morning had come. She looked at Billy; he was still asleep at his desk. Vicky tried to wake him up, but he didn't want to wake up at all. She sighed and pushed him so hard that finally he woke up completely.

"You have to go in to work right away," Vicky said, pointing to the clock. "The time is already past nine and you are supposed to be at work by now."

"Aw, I am too tired for work today," Billy yawned. "I'll call Vic and tell him so."

"You better call him right away," Vicky said.

She straightened Billy up in his chair, then went to the kitchen and dialed the phone for Vic.

Vic was in his office reading the paper when he heard the phone ring. He picked it up. "Good morning, *Lake Providence Sentry* newspaper," he answered. "May I help you?"

"Good morning, Mr. Stadden," Billy said. "This is Billy. I want to let you know that I can't make it to the office this morning. I will positively be back in the office tomorrow."

"Ah, that's OK," Vic said. "I was just wondering about you. How was your interview with Miss Nancy Williams yesterday?"

"I had a good time interviewing her," Billy said through a yawn. "We spent the whole day together. It went on until late last night. She invited me to her grandmother's roommate's house for dinner last night."

"I bet you got lots of information from her grandmother," Vic said.

"I'll give you the whole article tomorrow in the morning," Billy said. "I'm sure I'll be finished with it by then. I've been working on my notes all night."

"That's great." Vic was excited. "I can't wait to read your story about those women. I think you ought to go to bed and get some rest for today. Tomorrow morning is plenty of time for the finished article. Good-bye."

"Thanks, Vic," Billy said. He hung up the phone, went to his bedroom, took his clothes off and went to bed. Vicky went back to the dining room, picked up the papers from the floor and stacked them on the table. She collected their dishes, brought them to the kitchen and put them in the sink. She had planned to finish cleaning up, but she felt so tired that she decided she would have to go back and get in bed with Billy. She went to the bedroom, took her robe off, and slipped back into the bed.

They were awakened by a fire truck going by.

"I hate hearing that!" Billy complained.

"Why? That has to happen sometime," Vicky was yawning.

Billy looked at the clock; it was fifteen minutes to one in the afternoon. He looked at Vicky on the other side of the bed.

"Do you want to go back to sleep or are you going to work?" Vicky asked.

"I think I'd better get a shower first," Billy said. "I'll get freshened up and then I'll get back to work on the article so I can give it to Vic tomorrow morning."

"Can I join you in the shower?" Vicky giggled. "I got dirty too."

"Yes, sure, we can get together in the shower." Billy enjoyed that idea.

They went into the shower together. Sometime after that, Billy went back to the dining room and worked on finishing the story that was due the next day. Vicky went to the kitchen and got busy making a lunch for Billy.

Chapter 31

The next morning, Billy went to the dining room, collected all of his papers, stuffed them into his briefcase, and returned to the kitchen.

"Vicky, I'm ready to go back to work," Billy said. "See you later this afternoon. I love you. Bye-bye!"

Billy kissed Vicky and she gave him a bag with his lunch in it.

"Good luck getting your story published," Vicky said. "I hope the next assignment turns out as well. Bye-bye!"

Vicky was wondering whether the editor would like the story as much as she and Billy did.

Billy drove downtown to work. He arrived at the office and parked his car. He was sure that his editor, Vic, would like the article since it had been his idea in the first place. He got out of his car and went upstairs. Billy expected that Vic would be in his office as usual. He came into the office, but Vic wasn't there. Billy sighed, then took the article out of his briefcase and put it on Vic's desk. He left the office and walked to his own desk. He sat down and began checking galley proofs for the next edition.

At lunch time, Billy looked in Vic's office again, but Vic hadn't shown up at the office all day. Billy wondered whether Vic had gone out of town or what? He thought one of the other reporters might know what Vic's plans were for the day, so he turned back to the coworker, whose desk was hear his.

"Excuse me," Billy said. "Do you know anything about Vic's plans for today? I know this is a weekly, but we are going to have a deadline before long."

"I don't know what his plans are," the other reporter said.

"OK, thanks anyway." Billy sighed. He went back to his desk, took his lunch bag out of the briefcase and ate part of his sandwich. He wanted Vic to be here and read his story so he could find out if he liked it. Finally, Billy gave up on thinking about Vic and went back to his daily work of preparing the next issue.

Vic showed up at his desk at about three in the afternoon. He put his briefcase down on top of Billy's article and made a telephone call.

Billy kept on with what he needed to do for the paper until the alarm clock on his desk sounded. He looked at the clock; it was five in the afternoon. He was disappointed that he hadn't heard anything from Vic. He would have to check Vic's office again to see if he was there.

Billy saw Vic in his office, but he was on the phone again. He was relieved that Vic was there, but he saw that Vic's briefcase was still parked on top of his article. Billy preferred to leave Vic alone and let him find out for himself that Billy had left the article on his desk. Billy sighed, went back to his desk, grabbed his briefcase and started for home.

Vic was talking on the phone when he spotted Billy on his way downstairs. "I will call you back later, thanks, bye," Vic said to the person he was talking to. He hung the phone up and rushed out of his office, calling after Billy.

"Hey, Billy! Wait a minute!" Vic called loudly.

Billy heard Vic's voice and turned. "Yes, Vic?" Billy said.

"I need to talk with you a minute." Vic was breathing heavily. "Do you have the papers with you from your interview with Miss Nancy Williams two days ago?"

"Yes, I left that article on your desk this morning," Billy said. "But your briefcase is on top of it, so you probably didn't notice it."

"I didn't know you had finished the article." Vic was surprised. "Please, will you come back up with me to my office? I'll read your story right away."

"OK, I just need to call my wife Vicky," Billy said. "I need to let her know that I will be home a little late today."

"You can use my phone over there," Vic said. "Please come on back up and call your wife right away."

They came into the office. Vic took his briefcase off of Billy's papers. Billy dialed the phone to call Vicky and tell her that he would be home late. Then he waited for Vic to finish the story. Vic looked at Billy with a wide smile.

"It's an interesting story!" Vic said. "But I need a good title if we are going to get it in this week's edition."

Billy hadn't realize that he had forgotten to put in a title before he put the papers on Vic's desk. He tried to think of one, and what came to his mind was what Dorothy had told him she had heard from Mrs. Eloise Taylor.

"OK, I think the best title for this story," Billy said, "would be 'Margaret's last servant was Mary.'"

Vic didn't understand why Billy would choose that particular title for the article.

"Why do you think that is such a great title for this story?" Vic wondered.

"Well, it isn't just my idea," Billy explained. "Those were Mrs. Eloise Taylor's exact words about how the two knew each other."

"How did you get hold of that particular saying?" Vic wanted to know.

"Dorothy Datson was a servant along with Mary," Billy explained. "She had planned to meet Mr. Nelson Rhodes at his office, but Mrs. Taylor came in before her and told that to Nelson and his daughter, Karen. What she said was…"

"Margaret's last servant was Mary?" Vic said.

"Yes, you got it." Billy nodded.

"I got it?" Vic wondered. "I think that we have to know

why Mrs. Taylor said that. What was her job for Margaret?"

"She was a bookkeeper," Billy said. "Margaret and Eloise were very good friends and worked together for a long time."

Vic thought that the title sounded interesting, and he felt sure that people from this hometown area would want to read Billy's article in the newspaper the next day. He went to his office, took his pen out and wrote on the top of the first sheet of the article the title that Billy had given it. Then he circled the words and indicated a bold typeface for them. That meant that Vic was accepting the article along with Billy's idea of what the title should be.

"Sir, what are you writing there?" Billy was puzzled. "Does the title sound good to you? Can you tell me whether you think people will want to read my article? I guess it's possible they won't want to read this story because it has the colored family's history, not just the white family's."

"Why do you think they wouldn't be interested in reading this article?" Vic wanted to know. "You never know. Some people might like to read it and be more interested about the whole history of that family. Of course, it has to include the servants, too."

"Well, you know about the KKK members around here." Billy sounded worried. "If somebody reads this article and gets angry, they could try to destroy my job or even want to set fire to my house. If that happens, my wife and I will have to move back to my hometown up north."

Vic was upset and slapped the article down on his desk, frightening Billy.

"What do you think anybody would do to us?" Vic was angry. "I don't think what you are saying about people down here is the truth. In this day and age, both kinds of people ought to be brothers to each other. I know that some KKK members say they would like to hurt colored people, but if they actually do wrong things, I don't know about it. I am not a KKK member."

"Well, I don't know what to say," Billy sighed. "I am just warning you, but you know more about this society here than I do. Do you want to go ahead and put my article into the newspaper for tomorrow morning?"

"Yes, and it will not hurt you in any way," Vic said softly. "There is nothing wrong with this article. This story is about both sides. So you can trust me, all right, Billy?"

"OK, you can go ahead and publish the article," Billy said. "That is all that I need to know. I'll just go home now."

"You don't have to worry about it anymore," Vic said. "If you want to, you can stay home and see what happens during the day tomorrow. I will stop by your place tomorrow afternoon to let you know if we are having any problems from the town at all. That will be OK with you, won't it, Billy?"

"Yes, I appreciate your consideration. Thank you, Vic." Billy nodded. "See you later then. Bye."

"OK, take care of yourself, and your wife, too," Vic said.

Billy left the office and went downstairs to his car. He got in, still feeling unsure of what might happen to him after people read the newspaper tomorrow. He started his engine and drove back to his house.

Vicky was in the living room, sitting on a chair and watching through the window for Billy to come home. When he arrived she ran to the door, opened it and went outside.

"Billy! What did your editor think about your story?" Vicky was excited.

Billy got out of the car and closed the door. He came over to Vicky with a sad face.

"He didn't accept your story?" Vicky felt sad about it.

"No, he likes it and it will be published tomorrow," Billy said.

"Oh, that's wonderful!" Vicky was surprised. "Why don't you feel proud about it?"

"Yes, I am proud of myself," Billy said. "But I need to talk to you about it. Let's go inside."

Vicky was puzzled about what might be wrong with Billy. They went inside the house and closed the door.

Chapter 32

Early in the morning, the men came into the print shop and set up the roller press to run through the machine and make the newspapers. Other men took the folded newspapers out on the floor outside and then to the delivery trucks, which would drop the newspapers off at houses and stores.

The delivery service man placed the newspapers on the newsstand, and the first person who showed up bought a cup of coffee and the newspaper. Then he went to a bench and sat down. He opened the newspaper and noticed Billy's article. He read the article and it was interesting to him. He didn't feel like complaining about colored people in the story, and he kept reading the article.

One of his friends saw him on the bench. "Good morning, Henry," he said. "What are you reading in the newspaper today?"

"Good morning, Tim," Henry said, and he showed him the article. "I hadn't heard before about this story about Mrs. Rhodes' servant, this woman who worked with that one family for so many years."

Tim couldn't see it clearly enough because the paper was too far away from him, so he pulled the newspaper over closer. He looked at Henry and took the paper away from him altogether.

"Let me read it," Tim said. "Two brothers whose names were Robert and Ron Blackburn; they became enemies and each one took his own slaves. The family with Ron moved to this town, it says here."

"You probably remember when she got married," Henry was chuckling. "You know that Margaret couldn't keep her last name after she got married. Her relatives are from Mississippi. They will probably find out that a great grandfather or uncle from way back became an enemy against his own brother. I think that is a sad story. They all would probably want to meet their cousins one day."

"Yeah, probably you are right." Tim nodded. "But I don't know how those people will feel when they read this article. I was surprised to see that the three colored women weren't so stupid and that they could hear from family members all through the years. Unfortunately, a lot of colored people really lost track of their families since their masters bought and sold them and took them wherever they wanted them to work as servants or to pick cotton on the land they owned before the Civil War."

Tim looked back at the article and kept on reading the story. Henry nodded and left Tim alone.

Gina came into the printing area, took a newspaper out and went upstairs to Vic's office. She went into the office and gave it to Vic.

Vic smiled. "Thanks for bringing the paper," he said.

He opened the newspaper, found Billy's article and read it through again. He thought this really would be a valuable story about the lives of Margaret and Mary. Vic folded it back together and put the newspaper on his desk, then made a call about something else.

In another part of town, people sat in the restaurant and ate at the booths and read Billy's article in the newspaper. Some of the people knew the Rhodes family, and many of them had heard of Margaret. She had often visited downtown and been active in the church. People knew about her but didn't really know her family's background that well.

Dorothy took the newspaper from the front door, rushed to

the kitchen and opened it. She looked for Billy's article and found it. She read it all the way through and it made her feel so proud. It would give people good exposure to what it must have felt like for the families that were torn apart during, before and after the Civil War. Slave families knew about it, but now other people would, too.

Vic thought that he should go outside to hear how people were responding to Billy's article. He was planning to leave his office, but suddenly a man came in to see him. Vic looked at him and wondered who he was.

"Yes, can I help you, sir?" Vic asked.

"Are you the editor of this *Lake Providence Sentry* newspaper?" the man asked.

"Yes, I am Vic Stadden. Who are you?" Vic answered.

"I am Gerald Prine from New Orleans," his visitor introduced himself. "I am an editor the same as you are. I am visiting here for a few weeks. I just read the article in your paper, 'Margaret's Last Servant was Mary,' and I think that would be an interesting story for me."

"It is great to hear that," Vic said, feeling really surprised. "Please, have a seat. Would you like some coffee?"

"Nah, I don't need it, thanks." Gerald chuckled and sat back in his chair. "Can I have your permission to reprint this reporter's article for my newspaper in New Orleans? I think that people from my town would like to read it too."

"That is great. I can give you a carbon of the original article in our paper if you like," Vic said. "You can use it to fit into your newspaper format."

"Of course, I will take care of it," Gerald said. "When I get back to my office I will get my print shop to set up the type for my newspaper. Thank you very much for your permission to use it down in New Orleans."

"Yes, you are welcome. Anytime," Vic said. "Thank you for stopping by and seeing me here today."

Gerald shook Vic's hand. They stood up and left the office. Vic thought that what Gerald was doing would give the article a good chance to be republished nationally.

"Mr. Prine, do you think you could offer this as a spread to other cities in the state?" Vic asked.

"Yes, I can and will do that," Gerald said. "I have some friends who run papers in other towns besides my own. There probably should be some interest in other states like Mississippi and Texas, or even more."

"Oh, that is splendid!" Vic said, greatly pleased. "I have a business card at my desk."

Vic took a business card from his desk and gave it to Gerald along with a fresh carbon copy of the original article.

"Thanks, Mr. Stadden," Gerald said, giving his business card to Vic. "Here is my business card; you can call me anytime any of your reporters' articles would be good for our newspaper too."

"Yes, I will give you a call in a few days." Vic was excited.

"Thanks, and I hope to see you again soon," Gerald said. He waved good-bye to Vic and went downstairs.

Vic was thrilled and hoped that Billy's article would be republished in other states within a few weeks. He thought that he ought to stop by and see Billy at his house. He checked everything in his office and in the printing room downstairs in case anybody needed to ask him anything. He went back to his office, took a new copy of the paper and his briefcase, then went downstairs to his car in the parking lot at the back of the building.

Vic knew how Billy felt about being afraid of what some people might think or do when they read his article in the paper. When he reached Billy's, he got out of his car and went up to the front door. Billy opened the door and saw Vic standing there.

"I just brought a copy of the newspaper for you," Vic said, showing Billy the paper. "Probably you already have it, so you can take this one for your future children or grandchildren to read."

"Yes, I will take it. Thanks, Vic," Billy said softly. "Do you know anything yet about how people are responding to the article?"

"I guess there won't be any problems," Vic said definitely. "I would like to tell you something. An editor from a New Orleans newspaper, who happens to be visiting here, stopped by my office and is interested in reprinting your article in his local paper."

"Wow, that is wonderful news!" Vicky was delighted. "Billy, you should be proud of yourself!"

"Are you sure that the editor likes my article?" Billy asked.

"Yes, he likes it," Vic nodded. "Probably it will make a wide spread, maybe even nationwide pretty soon."

"WOW!" Billy didn't know what else to say.

He hugged Vicky, then shook hands with Vic.

"Thank you very much for stopping by to tell me," Billy said. "That's worth your taking the time, isn't it?"

"Yes, you are doing a great job!" Vic chuckled. "You don't have to worry about thinking that people might hurt you. I think I'd better get back to the office. It's OK for you to wait and come in tomorrow morning. Bye."

"No, wait a minute, Vic!" Billy said. "I would like to invite you to come out to dinner with us tonight, unless you have some other plans?"

"Nah, I don't have any plans tonight," Vic said. "I can join you for dinner. This can be a night to celebrate in your honor!"

"Yes, well, I have a plan for that, too!" Vicky laughed. "Please, won't you just come back over here later?"

"Yes, thanks, Vicky. I certainly will," Vic responded.

They did have the celebration dinner later that evening at the home of the successful feature writer and his wife.

Billy's article, "Margaret's Last Servant was Mary," was definitely being rerun in several Louisiana papers. Karen went into her father's office in Monroe and opened the newspaper on his desk. She showed him the article. He read it and was startled to learn that his mother had not told the story about the other branch of her family living in Mississippi all these years. Within a week, the article was already appearing in states other than Louisiana, even as far away as California and New York.

In Indianapolis, Indiana, more people knew Nancy now than ever before because of the interview Billy did with her while she was in Louisiana. Some of her friends and professors at the college told her that they had seen the article that described her grandmother's life as well as that of Mrs. Rhodes. Nancy was glad to hear about it, and hurried to the store and bought a few newspapers to look for the article. She found it in several different papers. That made her so proud of her grandmother.

NBC TV and radio heard about the story and were broadcasting comments about it. Most people from southern towns agreed that the story was true to life. Both white and colored people had something to say about what Mary's experience had been. There were many other such stories about whole generations of families continuing to work for their masters' families for many years even after winning their freedom at the end of the Civil War.

Chapter 33

Robert Blackburn's great grandson, Chris, worked as the manager of a cotton-fabric plant in Greenwood, Mississippi. He took a newspaper from the break room into his office, dropped the newspaper on his desk and sat down to look at it. He was reading through it when he noticed Billy's article from Lake Providence, Louisiana. Chris was surprised to read that Robert and Ron Blackburn had become enemies. He knew that Ron and his family had moved to Louisiana with a group of their slaves during the early 1800s. He didn't know any more about the history of his family. His father had not told him about all that had happened. Maybe he didn't know anything about it either. Chris thought that he should talk with his father, so he left the office, got into his car and drove to his father's house.

When Chris arrived at his father's, he went right in and walked through the foyer to the sitting room, but his father wasn't there. Chris thought that his father was probably on the porch or outside somewhere. He went outside and around on the porch to the back of the house.

"Dad, where are you?" Chris called.

In the greenhouse next door, Chris's father heard Chris calling him. He went to a small window and opened it enough to put his head out a little way.

"Chris, I am over here at the greenhouse," he said. "Please come on over and talk to me."

Chris entered the greenhouse and walked between the shelves of potted plants. His father was fixing a plant on a trellis and turned to look at Chris.

"What did you want to talk to me about, son?" his father asked.

Chris dropped the newspaper on the shelf beside the plant and showed his father the article that mentioned the Blackburn family.

His father had not known anything like this had happened, and he was surprised that his own grandfather, Robert, had not told him something about all this when he was a little boy, or even after he was old enough to understand things better. He had believed his grandfather had no brothers or sisters until he saw the newspaper article. He sat down on a stool and felt really confused. Chris came over to him and tried to make him feel comfortable.

"Chris, please listen me," he protested. "My grandfather didn't ever tell me about having a young brother."

"You didn't know that you had a great uncle named Ron?" Chris asked.

"Yes, that is correct," his father nodded. "I am glad that you showed me this newspaper, and I will talk with my brothers and sisters about this. But I am not sure if they will have read the newspaper this morning or not."

"Yes, I will talk with my wife about it, too," Chris agreed. "I need to get back to work now. I just wanted to make sure you saw the article at least. I'll talk with you later, Dad. Bye."

"Thank you for bringing me this article," his father said. "I want to keep it to show to my brothers and sisters. If they have it, then I will send this copy back to you, OK, Chris?"

"No, you can keep it after you show it to them," Chris said. "I will buy another copy of the paper before I go back to my office. Bye-bye for now, Dad."

"OK, give me a hug," his father said, and he hugged him. "Talk with you later. Bye-bye, son."

Chris drove back to his office and bought the newspaper before he went inside. He thought he might pick up another copy later. He and his wife would want one, and maybe somebody else in the family would like one, too.

Chris decided to leave work early. He arrived at home and found his two daughters, Missy and Bethany, playing cards in the living room. They noticed that their dad had come home early.

"Mom, Dad is home already," Missy called her mother.

Lynn was in the kitchen and heard her daughter telling her that she had seen her father drive up. Lynn looked at the clock; it was only four in the afternoon. Chris usually came home from work a little after five.

"Did you really see dad out there?" Lynn asked.

"Yes, he is coming in right now," Missy answered.

Chris came into the house and hugged his two daughters. "How are my girls?" he asked them cheerfully.

"Good. It's so nice that you came home early!" Missy said. "Mom didn't believe me at first that you were really here."

"OK. I'll tell her that I'm home," Chris said cheerfully. "Lynn, I really am home now. Please come out here and you'll see me in the flesh."

Lynn heard Chris's voice and realized that Missy had not been just trying to tease her. She went to the living room and hugged and kissed him.

"It's hard to believe that you actually came home early for once," Lynn said.

"Yes, it did happen," Chris said softly. "I would like to show you this article that was in the newspaper today."

"What are you talking about?"

He showed Lynn the article. She read it and was surprised to see that it was talking about the Blackburn family tree.

"Did you show your father this?" Lynn asked.

"Yes, I took it over to show him this morning."

"Did he know that this happened?" Lynn wondered.

"He didn't know anything about it," Chris sighed, "because his grandfather had not told him the truth. He never said anything about having a brother."

"Oh, what a shame!" Lynn was shocked and surprised.

"Yes, it certainly is a shame," Chris agreed.

Lynn looked at Missy and Bethany. They were staring at their parents and wondering what might be wrong. They certainly looked solemn.

"Chris, look at the girls," Lynn said, pointing at them. "I think that you ought to explain to them that we found some new information about the history of our family tree in an article in today's newspaper."

"That's probably a good idea," Chris agreed. "But they are still pretty young and might not understand what we are talking about in connection with the family history. Maybe I could just explain to them when they get to be teenagers. Then they could understand more about our family history than they would now. Do you think that's the right thing to do?"

"Yeah, I guess you are right," Lynn nodded. "But you probably need to tell them just a short story about it. You could just say that we found out we have some cousins in other states or something like that?"

"Um, that is a good idea," Chris agreed.

The girls had gone back to their game. Chris went over to them and told them that the newspaper had a story that might mean that their family had some cousins living in Louisiana. But neither of them really understood.

After a few years, Chris told Missy and Bethany a little more so that they could know that they really had cousins living in Louisiana, but the two family branches still had not even tried to reconnect.

Chapter 34

When Missy turned eighteen she was a freshmen at Mississippi College. All the new students and their parents arrived at the dormitory and took their bags and boxes into their rooms. The older students would arrive a week later. They would be glad to meet their friends again, having not seen most of them for three months.

Missy was nervous about meeting new students. She only knew people who had been students with her in high school, but she soon made some new friends, beginning with the first day of classes.

The first class Missy attended was a general course in history. In the classroom there was a large, dark brown, wooden lecture platform. Missy was sitting in the third row and could see the long blackboard on the wall behind the instructor, Dr. Eric Laiserin. He was a tall white man, about fifty-something years old. He seemed very friendly. He put his books on the lecture table and then looked at the students in the big classroom with a smile. He sat down and looked at the packet of registration cards for the students who were supposed to be here this period. He stood up and walked alongside the table with a book in his hand.

"Good morning, my name is Dr. Eric Laiserin," he said. "I have taught history classes for freshman students for almost thirty years at this college."

He pointed at a student in the first row. "I would like each of you to give your name and tell us where you come from. Will you please be the first one?"

The student had not expected that the teacher would choose him first.

"Don't feel stressed about it, OK?" Dr. Laiserin said. "Just tell us your name and what part of the world you come from."

"OK, but am I supposed to stand up tell them?" the student asked.

"No, you don't have to stand up," Dr. Laiserin said. "You can sit there and say it."

"OK, my name is Keith Gray," he introduced himself. "I am from Biloxi, Mississippi."

The next student looked around the classroom with a shy face. "My name is Kay LaPrarie," she said. "I come from Little Rock, Arkansas."

The students kept on introducing themselves one by one. Missy began to get bored listening to them. She looked down to check her schedule for the next class. Students in the second row continued to introduce themselves. Suddenly she heard one of the students say he was from Lake Providence, Louisiana. She looked at him quickly, but she missed hearing his name because the others were continuing to introduce themselves. Missy sighed. She couldn't figure out which one had said he had come from the town where she remembered her father had told her they had long lost relatives.

The third row kept on introducing themselves. Missy thought maybe it would work if she would ask someone in the second row what the boy from Louisiana had said his name was as she was introducing herself. The student next to Missy introduced himself. Missy already felt some nervous perspiration. She stood up and looked down the second row. The students were puzzled and looking at each other wondering why Missy was standing.

Dr. Laiserin was checking the enrollment cards when he noticed that the students were not as quiet and orderly as they had been. He looked at the third row and was puzzled to see that Missy was standing up to speak.

"I am Missy Blackburn from Greenwood, Mississippi," she

stated. "I want to know which one in the second row is from Lake Providence, Louisiana. Will you please raise your hand?"

One of the students in the second row raised his hand.

"That was me," he announced.

"Thank you," Missy said, and she sat back down.

Dr. Laiserin didn't know why Missy had asked the student what she wanted to know. He didn't realize that it was all because of the article that had mentioned her lost relatives. He had seen the article but had not figured out what the title meant to that particular family.

The students looked at Dr. Laiserin. He was thinking about what to do. He looked at the class.

"Ah, I am sorry we've had an interruption," Dr. Laiserin said. "I do remember that there was an article that mentioned that town about ten years ago, but I don't recall the reporter's name. It was an interview with a colored woman about the time her grandmother died."

"Yes, I know what you are talking about," Missy said. "The reporter's name was Billy Vangslia and he interviewed a young woman named Nancy Williams."

"Yes, you have that right!" Dr. Laiserin was surprised. "Miss Blackburn, I would like to know what the title of the article means? Probably you remember the title?"

"Margaret's Last Servant was Mary," Missy said.

"Yes, that's what I recall about it too. Thank you!" Dr. Laiserin said.

The students looked at each other for possible explanations. They had never heard of the story, of course. Dr. Laiserin looked out at students in the auditorium and could guess that they didn't know anything at all about the subject.

"Well, that was ten years ago," he said. "You were young and your parents might not have read the article. I would like to talk more about this at a later time. Please, will you continue to introduce yourselves."

The students kept on with the process, which took most of

the assigned period for the opening class. The bell for dismissal rang and the students left immediately.

Missy tried to catch up to the student from Lake Providence. She looked for him outside but he must have hurried away. She was unhappy about it and sat down on the steps to think of a way to find him. Somebody from the class came over to her.

"Excuse me, Missy Blackburn?" he said.

Missy looked at him and stood up to shake his hand.

"Tell me what your name is, please?" Missy asked eagerly.

"I am Brian Kelley," he said.

"Oh, good," she said. "I would like to know about yourself and about your family. Do you all come from that town?"

"Mrs. Margaret Rhodes was my great grandmother," Brian said.

"Then I bet I can guess that Ron Blackburn was your great-great grandfather?" Missy stated it as a fact.

"Yes, that is right," Brian said. "Then it must be true that Robert Blackburn was your great-great grandfather? We are long-lost relatives? But now we have really found each other, right?"

"Yes, that's what I think too!" Missy was pleased to hear him say that.

"We are more likely distant cousins or something like that?"

"Yes, we are!" Missy agreed.

They hugged each other and talked about their relatives. They each had pictures of other relatives in both families.

That first weekend of the term, Missy stayed at school. On Saturday evening she thought that she should call her parents and tell them that she found these long-lost relatives. She went to a phone booth at her dormitory and dialed a direct call to her parents.

Chris and Lynn were in the living room. Lynn was reading book and Chris was watching sports on the TV. They heard the phone ring. Lynn got up and answered it.

"This is the Blackburn family. Who is this calling?" Lynn asked.

"Hello, Mom, this is Missy."

"I am so happy to hear from you!" Lynn said. "How are your classes? Are you meeting new friends?"

"Yes, I like the school," Missy said. "Can I talk with Dad, please?"

"Yes, I'll call your father to come to the phone," Lynn said. She told Chris, "Missy wants to talk with you about something."

"OK, I'm coming right away," Chris said.

"Hello, darling, how's my girl?" Chris asked.

"Hello, Dad, I'm doing fine and I like the school," Missy said, "but I want to tell you something interesting that I found out."

"Well, that's good to hear," Chris said. "What did you find out?"

"I met Ron Blackburn's great-great grandson," Missy said. "His name is Brian Kelley. He is in one of my classes here on campus."

Chris was surprised that Missy had found a lost relative. He looked at Lynn with some shock in his expression.

"What is that matter?" Lynn wondered.

"Do you remember about that article in the newspaper?" Chris asked.

"Yes, sure, I guess so," Lynn wondered. "What are you talking about?"

"I am sorry, Lynn, I thought you would remember right away." Chris sighed. "Missy found Ron Blackburn's great-great grandson. He is in one of her classes at the college."

"What!" Lynn was really surprised. "She told you that she found him?"

"Yes, that is why she is calling us now," Chris said.

"How wonderful!" Lynn was excited. "I think we ought to

meet him. What is his name?"

"Ah, I think she said Brian Kelley," Chris said. "Missy, his name is Brian Kelley, is that right?"

"Yes, that's it," Missy said.

"Yes, that is his name," Chris told Lynn. "We are thinking we would like to meet him when we come to visit you there?"

"Yes, that is a good idea!" Missy was excited. "Why don't you come and visit me tomorrow afternoon? If you can come, then I will talk with Brian about it. I am sure that he would really be pleased to meet you, too."

"She wants us to meet him tomorrow afternoon," Chris told Lynn.

"Yes, certainly, we'll be able to go and meet Brian at the college tomorrow afternoon," Lynn said. "I think it will be interesting to meet a lost relative!"

"Yes, we will go for sure!" Chris agreed. "Missy, we will see you at your room tomorrow at about three in the afternoon and hope to meet Brian then, too. Will that be OK?"

"Yes, I'll talk to Brain after we finish up here now," Missy said. "I'll ask him over to my dormitory and we can wait for you here, so whenever you can get here will be fine. OK, Dad?"

"Sure," Chris said. "Thanks for letting us know that you found him. We'll see you tomorrow afternoon then. I love you, good-bye."

"I love you, too. Bye," Missy said.

She hung up and the phone up and walked across the quadrangle to the freshman boys' dormitory. She called Brian from the lobby and told him that her parents would like to meet him. Brian said he would be thrilled to meet them, too.

The next day, Missy and Brian and a few of their friends ate lunch together at the campus cafeteria. After that, she was supposed to go from the cafeteria to meet with her parents at her dormitory. Missy told Brian they should leave right away. He agreed with her and left the table after saying good-bye to their friends. They were walking on their way to her dormitory when she saw that her parents had already arrived and were coming into the entrance area of dormitory.

"There are my parents; they will probably go right up to meet me in my room," Missy told Brian. "We can probably catch them before they go upstairs. Let's go now!"

"Cool!" Brian answered.

They ran over to the building and called to her parents just as they were going upstairs. They heard Missy's voice and looked down at her.

"It's a good thing that you caught us!" Chris laughed.

"I am so glad to see you," Lynn said with a smile.

They all hugged each other and then they looked at Brian.

"This must be Brian Kelley?" Chris asked.

"Yes, that's him!" Missy said. She turned to Brian. "This is my father; his name is Chris Blackburn, and my mother's name is Lynn."

"Oh, it's so nice to meet you," Lynn said. She hugged Brian. "We are glad Missy found out about you!"

"Yes, thanks, I'm glad to be meeting both of you, too," Brian said. He looked at Chris. "Your great grandfather was Robert Blackburn?"

"Yes, he was my great grandfather." Chris nodded. "We would like to meet your father. Probably we can visit your family in Lake Providence, Louisiana, someday."

"Yes, I would like that," Brian said. "But I haven't talked with my mother to tell her that I met a lost relative here."

"That's all right," Chris said. "What is your mother's name?"

"Karen Kelley. Before she was married her last was Rhodes," Brian explained. "My grandfather was Nelson Rhodes, but he died of a heart attack when I was about ten years old. My great grandmother was …"

"Mrs. Margaret Blackburn Rhodes," Chris said.

"Yes, that's exactly right." Brian still felt surprised by the situation.

"I read the article in the newspaper ten years ago," Chris explained. "My father never heard it from his grandfather, Robert, that he had a younger brother named Ron."

"What a shame," Brian sighed. "My mother told me that we have some lost relatives in Greenwood, Mississippi. I'm not sure how she knew it. But I am certainly glad that Missy found me in that class the first day we were there."

"Yes, it was a funny thing; I was getting bored listening to students telling their names," Missy said. "Then I heard someone say that he came from that town you had told us about a few times."

"I am glad that you never forgot what I told you." Chris smiled.

Missy smiled back at her father, but something was missing. She looked around at her parents.

"Where is Bethany?" Missy asked.

"She is out of town on a trip with the school band," Lynn said. "Bethany is supposed get home late this evening after they have their dinner."

"Oh, that is great. I want her to meet Brian, too," Missy said. "I'd like to take Brian home to our house so he can meet Bethany and my grandfather. Maybe for a weekend? Does that sound good to you?"

"Sure, you can bring him to our place," Lynn said. "He is part of our family tree."

Brian met Missy's family at her home one weekend later. Beginning with the Thanksgiving holiday, Missy's family visited Brian's family at Lake Providence for a week. They needed to share information about each other's relatives for the first time in almost a hundred years.

Chapter 35

During the 1970s, many of the farming families were no longer interested in keeping on with the business of planting cotton. They mostly sold their acres to another nearby farmer who was willing to buy the land. Farmers needed more land to bring their holdings up to a thousand acres or even two-thousand. It was no longer possible to make a living if the farmer only had forty acres.

Before the Civil War had come into the South, the plantations often had more than two thousand acres, and enough slaves to do the hard labor involved. In the 1920s, the federal government ordered the plantation owners to reduce their holdings to forty acres. The government divided the acreage among small farmers, who were supposed to be able to plant cotton and sell it for enough profit to support them.

In Lake Providence, there is a house with about twenty acres of planted cotton. There are a few good-sized barns and a smaller one for the sharecroppers. But no one lives there. Under the auspices of the office of the secretary of state, this set of buildings and the grounds around them are kept in good order to preserve the history and heritage of cotton cultivation. The house and barns have been remodeled. The Louisiana Cotton Museum opened in March of 1995. Visitors come to the museum from the United States and many other countries.

Downtown Lake Providence is a few miles south of the cotton museum. The town has a few businesses left and a small restaurant. Some of the buildings were destroyed during a riot in the early 1970s. That community and others have been trying to build a better economy since the Louisiana Cotton Museum was opened.

Margaret Rhodes' great grandson, Brian Kelley, sold her old house to another family. He married and moved to California and has a family. His distant cousin, Missy Blackburn, got an MS degree in history. Her thesis discussed the impact of cotton on society and culture, specifically in the city of Greenwood, Mississippi. She also married and had a family. She and Brian have become the best of friends since they met while attending undergraduate college.

Nancy Williams earned a Doctor of Philosophy degree from the University of Indiana. She has specialized in the study of black history, with a special interest in the southern social life of Atlanta, Georgia.

Billy Vangslia retired as the editor of the *Banner Democrat*. He had also worked as a reporter for the *Lake Providence Sentry* and *The Pelican* newspapers. He has retired to Sarasota, Florida, and lives near his children and grandchildren.